W9-AOP-382

BLOOD CELLAR

Ed raised his eyes and squinted at what he thought was a shadow against the back wall. Gun raised, he stooped under a heat duct and walked slowly toward the shadow. "C'mon out!" he yelled. "I'm armed!"

The shadow grew larger, and seconds later the deputy was looking into the face of a young boy. Holstering his gun, Ed breathed a sigh of relief. "What the hell are you doing down here, kid?" he asked. "You live here?"

Ed squatted and cupped the boy's shoulders. It was then he saw the trace of blood at the side of the boy's mouth. "What happened kid?" he asked, feeling anger swell within him. "Your parents do this?"

The boy said nothing.

"C'mon, son, don't be afraid. Answer me."

The boy curled back his upper lip, and Ed could not believe what he was seeing. The boy had . . . fangs, long, white, pointed fangs.

Ed fell backward and scuttled crablike across the floor. But the boy was too fast and too strong. He forced Ed's head back to the cold cement, sending a shock wave of pain down his back. Semi-conscious, Ed Land did not realize that the horror had only begun. . . .

PINNACLE'S HORROW SHOW

BLOOD BEAST (17-096, $3.95)
by Don D'Ammassa
No one knew where the gargoyle had come from. It was just an ugly stone creature high up on the walls of the old Sheffield Library. Little Jimmy Nicholson liked to go and stare at the gargoyle. It seemed to look straight at him, as if it knew his most secret desires. And he knew that it would give him everything he'd ever wanted. But first he had to do its bidding, no matter how evil.

LIFE BLOOD (17-110, $3.95)
by Lee Duigon
Millboro, New Jersey was just the kind of place Dr. Winslow Emerson had in mind. A small township of Yuppie couples who spent little time at home. Children shuttled between an overburdened school system and every kind of after-school activity. A town ripe for the kind of evil Dr. Emerson specialized in. For Emerson was no ordinary doctor, and no ordinary mortal. He was a creature of ancient legend of mankind's darkest nightmare. And for the citizens of Millboro, he had arrived where they least expected it: in their own backyards.

DARK ADVENT (17-088, $3.95)
by Brian Hodge
A plague of unknown origin swept through modern civilization almost overnight, destroying good and evil alike. Leaving only a handful of survivors to make their way through an empty landscape, and face the unknown horrors that lay hidden in a savage new world. In a deserted midwestern department store, a few people banded together for survival. Beyond their temporary haven, an evil was stirring. Soon all that would stand between the world and a reign of insanity was this unlikely fortress of humanity, armed with what could be found on a department store shelf and what courage they could muster to battle a monstrous, merciless scourge.

Available wherever paperbacks are sold, or order direct from the Publisher. Send cover price plus 50¢ per copy for mailing and handling to Pinnacle Books, Dept. 17-477, 475 Park Avenue South, New York, N.Y. 10016. Residents of New York, New Jersey and Pennsylvania must include sales tax. DO NOT SEND CASH.

The Hunt

T. LUCIEN WRIGHT

PINNACLE BOOKS
WINDSOR PUBLISHING CORP.

To Shirley for her faith
and for one very appropriate comment

PINNACLE BOOKS

are published by

Windsor Publishing Corp.
475 Park Avenue South
New York, NY 10016

Copyright © 1991 by T. Lucien Wright

All rights reserved. No part of this book may be reproduced in any form or by any means without the prior written consent of the Publisher, excepting brief quotes used in reviews.

First printing: February, 1991

Printed in the United States of America

PROLOGUE

Cynthia Lucas stared at her weakening reflection and thought about the sequence of events that had brought her to the precipice of immortality.

Very soon after the first visit, she had noticed an increased level of apathy, toward her husband, Judd, toward her charity work, toward her seven-year-old son, Jeffrey. Toward life itself. Soon after that first visit, what had been central in her life only entered her thoughts in purely diversionary ways.

She remembered—again very soon after that first visit—feeling like someone caught in the mystical grip of evangelism, swayed to the Mighty Word by some silver-tongued purveyor of "truth" whose only purpose was the systematic fleecing of an ill-informed, cross-wielding and usually gray-haired audience. Never had she considered herself capable of being numbered among their kind. Never had she seriously considered blind faith or the giving of unlimited trust. Not to anyone. Not to Judd, not to her parents. Not to anyone. And least of all, not to him.

But dammit, he had those eyes; ever since she had known him, he had had those eyes. There was comfort and an almost orgasmic warmth in their depth. There was the promise of a winterless life. There was apathy. Oh, there was that, masked as disdain. Even loathing—if the truth be known. Why hadn't she seen it before, when they were kids? Why had she chosen now to accept him?

"Oh, God!" she mumbled as the flood of memories seemed to suddenly weaken her wall of apathy. "Oh, God, what's happened to me? Oh, God!" But since that first visit, the word "God" had grown pointed and penetratingly sharp, a little three-pronged dagger ready to slip quietly into her heart and . . . and . . . and what? she thought confusedly, the same confusion that had been plaguing her since that first visit. What, dammit, what?

But then, finally, thankfully, the confusion slipped quietly and irretrievably away, and she felt her body suddenly become rigid, as if guarding against its return. And with a haughty, very self-assured smile she simply let that word—"God"—fall into the basement of her mind, deciding with profound finality that dredging it up any time soon would serve no useful purpose. None whatsoever. He wouldn't like it. Her large eyes opened wide at the truth of that thought, and she felt as if a huge weight had been lifted off of her.

She studied her unfocused, almost transparent image and delicately traced her long-nailed fingers over her wounds, remarking to herself how perfect they were, like tiny, symmetrical volcanos. Tiny, dead, perfect volcanos. Then she got up, went to the window and peered at the quiet darkness through an inch-wide opening where the plywood met; a darkness that had become ever so relaxing to her, ever so inviting.

Jeffrey Lucas squeezed his eyes tightly together. His dream did not lack for clarity.

He was walking with his mother through Soldiers' and Sailors' Park, even though it wasn't time for a walk. It was late. The sky was black and starry, and the streets were quiet. *Why didn't Dad come, too, Mom? Is he asleep? Is Dad asleep?* But for some reason she ignored him and walked very fast. And she was hurting him, squeezing his hand much too tightly. His feet pistoned along to keep up, barely touching the ground, and all the while he said to her, "Where are we going, Mommy? Where are we going, Mommy? Where are we going, Mommy?"

She whisked him past the cannon, and he thought of how his dad had taken his picture there, astride the thing like it was some big, cold, dead black horse without a head. And he vaguely remembered his picture being taken on a real horse once, with his "real" mother standing next to it. *His real mother.*

"Where are we going, Mommy? Where are we going, Mommy? Where are we going, Mommy?"

She glared at him. *Shut up, you little shit!*

It was that word—"shit"—a word he had used only once, resulting in a mouthful of Palmolive soap, that fetched him from his dream just as surely as a ball-peen hammer upside his head. *Shit,* his mother had said—or thought—he couldn't be sure. *You little shit!* Was she talking—thinking—about him? Was he a little shit? Had he been bad? Was that why he was a "little shit?"

He lay there in the gray-black darkness, eyes still closed . . .

Why? he thought remotely, *why don't I open my eyes?*

. . . and tried to resist the dream—nightmare—but he couldn't. It played back to him in a thick layer of sweat, in the *ka-thump, ka-thump* of his heart and the contrapuntal pounding ache inside his head as the air about him seemed to move, lying over his body like a lacy cerement of death.

Earlier it had come to Cynthia that she must find some way to thank him. A display of gratitude, her mother had always insisted, was the cornerstone of good breeding. She thought of Jeffrey and her face hardened with stony resolve. *There's no room for you here anymore!*

Oh—God!

But this time the word was dead, not simply remanded to some dark corner, but dead; just as dead as—she laughed quietly—the heavenly Father, the dead heavenly Father! There was another god now, and this one had nothing at all to do with purity and righteousness and making sure one did not covet thy neighbor's wife. This god was born of death, even fertilized by it. And this god needed . . . gratitude.

The word "sacrifice" had come to her, but only because she had not as yet fully evolved. The act of gratitude had already been completed, leaving only semantics. Her time, however, was near; her fight was almost over.

She turned away from the window and started for the door.

With sleep only seconds away, Jeffrey heard what he thought was a door opening. He turned onto his back and saw his mother standing there, holding on to the knob, her form solidly black, backlit yellow by the hallway light.

"Come with me, Jeffrey," she said flatly.

He pushed his small body backward, half wondering if she was part of a new dream—a new nightmare.

And then he opened his eyes wide enough to see—to really see. His mother was not standing in the doorway—no. There was no doorway; instead there was a man, a large, hulking, hunched-over old man, lantern light reflecting in dirty yellow patches off his body, glinting dully off teeth that seemed overly long and sharp. And this was not his room; this was a stinking rathole of a cellar, and he remembered then, remembered it all, the other man, the large man that his mother called Robert, and how she had said, "Take him, I've no further use for him!" And then his racing blood stole his sight and left only panic and numbing fear in its place. "Mommy, Mommy, Mommy!" he cried as the old man shambled closer, as his mouth yawned wide and he bent down over Jeffrey and whispered, "Welcome." A moment later the man's bared teeth penetrated his neck, and Jeffrey began his trip to immortality.

Across the room, Cynthia Lucas opened the door

and smiled.

Ten Years Later

Steven Lucas, alone in the backseat, turned the page of his book, *Tropical Fish,* and stared into the round, silver, black-centered eyes of a red wagtail platy. Just then the car hit an unusually large pothole and caused the page to turn, revealing a quartet of long-finned black tetras swimming in jetlike formation. He turned the page back and remotely heard his father say something about "In an hour or so," which he thought was how much longer he'd have to suffer this ride. He hated being cooped up in the backseat. The only thing more boring than a drive was meatloaf, especially the unimaginative way his mother made it: a little salt and pepper, a splash of ketchup, and an hour and a quarter at three hundred fifty degrees. *Yuch!*

As he turned the page, he saw the first drops of rain splatter lightly onto the side window. He looked out at the sky and thought that his dad was probably glad he got those new tires. He had gone to the tire store with him and heard the salesman say that he was smart to come in when he had because his right front tire had gotten weak—the man had used some big word; he couldn't remember what—and that just a few more miles and they would probably have had a blowout. "And you know," the man had gravely added, "what a blowout at sixty will do!" Steven imagined a racehorse cruising nicely along at about forty and then having one of his skinny legs break.

There you go—jockey crushed, horse's neck broken, a real mess! And a car doing sixty would probably be just as bad; there was no doubt about that!

"You got your belt on, son?" his father said as he glanced into the rearview mirror.

"Sure, Dad," Steven answered. "You, too?"

Bruce Lucas smiled condescendingly. "Don't you worry about us, son. We're fine."

Steven grimaced. Just because they were adults didn't mean they weren't supposed to follow the same rules he had to follow. He'd sure hate to see anything happen to them because they got careless or felt like they were—what was that word—immune? That was it, immune. He had heard his mother use it and liked the sound of it, so he'd stopped her in mid-sentence and asked her what it meant, cementing her response into his memory. He knew that his habit of stopping his parents in mid-sentence sometimes annoyed his father, but how else could he tell sometimes what they were saying?

His father said, "Oh, hell," and leaned a little forward to get a better look at the blackening sky. "Looks like a real beaut." Steven's mother only nodded and mumbled, "Hope it doesn't last too long." She, Steven knew, hated to drive in bad weather. She'd get all white in the face, and she wouldn't say anything. One time, during what his dad said was "A storm of biblical proportions," he saw her hand on his father's leg, the fingers just as white as snow. When the storm stopped, she let go of his leg, and the color came back into her face. But Steven had a lot of faith in his dad's driving ability. His father even knew how to drive a school bus, which he had done part-time when he was going to college. Well, Steven assumed, anyone who could drive a bus could certainly drive a car. That was like Mike Schmidt going down to the minors.

The road ahead began to sheet with rain, and the sky erupted in a web of lightning. Steven flinched as an especially tumultuous clap of thunder exploded nearby. His father smiled and said, "Anything this heavy can't last long," and shot a calm look at Steven's worried mother.

But during that fleeting second of interrupted concentration, that moment of loving reassurance, the car drifted just ever so slightly to the left, toward the solid white line indicating a NO PASSING ZONE. It was not something his school-bus-driver father could see very well, not with the rain obliterating almost everything in a gray wet fog. So, Steven would remotely think later, after the accident, it wasn't really his father's fault that he was now an orphan. It wasn't really his father's fault that their car crossed over that stupid line and just barely grazed that pickup truck full of driveway stone. And it wasn't his father's fault that their car careened out of control and skidded all over the wet pavement and finally broadsided a great big tree, killing both his parents immediately and leaving him almost unhurt. It had been that storm, that big, stupid summer storm.

As he lay in his hospital bed, thinking about the fact that he would be getting out that morning, he again thought of the word "immune." No one was. Not even school-bus-driver dads and scared-to-death mothers.

Then he cried.

CHAPTER ONE

Judd Lucas nodded to his right, out the passenger window of the Jeep Cherokee. "See that pukey green place?" he said to his nephew, Steven.

Steven, age eight, turned and nodded with feigned interest as the Cherokee rolled past the long-since abandoned restaurant on the outskirts of town.

"That's where your aunt and I went on our first date," Judd continued. He glanced toward Steven. "I think it was called 'Something Different' back then, but they changed that to 'September Place.'"

Other than, "I'm your uncle," a greeting punctuated by a forced smile at the Rochester International Airport an hour earlier, those were the first words he had spoken to the boy. He would have spoken earlier, and more often, but he hadn't known what to say. What do you say to a kid whose parents have been killed in a traffic accident? Do you make small talk? Do you try to see where the kid's head is at, or maybe act like it never happened? These were questions Judd Lucas pondered at length, finally deciding small talk was better than a full-blown inquiry or mile after mile of stony silence. As he spoke, he wished he hadn't waited so long.

Judd managed a smile. He was a modestly handsome man of forty with a full head of graying blond hair, who had always wanted to be taller than his five feet ten inches. "I'll tell you, Steven, I spilled my guts out that night. I mean, I so wanted to impress her that I told her anything I thought she wanted to hear. Back then I thought that was what you had to do to win a lady." The memory made him laugh. "Years later she told me I made a real horse's butt out of myself that night. Looking back, I guess I did."

Judd's monologue had little effect on Steven. Judd again nodded to his right and continued. "See that Mobil station? Well, when I was a kid, sixteen or so . . ." he paused, wondering if he should relate this sliver of the past to Steven; technically it involved a theft. But his tone, that of someone with a deep secret on the tip of his tongue, caused Steven to slowly turn his head. He looked directly at his uncle for the first time. *Got your interest, huh, kid?* Judd thought. "Truth is, I, well, I 'borrowed' my dad's Chevy Biscayne one night."

Judd was positive he saw it, a smile slowly rising at the edges of the boy's mouth. "Borrowed?" Steven said in a barely audible voice.

"Euphemistically speaking," Judd added, noting that Steven had inherited his dad's keenness and expecting to be questioned about the word "euphemistically."

"What's 'euphemistically'?" Steven asked, enunciating with perfect clarity.

Judd fidgeted and did a mental backflip. "Well, it's like when you say one thing but you mean something else." *Good, that's good, Judd. A little vague. . . .*

Steven's smile grew larger. Judd returned it, realizing then that this kid was pretty bright, that with him the truth was probably the best option.

"Okay, so I stole my old man's car—but only for a little while, just a few minutes. Anyway, the damn thing ran out of gas."

For the first time in a week, since his parents' deaths, Steven Lucas laughed. Judd felt warmth rise unbidden within him. Laughter and eight-year-old kids—a natural. Sure, he'd have a real battle the next year or so, depression, grief . . . memories. But this laughter was a start, something to build on.

Cranking up the laughter now, Judd added, "I had to hike all the way over here and beg some gas from these guys. And you know what? My dad never was the wiser. Mom knew, but the old man never did! Great start for a cop, huh?"

Laughter suddenly filled the Cherokee, and as they rolled past a sign that said, "Welcome to Hunt—where living is worthwhile," Judd Lucas pictured himself and Steven as friends, not just relations, an uncle helping out, doing the right thing. He looked forward to that happening; more than anything in the world, he wished for that.

The town of Hunt, population 11,345, or thereabouts, thirty-five miles east of Rochester, had been Judd's home for most of his life, a life that had more than its share of loneliness and tragedy. But there were pleasant memories too. There was Cynthia and Jeffrey. At least their memory. Both had disappeared ten years earlier.

"And this, Steven, is the only place in the whole United States where there's a church on each and every corner."

Steven looked away, having missed most of what he'd said, because he'd been thinking about his own parents. Judd's reminiscense had backfired.

"On your right you got a Presby, across from it a Catholic, then an Episcopal and a Methodist on the other side. We used to have a youth group in the Episcopal. I remember one time a bunch of us got together and carried Father Sloan's bug into the graveyard behind the church."

"Bug?" Steven said, his interest slightly piqued.

"Yeah, you know, his Volkswagen, little German cars that look like beetles?"

"Oh."

"And see that park on your left? The town has a huge bake sale there every summer. That cannon seats about twenty kids."

A black, wrought-iron fence ran across the front of the small, grassy park. To the left of the park was the Methodist Church; to the right, the Masonic Temple.

With a look of fond remembrance, Judd added, "I kissed Cynthia for the first time on that bandstand."

Other than the four churches, the main drag of Hunt was a clone of a thousand other small towns across the United States. The four churches were on the corners of Market and Main, and about a hundred yards farther down were two alliteratively named banks, First Federal and Marine Midland. The only building along Main taller than three stories was a white, pillared building that housed three small businesses. Almost all of the homes along the main drag were painted a different color to distinguish each from its neighbor. Judd slowed at the corner of Cuyler and Main. Johnson's Prescriptions and a place called The Settler's Post—a florist shop, owned by Rosemary Hamilton, Judd's high school sweetheart before he married Cynthia—were on the other side of the intersecting street. Most of the homes along the side streets behind Main were old and bland, purely functional. There were a few larger homes, a sprinkling of Victorian mansions, but they were either apartment houses or funeral homes now. The town itself had stagnated, but on the outskirts, new subdivisions had started to pop up like mushrooms in a graveyard.

Judd pulled over, parked diagonally and nodded toward a two-story, faded red brick house with dark brown trim. The yard was small with knee-high hedges along the front. "This place has a lot of historical significance, Steven." He leaned to his right, then squinted. "What's that sign say? I can't make it out. Gettin' old, I guess."

Steven hesitated, then said, "Uncle Judd, I can read, you know. You don't have to trick me like that."

Judd dissected the tone, the look on the kid's face. He hadn't spoken angrily; he'd just issued an emotionless statement of fact.

"Sorry," he said.

Steven turned, then began to read, "This house, built by Pliny Sexton in 1827, was a station of the underground railway in the days of slavery." He shrugged. "Neat."

Judd took a deep breath and let it out. "The town hasn't changed much, not in all these years, the names, but not the buildings. That bar over there, The Krohbar, that was there when I was a kid."

Judd pulled out and started down the road again. They drove past The Video Marquee, a fitness studio, and a huge pet shop called The Kritter Korner, the name bringing a smile to Steven's face. On their left now was Marifiotti's Shoe Service and to the left of that Pearsall's Style Shop. The four windows in Pearsall's, two up, two down, had 1920's-style caricatures of smartly dressed women etched into black paint.

They took a right just outside of town near a supermarket called Breens and found country again after they had crossed the Barge Canal. Home for Judd was only a few minutes and a shift into four-wheel drive away.

The cabin was surrounded by tall, lusty evergreens that protected it from winter winds and provided a good deal of shade during the hot, humid summers. It was small, but size didn't matter when you were alone. Now that he had Steven, he'd have to do something about another bedroom, though. He couldn't have the boy sleep on the sofa for the next decade. One thing he did have was privacy, which was why he had built the cabin here in the first place. Hunt was five miles east, the cabin's only access a one-lane dirt road intersecting Route Eight, itself a narrow two-laner in constant need of repair.

Five years back he had picked up a dog from Lollipop Farm near Rochester, a dumping point for unwanted pets and strays caught by the dog catcher. Sam, a shepherd and Lab mix, was around somewhere. He had a routine, out of the house by dawn and home by dark. Judd had installed a pet door in the kitchen, modifying it for exit only. Two playful yelps around dusk was the signal. *I'm home, boss, just me and my appetite, maybe a few burrs.* First some food, then a good brushing. Afterward Sam would curl up in front of the fireplace and doze off, a practice Judd didn't at all like; why own a dog if he didn't keep you company? But Sam was always too exhausted from doing whatever it was dogs did in the woods to offer Judd much more than a glance, let alone companionship.

Judd got out, opened the back door, and removed Steven's luggage. He drew a deep breath, letting it out slowly. "Smell it, Steven?" he asked. "The air? Probably hasn't changed in a million years." The apprehension on the boy's face was unmistakable—and predictable. Hell, these woods, Judd knew, could frighten a grown man. He glanced at the treetops. Sometimes the wind got trapped up there and made a fiercesome racket, like a wild thing in a cage.

"You tired, sport?" he asked.

Steven replied with a loose shrug.

"Well, c'mon, let's grab something to eat and hit

the sack; what do you say?"

As soon as the door closed behind them, Steven asked, "Got any Apple and Cinnamon Cheerios?"

"Isn't that breakfast stuff?"

"It's my favorite. Mom said it's good for me."

"I got some cereal, but not that stuff. Have a look; see what you can find."

Watching Steven, Judd saw his own son flipping open cupboards and slamming them closed. Jeffrey had had little patience when it came to satisfying his appetite. It was the one thing about the kid that always struck Judd as odd. Jeffrey always ate as if he had sat down to his last meal. He had been a normal kid otherwise, but that quirk . . . well, it was *strange*. Over the years Judd had come to see it differently. Now he was almost grateful for that peculiar aspect of his son's behavior—it brought the boy into fuller focus.

"Uncle Judd?"

Jeffrey faded. "Find anything? I should have stocked up; sorry about that."

Steven turned, a package of tainted bologna in his hand and a faint look of disgust on his thin face.

"Oh, yeah. I, uh, I've been saving that for Sam. I think there's some chipped beef in there somewhere."

Steven grinned mischievously. "Shit on a shingle?" he said, barely audible.

"Excuse me?"

"Nothin'."

Judd smiled and silently chastised himself for being thoughtless. *Mental note—get something good! And nutritious.*

He joined Steven. The chipped beef—aka, shit on a shingle—had been reduced to a few bites. He pulled out a handi-bin. Two large pink grapefruit tumbled toward the front.

"Powdered sugar's great on these," Judd said, pulling one out and tossing it into the air a foot or so.

"Not exactly the Ritz, huh, Uncle Judd?" Steven said, smiling.

They ate on the sofa, in front of a huge, fieldstone fireplace. Blueprints had called for something smaller, about half the size. Above the imposing oak mantel hung a painting of Cynthia and Jeffrey, done cheap by a local woman, one of those "artisans" just creative enough to sell, but not talented enough to make a living.

He had found the woman during a bazaar at Soldiers' and Sailors' Park in town. The painting was typical of the semi-talented; Jeffrey's features were too large, and Cynthia's too small. But they were together, and that was how he would always remember them . . . how he had remembered them these past ten years.

"We just got nothin' to go on," Bill Rupples had told him back then. And that was pretty much true. There had been reports of prowlers, but little else. But Rupples was notoriously lazy and just waiting until he could retire on the county. He put the case into the inactive file within a year and just repeated what he had told Judd the year before: "We just got nothin' to go on." It came to Judd one night that maybe as sheriff he could get something done.

Simple enough, throw your hat into the political ring, rely on your military police background, hope the townfolk had had enough of Rupples's armchair way of doing things. As it turned out, they had. Rupples left town quietly and quickly after the loss, with just a note on the office swivel chair. "I hope you find them. I really do." Rupples wasn't all bad, just lazy.

But even as sheriff, Judd learned little more. Clues in the case were scarce: a scarf belonging to his wife found in the woods on the other side of town, some bones—a femur, metacarpals, a sternum with two attached ribs—nothing, really. It was as if his family had simply ceased to exist, as if they had been spirited into another realm of existence.

In the painting, Jeffrey sat atop a blind black-and-white pony while Cynthia stood in front holding the reins. The painting had been done from a photograph taken on Jeffrey's second birthday. He had been a chunky kid, his cheeks fat and rosy, healthy looking, his lips puckered as if he had just tasted salt. And Cynthia, dear sweet Cynthia. Her hair was blond and swept back, and she wore a blue, flowered print dress and the most beautiful smile he'd ever seen. Judd felt his eyes water and looked away. *"Best not show 'em what's in ya, Judd, boy. Best keep it in there, keep 'em guessin'." Good old Dad.*

Right after they had finished their grapefruit, Sam gave a crisp yelp from the front yard. Judd let him in and smiled as the dog ate and then curled up in front of the cold fireplace, offering Steven only a dark-eyed, half-interested glance.

"Hard day at the office," Judd told Steven. "I think he's got the right idea, though. Tell you what, you take my bed tonight, up there in the loft. I'll sack out here on the couch." A week's worth of having his emotions torn from here to Friday had left Steven physically drained. Judd's offer was like Rocky Road ice cream on a hot day.

That Night—Hunt

At the Sports Odyssey Store on Main, the owner went over his books and contemplated bankruptcy. At Nina's Pizzeria across the street, three teenagers waited for their deluxe supreme. At the same time, at Canaltown Video, a disgruntled clerk angrily eyed a middle-aged man and woman as they casually searched for a movie. It was already past closing time. While all this was going on, Adrian Foote, local felon, walked briskly toward the 102-year-old All house on the other side of town. What had been impregnable was now pregnable. The night before, on his way home from a "job" in Hidden Valley, he had stopped to rest near the All house. During that rest he had watched while a man—a very large and tall man—withdrew a key from a hiding place under the steps and then went inside. He hadn't stayed long, a couple of minutes or less, but he had redeposited the key afterward. Luck, Adrian thought then, had just stepped up and kissed him right on the mouth.

Now boarded over, the house had been owned by

the All family until 1968, passed down from generation to generation for seventy-one years. Jacob All, an immigrant from England, had built the house with monies earned in the dry goods business. There were rumors at the time that Jacob's wealth had been obtained by less than honest toil, but those rumors were never proven.

The house Jacob built was actually somewhat modest for the time, when gargantuan homes were more the rule than the exception. But Jacob had not been an ostentatious man. He enjoyed his privacy and died on the front porch one Easter morning, a glass of lemonade on a table beside him. The house fell to his son, Robert, a tall, sinister-looking man with dark, mysterious eyes, which made him a favorite with the ladies. Robert, it was said, fell victim to the husband of one of those ladies. The joke that followed had something to do with cocking your weapon and making sure the lady's husband didn't do likewise. But Robert's body was never found, and the deed was filed under the category of rumor. Soon after, the house became the permanent residence of Robert's son, Robert Jr., and his daughter, Becky. When she died in 1978 the house was boarded over because no heir could be found. Because of a delinquent tax bill, it became the property of the state.

Adrian passed through the business district, checked out the latest offering in the front window of the Video Marquee and then walked through the park off Main, traveling the remaining distance through backyards. He had to climb a couple of fences and hustle away from a leashed bloodhound, but he didn't mind—it kept his reflexes sharp.

It was nine-thirty by the time he arrived. The moon, not as large or as orange as it had been earlier, was almost overhead now, clearly visible from Adrian's vantage point behind the house. There were railroad tracks across the street, dense woods beyond. The Barge Canal ran behind the house about a hundred yards back. Occasionally, canal rats found their way into the basements of these homes, a malady that kept the local exterminator well-heeled. There was no driveway at the All house, only tall hedges on both sides in dire need of a trim. Adrian had had to fight through them to get behind the house. But although the hedges needed attention, the lawn was always mowed. The neighborhood association paid Stanley Crimmons five dollars a week to see that it was. And Stanley did it faithfully every Saturday afternoon around two, weather permitting, and if his homework was done. The neighborhood association figured that just because the house was boarded up didn't mean the yard had to grow wild—there were property values to consider.

Adrian scurried toward the back of the house and braced himself against it. Stepping lightly, he peeked around the corner. The moon shone down at him like a giant flashlight. He pulled back, drew in a deep breath and held it. The quiet was dreamlike, only silent mental messages racing along his synapses, and now and then the distant blare of a car horn. Adrian let his breath out, stepped into the moonlight and squatted down beside the steps. They were made of wood, and at first Adrian wondered if perhaps he had been seeing things because there was just no way to get behind those steps. But then, inadvertently, he pushed on the right board. He pushed harder and it fell inward, flopping quietly onto the soft earth. Within seconds, and with a little groping, he had palmed the key. He clutched it in his fat little hand and hoisted himself onto the porch, peering through breaks in the railing at the street beyond, toward the tracks and the ominously dark woodline. There appeared to be two boys hiking along those tracks. He watched as they took a left, toward the woodline. After they were out of sight, he stood, put the key into the lock, opened the door and stepped inside, shutting the door carefully behind him. Instantly his nose wrinkled—there was an odor here, the smell of something freshly killed, he decided. The movie *Young Frankenstein* flashed through his mind, the six-month, three-month and freshly dead scene, and it brought a smile to his face. *But, hell,* he told himself, *the place has been boarded over for a lot of years. It's not about to smell like Clorox 2.* Despite the smell, a shiver of raw power crawled through him. Whatever that guy had locked up in here would soon be his, all his. He flicked on his flashlight and drew it around the room. Just to his left was a passageway bordered on either side by pillars; on his right, just a few feet farther, a staircase. The kitchen was in front of him, the door hanging only by the bottom hinge. He aimed the flashlight toward the stairs and ran the light upward toward the landing. Looked safe enough. If there was anything valuable in this old house, it was probably up there. His gait was slow yet steady—practiced. More than once he'd had to tippy toe through an occupied bedroom to lift something—shadows didn't make a sound, and neither did he. He swiped a line of sweat off his forehead and noticed that it was considerably warmer here than outside, and even warmer than downstairs. There were three bedrooms, each door open and, as downstairs, only sheet-covered furniture. He stuck his flashlight into one of those bedrooms and ran the light across the back wall. He paused briefly when the beam passed over a boarded-up window, the light-colored wood momentarily drawing his attention. *There's nothin' up here,* he thought with a sigh, *not a damn thing!* His hopes fading, he went downstairs and into the kitchen. The first thing he saw was a locked door, a door that he thought led to the basement. Without hesitation, he jimmied the lock with a crowbar he'd found lying nearby and opened it.

Playing the light down the stairway, Adrian watched as it passed over the bottom halves of two more doors, one on either side. He started down the stairs and realized that the door on his left was barricaded by a thick beam, slotted on either side. Smiling broadly, he stepped closer. A good deal of money had been spent on locks and barricades—what were they hiding? How much would he be worth after this evening?

Just as he was about to find out, he stopped. He had heard something. The first thing he thought of was the shuffling of feet—he paused—no, couldn't be. Animal, maybe. Some squirrel got in there and couldn't get back out. He thought about that awhile. No, something bigger than a squirrel—squirrels didn't make a lot of noise. Definitely something bigger than a squirrel. But then he thought that maybe he'd only been hearing things. It was as dark as the inside of a well down here, and this old house with all its boarded-up windows and putrid smells would sure go a long way toward making you hear things. With no other explanation available, he shoved the crowbar into his belt. Its dangerous heft brought a grin to his face. He was a man with a weapon; it didn't matter what was in there—if anything. Nothing was going to keep him from his prize. Nothing. With a strong sense of finality, he put his hands under the six-by-six and pushed upward, the weight of it surprising him. With a scraping wooden sound, the six-by-six lifted out of the slots. He heaved it onto his shoulders, turned and let it fall behind him. The first thing he noticed as he opened the door was that the smell was even stronger here than upstairs. It made his eyes tear and his nostrils sting, and brought to mind a recently drowned friend, yellowed and bloated and stinking all to hell. The smell almost drove him off, almost made him forego any dubious prize this stinkhole had to offer. But, he reasoned, he'd come too damn far to leave just because the place stunk. He drew the light around the basement room. The walls were made of stone, the cement floor cracked and slimy. There were a number of wood braces, and even a few tall jacks. And to his front a wood partition jutted about halfway into the twenty-by-twenty-foot room. Suddenly, he heard what he thought was the strike of a match. Instantly light communicated feebly throughout the basement room, light emanating from behind the partition. *Lantern light,* he thought. Then, silently, stepping out from behind that partition, he saw three boys, three young boys. "Holy shit!" Adrian whispered, feeling as yet no sense of danger. The tallest boy, blond and a shade over five feet, was on his left. Barefoot, he wore a faded red sweater and worn jeans. The boy in the middle, dark-haired and with large features, wore a tan bathrobe, open in the front, over old-looking underwear and lop-eared bunny slippers. The last boy, the same height as the boy in the middle, wore jeans and a New York Giants jacket. The word "GIANTS" had fallen off, leaving only the outline arched ghostly in the front. He had an almost angelic quality, his features small, perfect. They stood side by side and simply stared at him until Adrian heard what he thought was the name "Robert?" spoken from behind the partition, the voice gravelly and old with a hint of vibrato. The tallest boy turned, looked in the direction of the voice, turned back and looked again at Adrian. In a soft, weak voice, he said, "Martin," as if in introduction. Immediately Adrian moved to his left so that he could see this "Martin." Slowly, an old man, a thin gray blanket pulled to his chest, his large, hairy arms at his sides, came into view. He turned and looked directly at Adrian. Instantly Adrian understood that it was the man's look of extreme old age—*a man too old to live*—that brought his pulse to a maddening pace, that puzzled his thoughts and made his fear as profound as any he had ever felt. *Leave, just get the hell outta here,* he told himself. *This is crazy, something that happens down at the movie house!*

He wheeled, blinded in the flurry of lantern light and sudden fear, and instantly slammed into a bracing, his forehead taking the full, thudding force of the blow. He fought for balance, his head throbbing with pain, his eyes straining to focus as he reached for something—anything—to steady himself, and finding nothing. Then he fell heavily to the floor and rolled onto his back, moaning from the dull, pounding ache inside his head. Only seconds later he forced his eyes open and looked toward the boys. Slowly his focus returned, but he was still very weak, too weak to stand. As he looked more closely, Adrian could see that their eyes lacked the sparkle of youth that should have been there, as if their tear ducts were missing, which only fueled his fear. Again he thought about getting up, but as he tried, the pain in his head rose maddeningly and quickly drained his strength. He was going to try again—despite the pain—but then, with a suddenness that drew a quick scream of surprised fear out of Adrian, the tallest boy did something that indeed made him think about things that happened only in the movies. And the more he watched the boy, watched as his teeth lengthened, the faster his surprise turned to paralyzing fear. Within seconds after each boy had peeled back his colorless lips to reveal razor-pointed canines, Adrian felt a warm trickle of urine down the inside of his pant leg. He cursed his fear now, the damnable unknown, yet there was precious little he could do as the old man pushed himself into position behind the boys as they pressed forward, their fangs glistening. They moved with merciful swiftness, and within seconds they had torn away most of Adrian's clothing and had lain him open like room-temperature cheese, despite his feeble plea for mercy. Even through this haze of fear and pain Adrian saw the old man. A wide, nasty grin had parted his lips as he watched the boys sink their teeth deep into this new victim, his legs, his stomach, his now quieting carotid. They sucked contentedly, quickly and effectively draining Adrian of his blood; the squirt of it leaving sounded like water down a drain. It was then, through fogging eyes, that Adrian saw the girl; a dark-haired girl, her jeans and pink blouse almost unrecognizable, just bits of rag hanging from her body, lying at the foot of the old man's bed. A huge canal rat standing on his hind legs, his forepaws drawn prayerlike together, his nose twitching, stood close by, his focus shifting slowly from the girl to Adrian.

The last thing Adrian saw was the old man as he leaned over him, hands on knees, his craggy, white-gray face only inches away, his dark eyes inexplicably pointed with light. And the last thing Adrian heard was a deep, rolling, old-man laugh, the laugh of a man who had not had reason to laugh for a very long time. And he didn't stop laughing, even after Adrian rolled onto his stomach and died, his body shredded yet bloodless.

* * *

Locked up with Martin for more than ten years, it didn't take the boys very long to leave once they had been sated. By the time they found their way out of the house, their strength had doubled. Pausing only briefly, each went in a different direction, two toward Hunt, and the third away from town, toward the woods beyond the tracks and farther, toward Hidden Valley Subdivision.

Seconds later, having stumbled his way past Adrian to the bottom of the stairs, Martin recognized a growing fatigue. He knew he could not leave, not yet, not without the promised cure. So he shut the lantern down, returned to his bed, and drew the tattered gray blanket over him. Within an hour, Robert All Jr. had once again barricaded Martin's room and locked the house up tight.

CHAPTER TWO

At Hidden Valley Subdivision

Ben Ferguson glanced around the moonlit neighborhood; at completed homes, at wood skeletons, at freshly dug basements yawning like giant lion snares. His own gently sloping yard, a fine fuzz of young grass tentatively binding the rich, dark soil, stretched out to his left, thinning grass cascading into a drainage ditch, glossy black asphalt just beyond. The home across the street, completed the day before, awaited its proud owners like a huge, shiny toy. The home to his right, similar to his own two-story colonial, was dark, save for a light in an upstairs bedroom. He glanced to his left and remembered the black couple flitting about their wood skeleton like ants at a company picnic, hearing her soprano squeals of delight, his tenor promises, sharing an occasional hug. Someday maybe he'd say hello.

He stared into the semi-darkness and remembered,

with a small measure of anxiety, something his next door neighbor Lenny had said about the nights being quieter than the days. What was that Belushi line? he wondered. So quiet you could hear a mouse get a hard on. Sure, it was that quiet.

A floodlight illuminated the driveway and part of the front yard. His son, Brian, sat beside him. They were drinking iced tea and enjoying a little "quality time," something Ben told himself he was going to make a concerted effort to do.

Brian had just returned from a jaunt down the tracks on the other side of the main drag with Lenny Swartz's son, Andy, the next door neighbor on the right. He hadn't pressed him about just where they had gone, but Ben suspected that down those tracks, somewhere, Andy had built a fort. Why else would he have carted off all the leftovers from the Swartz's addition: shingles, tar paper, two-by-fours, anything they could beg or steal, or so Andy's dad had told him. Forts, hell, they were a kid's second home.

"So, how you like it here, Brian?" he said as he raised the glass to his mouth, fully expecting a glowing report about the house, the neighborhood, the rarified country air; Brian simply echoing his mother.

"It's okay, I guess," Brian mumbled.

"Well, you'll make more friends, you'll see."

Brian looked at him for a while, "Dad, why'd we move? I mean, it would have been okay with me if we stayed in the city. I wouldn't have minded, honest."

Ben thought a moment and said, "Well, we just outgrew the other place. And it's only normal to want the best." He paused, drew in a deep breath, then exhaled. "You know your mother and I worked pretty darn hard for all this . . . you will never know just how hard!"

"I had all those friends, Dad!"

Where the hell'd that come from? Ben wondered. *I thought he liked it here. Advice, Ben, a little good, fatherly advice.* "Brian, friends are like . . . well, like weeds in a garden—every year there's a new batch. Making new friends—weeding your garden—is just part of growing up." He wanted to smile, overly pleased as he was with his analogy, but he didn't, at least not outwardly.

"I guess."

"And what about Andy? He's a nice kid!"

"Yeah, he's okay."

"Just okay?"

Brian shrugged.

"Brian?"

Just then Andy Swartz walked out his front door, waved, walked down his driveway and then up Ben's. He stopped a few feet away, his thin, pale face even more pale in the white glow of the garage floodlight. It was warm, too warm for his blue spring-weight jacket, the same jacket he'd had on earlier. He looked at Brian as if he were gathering his thoughts, but Ben spoke first.

"You took the long way, Andy."

"Yeah, my dad said not to walk on your grass 'cause it's new."

Ben nodded approval. "Well, that was considerate. I suppose I'd ask Brian to do the same."

Andy looked back at Brian. "I was gonna take a walk around the neighborhood. You wanta go?" he asked hopefully.

Ben glanced quickly at his watch. "It's pretty late, Andy; besides, you boys just got back—"

"Just around the neighborhood, Mr. Ferguson. Just for a little while," Andy interposed.

Ben sighed. "Sure, go ahead," he said. "But watch out for the cars."

Denying his son had been difficult lately, what with the image of the kid's blistering backside playing through his mind so many times each day. He had lost it that day last month, lost it totally, and Brian had paid the price. He just prayed the boy wouldn't piss him off that bad again. Just prayed to God. Kid would probably run away if he thought for one minute that he was going to get another whipping like that one. Ben shuddered. He'd probably run off, too, if he were the boy.

Andy and Brian strolled down the driveway and turned right, toward the main road. "Be home in an hour, okay, son?" he yelled after them.

Brian turned and waved. "Sure, Dad, an hour. See ya."

Ben stayed in his chair and watched them take a right at the main road of the subdivision; they were shadows now, anybody's kids from a distance. He wondered what they were talking about; sports maybe, girls . . . probably not girls, not yet. The fort, more than likely, what to name it if they hadn't already.

Andy spied an egg-size rock in the road, kicked it hard, and watched as it tumbled into the dirt yard of a house under construction. Without looking at Brian, he said, "If I tell you something, you gotta promise not to tell."

"What?" Brian asked.

"You gotta promise—on your mother's boobs you gotta promise. On your mother's boobs!"

Having Andy talk about his mother's boobs left Brian feeling strangely anxious, but he didn't want to lose this friendship before it got going, even though Andy was probably just another weed in the garden.

"What's my mom's chest got to do with it?" he asked, hopefully nonchalant.

Andy regarded Brian with his eyes only, then looked back down the road. "Okay, okay," he said, "swear on your balls, then. Swear on your balls you won't tell."

My balls? Brian thought. *Somethin's wrong with this kid. First mom's boobs, now my balls.* But his balls weren't nearly as sacred as his mother's boobs.

"Okay," he said tiredly.

"Swear it!" Andy stopped abruptly and shoved a finger into Brian's chest for emphasis. "C'mon—swear it!"

"Okay—okay! I swear—all right?"

Andy slowly removed his finger. "See that house up there, the one on the end?"

Brian squinted through the darkness. "Yeah, I see it—what about it?"

"I know a way in—that's what! I've been goin' in there for a week now. All by myself, too!"

The rollercoaster ride at Seabreeze Amusement Park—now there was a real heart stopper, especially at night. And sometimes, when he was under the covers with a penlight and a horror comic, Brian's body tingled. But this—this was something else altogether. He had dreamt about their house, about what went on inside while it was being built, when the workmen weren't there hammering and sawing and making lots of noise, scaring off whatever. . . . Maybe, just maybe, someone—or something—had lived there at night. Of course, there had been absolutely no way for him to find out. But now, he was actually being given the opportunity to go inside one of these houses at night. He stared at the place, looming before them like some huge, darkly majestic headstone. Sure, he had a chance, but would he have the nerve to actually follow Andy inside? The more he stared, the more he wondered about that.

"C'mon," Andy said, "piece a cake! 'Less a course you're chicken. You chicken, Brian? Yeah, I'll bet you are—just like you were chicken to go into the woods tonight, just like then!"

Yeah, Brian thought loudly, *you're a weed, Andy, and you got a stupid smile, too!* He looked at the house one more time and said, "C'mon, let's go," although he had a bad feeling about the whole thing.

They walked quickly yet almost soundlessly, their sneakers squeaking against the asphalt, and entered the property via the stone-filled driveway. They went around back and stopped near the back door of the garage.

"Not much of a yard," Brian said.

And it really wasn't. Thick, tall bushes, as close as ten feet in spots, framed the area. A large maple near a bowed window cast a shadow onto the house, the shadow angled to the left by the full moon at their backs. The uneven ground was littered with the detritus of construction: chunks of wood, cinder blocks, a bucket lying on its side a few feet away. From here they could see a long two-by-eight leading to the back door of what would eventually be a family room.

"Neat, huh?" Andy said, not really wanting or expecting a response. Neat about covered it.

In the days to follow, a deck would be built off the family room, but for now the two-by-eight was a quick way in and out for the workmen. The boys stepped onto it, Andy in the lead, and took a few steps. As the board sagged under their combined weight, Brian lost his balance. His arms slowly circled as he fought for control, visions of his head smashing open against one of those cinder blocks flashing through his mind. But just as quickly as he lost his balance, he found it. He looked at Andy, at his ugly smile, and felt his face flush. *You wanted me to fall, didn't you, Andy, didn't you?* he thought. Still smiling, Andy turned and continued his balancing act.

When they were within a few feet of the door, Andy stopped, his arms horizontal, and said, "Look, see there?" The glass had been broken near the doorknob, a piece of cardboard shoved into the opening.

"Did you do that?" Brian asked, remarking to himself what a stupid question that was—of course he had.

"No, I didn't do it; it was like that before."

"Why don't they fix it, then?"

Andy shrugged heavily and again wobbled the

board. Brian put his hands out farther and glared at Andy, who, it appeared, had better balance. "I don't know," he said. "Guess they figure no one round here's gonna wanta go inside, you know?"

"Yeah, I guess, but they gotta fix it sometime, though."

"I suppose," Andy said. He turned, flapped the cardboard, reached in, unlocked the door, and stepped inside. Brian hesitated a moment, then followed.

A puzzle of odors greeted them: recently installed drywall, wood stain, and sawdust, a decidedly new smell. Brian glanced to the right. A round window beside the white brick fireplace caught his attention. The moon had slivered into the top left corner, as if the window were the business end of a telescope, an effect that Brian appreciated far more than Andy.

"Look at that," he said.

"Yeah, so what?" Andy replied.

But Brian had become entranced. He watched intently as the sliver of moon grew and grew until it filled half the window. At the same time a noise in some distant corner of the huge house brought him back to reality. "Andy" he said turning, "where are you, Andy?"

No answer.

"Dammit, Andy—where are you?"

He stepped toward the doorway; the stairs stood just beyond. Once he reached the hallway, he could see the sunken living room to his right, tall windows spaced every five feet or so, nothing visible through them except the hulks of other unfinished homes across the street. He had a sudden urge to leave. Andy was obviously trying to scare him—and he probably would. But he also realized that if he did leave, Andy would never let him hear the end of it. He moved to the bottom of the stairs and looked upward, toward the considerably darker landing.

"C'mon, Andy!" he yelled, unconcerned that someone might hear him, someone walking a dog or simply passing by.

Still no answer.

"I'm gonna leave—I promise, I'm just gonna leave!" he continued, glancing around nervously as his voice echoed through the rambling structure. He looked back up the stairway, took a deep breath, then let it out. "Okay, I'm leaving!"

But as he was about to do just that, he heard, "Over here, over here."

"Andy?" he said, almost at a whisper.

"C'mon, over here!"

The voice had a multi-directional quality, as if Brian were thinking rather than hearing it.

"Where are you?" he said, a little louder this time.

"Over here, over here!"

He thought for a second and guessed the voice had come from the second floor. He started up the stairs.

"You up there?" he hollered.

Nothing.

Once he had reached the landing, he stopped. There was a window to his right, at the end of the hall. He walked over to it and looked out. Beyond a hayfield, a woodline rose toward the dark purple sky. The field looked like a painting, although a wind had risen, gently waving the dark yellow stalks. As he watched, Brian wished mightily that he were out there instead of in this big, new house, with all the strange smells . . . with Andy. And as the image of that scene—the hay, the woodline, the dark purple sky—grew and grew, imprinting itself onto his brain, he knew that the longer he looked, the longer he wished, the worse it was going to be. Simply turning around would be an exercise in terror. Why? Because Andy was behind him . . . waiting. He had hidden some stupid costume, some skeleton thing or something, and he was going to scare the shit right out of him. His heart hammered against his chest wall. His body dripped sweat. His mind raced—*don't be there, Andy; please, oh, God, please don't be there! Maybe . . . maybe I can stay here till morning. It'll be okay then; the sun'll come up and it'll be light out. . . .* But, his thought continued, he was eight now, old enough to face up to demons, kid demons or Andy demons or any kind of demon. It didn't matter. So with all the bravery he could summon, he clenched his kid fists, filled his kid lungs with nerve-steeling oxygen and wheeled. For a moment, for just a silly millisecond, he thought he saw something, a form, a big kid maybe. But he hadn't. He couldn't have. There was nothing there now, not a damn thing, just four closed doors, one at the end of the hall, one to his left and two to his right. Again he considered leaving, but again he understood that leaving wouldn't do him a lot of good in the long run, not with Andy. Not with a weed. Even though Andy was a jerk, he really was pretty good at scaring people. He thought about that, thought hard on it, remembering how Andy had scurried off while they were in the woods, leaving him alone and afraid, so afraid. No time to think about the woods; he had to think about the here and now. Obviously Andy was in one of the four rooms, behind one of those closed doors. If Brian was quiet enough, maybe he could find him before he could leap out at him or sneak up behind him or whatever it was he had planned. Brian felt a smile gather at the corners of his mouth. If Andy was good, then he was going to be better, lots better! He moved as silently as possible toward the first door on his right, gripped the knob and slowly pushed it open. Because it was new it made no sound whatsoever. He stepped inside. There were windows on the back and right walls, and a double-wide closet with sliding doors to his left, the doors closed. He glanced out the back window. From here he could see what he thought were the starlike lights of Hunt twinkling in the distance. He looked to his left, at the closed closet doors. If Andy was here, he was in that closet. A heat vent to the right of the closet reminded him of how his dad would yell down to him through the vents in the old house, his dad's voice like the voice he had heard earlier. *So that's how Andy made his voice sound like that,* he thought. *Who's going to scare who—huh, Andy?*

He stepped toward the closet, unable to suppress a smile, yanked the door open and stuck his head inside. "Gotcha!" he yelled.

But as his eyes adjusted and he saw that the closet was empty, he took a halting step backward, halting because at the same time, he felt a presence—somebody . . . something was nearby, here in the room or—

The door slammed shut, and Brian screamed a very

small, frightened scream as his gaze focused on the closed door, his heart rebounding, pounding like it had at the window.

And from beyond the closed door, a boy laughed, not a full-blown belly laugh, more a titter.

"Dammit, Andy!" Brian said, angrily yanking the door open just in time to see a thin, dark figure move swiftly down the stairway. "Hey!" he added, giving chase.

When he got to the bottom of the stairs, a door opened to his right. He watched as Andy stepped into the dark hallway and walked toward him, hands up in bewilderment.

CHAPTER THREE

About The Same Time In Hunt

Walter Higgins pulled his wrist to within a foot of his eyes, waited for his focus to sharpen and checked the time: 10:04. "Damn her!" he said, his words slurred, his head rotating slightly as if his neck muscles had begun to atrophy. "Why'd she hafta do that? Bars don't close for a coupla hours!" Suddenly he heard the voice again. "Sure, Walter, coupla hours—you'd be comatose by then." Walter hated that voice, that hitchhiker from his sober past. One of these days, one of these so very quickly passing days, he'd grab that voice by the throat and. . . . "Sure you will, Walter, sure you will. You do that, you might as well go down to Murphy's Hardware, buy a spade, go on up to that cemetery on the hill and start digging your own grave." And Walter knew that if he did sever that sobering umbilical, then he might as well dig his own grave. Being a drunk was one thing. Being unable to face reality was quite another. And he could still face reality, at least part time.

His customary hangout was The Krohbar, just down the street from the corner of Market and Main, where he now stood bathed in the glow of a streetlamp, his body gently swaying, as if he hadn't yet got his sea legs. While at The Krohbar, his wife had called with some wild story about prowlers. "And get your ass home pronto!" she had ordered—adding, in a somewhat mumbling voice, that he probably wouldn't be much good anyway, but at least he was big and ugly, which might help. Walter wasn't really ugly though, just very ordinary-looking. Sure, the booze wreaked havoc with his capillaries, making his face look like a bloody pin cushion, but he wasn't really look-away ugly. And Walter knew that whenever she took her Valium she didn't know what she was saying anyway.

Walter and Barbara lived on Fitzhugh Street, off Sexton, in a house they'd bought cheap from her brother-in-law, Judd Lucas, the town sheriff, after Judd's wife and son had disappeared. The house, a century-old colonial, was in constant need of repair, repairs that wouldn't get done because Walter and Barbara were broke. And they'd probably never be done because Walter just couldn't keep a job.

Nightfall usually found a few cars parked along the street, and tonight was no exception. Walter shuffled past an '82 Belvedere parked three houses down from his own. The car belonged to Teddy Dorsey, a math teacher at the local high school. Walter grinned as he glanced to his right at Rosemary Hamilton's house, white sheers dulling the triangular glow from a living room light. As he did, he wondered vaguely why she and Judd hadn't gotten back together since his wife's disappearance. They'd been an item in high school, all those years ago. They still saw each other every now and again, and Judd had even mentioned to him that he still thought of her as "a very attractive woman." Still, he hadn't done a thing about it, not more than an occasional lunch or a stop by her shop. But Teddy Dorsey sure had. And they were at it again tonight, like most nights Teddy's wife, Sue, caught the B shift at the paper factory. Walter smiled a silly, drunken smile. *Sure takes balls to leave his car parked right out in front like that,* he mused. But Rosemary Hamilton, every sultry inch of her, could make any man's brain turn to mush—follow the lead of their loins, as Walter liked to put it. She sure was a stunner, as pretty as the silk flowers she sold two doors down from The Krohbar.

"Plug her one for me, pal!" Walter mumbled as he shambled past.

At his own front door now, he fumbled in his pants pocket for the house key. Like everyone along Fitzhugh, Barbara Higgins kept the door locked and the porch light off. *Spiteful bitch,* Walter thought. *She knows how hard it is to find that goddamn keyhole, 'specially when you got a snootful.* And tonight the keyhole may as well have been filled with cement. "Damn her," he spit as he dropped the key back into his pocket and groped for the nipple of the doorbell, succeeding on the third try. He grinned as he held it in, picturing Barbara cursing him all the way down the stairs. And she was most certainly upstairs, sitting in front of her precious mirror, Walter thought. Christ, she spent most of her life there!

And he continued to hold the nipple in as all three hundred and twelve pounds of her yanked open the door and glared down at him glassy-eyed.

"Where you been, Walter Higgins? I could have been violated for all you care!" she fumed.

Walter's unsteady gaze found his wife's small, dark eyes.

"Violin?" he said.

"That's right, Walter, vi-o-la-ted!" She enunciated with profound clarity, purposely sending out a mist of spit on the last syllable. She had taken not just one, but two Valiums only a half hour ago, leaving her as foggy-brained as Walter.

A smile whispered along his mouth as he mopped his forehead with the back of his hand. The thought of anyone wanting Barbara for *that* purpose brought on a low chuckle. "You mean . . . raped?" he whispered.

Her eyes slit with anger as she bent toward him. His own drunkenness, the lack of light, and his flippant mood all came together and made her look like a reflection in a fun house mirror, her fat face twice as large as the one he saw when sober. A chubby index finger, surprising him because all he could see was her clown's face, pistoned into his chestbone while she spoke. "You just better put a real tight lid on it, Walter Higgins! And get your drunk ass in this house—what we got to say don't concern the neighbors!"

Still chuckling, and not really understanding much of what she'd said, Walter slid past her. Barbara, still certain that a prowler lurked about, looked beyond him toward the dark street, her drug-numbed brain even momentarily conjuring up a shadow-shrouded prowler, causing her to slam the door behind her.

With Barbara following close behind, Walter stumbled into the living room and plopped heavily into a faded green recliner, a chair he unwillingly shared with the family cat, a tabby named Carl. Having deftly avoided Walter's fat ass, Carl glared at Walter from an arm of the sofa to Walter's right. Walter just glared back. He hated Carl as much as Carl hated him.

"Well, aren't you going to check?" Barbara asked, the fat under her arms shaking muddily as she spread them wide in mock bewilderment. She'd been lucky just to get him home; having him check for what he probably considered to be a phantom prowler was a little too much to ask.

Walter turned with a stuttering grace indigenous to drunks. "For what?" he said.

"For what?" She had to stop and think a moment, temporarily having forgotten herself. A lot went on in her brain. "For the goddamned prowler—the goddamned prowler I called you about!"

Walter looked at Carl. "You seen any of them prowlers?" he asked.

The cat didn't budge. His eyes faintly hooded, Carl regarded Walter suspiciously, as he did anytime Walter spoke.

Walter looked at Barbara again. "There ain't no prowler. Carl told me!"

Barbara rolled her eyes, sighed heavily, and slapped her hands onto her wide hips. "Okay—just sit there then, you old drunk! Just go ahead and sit there while some pervert has his way with me!"

Walter let that thought bang around in his brain for a while. Finally he said, "You been readin' them harquins again?"

Barbara sighed with exasperation and turned away from her husband. She had been reading a Harlequin romance.

Walter regarded her with a semi-steady gaze. "Hah! Thought so!" he said.

With that, Barbara turned and huffed off angrily. At least she could now enjoy her coveted private time in peace. Walter would probably fall asleep right there where he sat. Maybe catch cold, she thought. Maybe a bad cold . . . maybe worse.

She marched up the stairs, sending shock waves into the stairway, went into their bedroom and flipped on the low-wattage overhead light. The bed, a queen-size sans headboard, was still unmade, the sheets and spread shoved around as if frenzied lust had recently invaded their marriage bed—it hadn't—not for the last five years. Lust and booze made strange bedfellows. In truth, Walter slept like electricity was being shot through him every twenty seconds and customarily kicked the covers to the foot of the bed. The smell of his booze sweat lingered in the sheets, but Barbara was used to it by now, her own smell not much better at times.

But even though their bedroom, like the rest of the house, was essentially a pigsty, the top of her antique cherry wood dresser and the mirror—especially the mirror—remained remarkably clean. One of the joys of Barbara's life, something she had been doing ever since she had put on the weight, was to spend some quiet time in front of her mirror running a brush through her long, radiant brown hair. Each night she stroked her hair at least two hundred times, each stroke as slow and as methodical as the last, as if she were under a trance, which, thanks to her Valium, she usually was.

She slipped out of her pink and white flowered house dress and panties, left them on the floor near the foot of the bed and shrugged into her red terry cloth bathrobe. Leaving the robe open, she sat down before her beloved mirror and picked up her brush. She wasn't smiling yet, at least not outwardly. But a ground swell was building.

At about the tenth stroke a light came on in the Martin's house across the street, a house reflected in the mirror. But because she had started her slow transformation, she didn't consciously notice. To her it was just another star blinking on during a foggy night.

Blinded to anything but her own miragelike reflection, she began her ritual. And once again, at stroke fifty, her chin line strengthened, becoming what it had been twenty-five years ago. A few minutes later the fat around her eyes melted away revealing a clearness, a youthfulness—a sultriness—that had not been there just a few minutes earlier. And so, by the hundred and fiftieth stroke, there once again appeared before her a woman of rare and delicate beauty. She even had recognizable breasts now, not simply fatty extensions. And no longer were her size ten, extra-wide feet straining against size eight and a half medium slippers. The transformation, blessedly, was complete.

Because she was so consumed by pleasure, she didn't notice the tapping, not at first. And when she finally did notice, it was only a gentle, soothing sound, a small branch leaning into the window from the large elm in the front yard. She put the brush down and looked slightly to the left of her reflection. Against the totally black backdrop, she saw only the light in the Martin's house across the street, and that only as a faint blip on the darkening radar screen of her mind. But the tapping continued. And even though she dismissed the tapping as pill-produced, she smiled demurely at her still beautiful reflection and turned in her chair to see what it could be.

His memories were vague, some pleasant, most not. The woman looking at him bore some resemblance to his mother—the hair, the eyes a little—but his mother had been . . . smaller. Not as fat! He was confused, awfully confused.

Her first thought was of Jeffrey, her missing nephew. Because she had loved Jeffrey very much, it did not occur to her to be frightened. Strange things occasionally happened after she'd taken her pills and brushed her hair, after she'd left reality behind. She had envisioned a brass bed last month and a slim-waisted, red dress lying on the coverlet. So why couldn't Jeffrey be standing at her window? Why couldn't her lovely nephew return to her for just a little while?

Snatches of an earlier life came back to him as he looked at the woman sitting in front of the mirror. He could see his mother handing him an ice cream cone; could see her pushing him on the swing at the park. And he could see her looking at him as if he were a stranger just before the old man. . . .

Barbara thought, *Ten years ago I was a very beautiful woman, and Jeffrey, my dear, sweet Jeffrey, was alive—so why can't he be alive now, now that I'm beautiful again?* She considered that for a moment, and her thought continued. *Yes, Jeffrey and Cynthia—it would be nice to see them again.*

"Jeffrey? Jeffrey—where's your mother, Jeffrey? Where's Cynthia?"

Her words made his head spin. He pointed at her.

Barbara smiled and shook her head lightly—this daydream was progressing nicely. She would gladly be his mother, given the chance. "No, Jeffrey," she said. "I'm your aunt, your aunt Barbara. Where's your mother? Is she with you?"

He looked to his left and right and then at the street, twenty feet below. Then he looked back at Barbara—back at the woman he thought was his mother. He pointed at her again, more rigidly this time.

"Dear, sweet Jeffrey—I'm not your mother, even though I wish I were."

There was an ache inside of him, a longing. Something was missing, something that had been here, in this house, something she alone could give him. He tapped again, harder this time, then again and again, quicker still, until his finger was being jammed into the window with such blinding speed that it no longer sounded like tapping. Now it was a steady, tenor thunk.

Barbara rediscovered reality with a numbing finality. She thought of her reflection, of the brass bed and the slim-waisted dress—all mirages, scabs of the truth. Even when she became transformed, she always could see a ghost of what really was, a double image—the truth beneath, what she wanted to be the truth lying over it—her house dress lying beneath the red dress, their simple bed beneath the brass bed. But this boy at the window did not present a ghostly image. Though she squinted and tried, she could not see through him. He was real, just as real as the jowly, ugly woman who customarily stared back at her from the mirror. With one last look into his large, brown eyes, she turned away and looked back into the mirror, fully expecting Jeffrey to be looking back at her. But he wasn't. He was gone. The mirror, save for her reflection, was empty. The tapping continued, but certainly it was nothing more than old pipes, or the gutters. *Sure,* she thought, *the gutters, that's all. Jeffrey's gone. Dead, probably.* She stared at her reflection for a very long time, then took a deep breath, let it out and pushed herself up. As she turned toward the window again, the numbing fear she instantly felt was muted by the prospect of insanity. If she were crazy, after all, then what she saw at the window—Jeffrey, his head cocked queerly to the side, his handsome little face too damn pale, his sad eyes too shot with blood—could be explained. "Just a hallucination, Mrs. Higgins, just the past playing silly little games," a shrink would tell her. And so, in his clinical, detached way, he would make it all better. She was crazy. Pure and simple. Alive, but crazy as hell. The sweat rose on her body and made her face gleam as if Vaseline had been smeared on it.

* * *

Rosita and Julio Vasquez, both in their early thirties and relative newcomers to the United States, walked casually down Main Street, past closed shops, past the fire station at the corner, and turned right onto Flint. They had stayed late at their restaurant, Antonio's, because business (thank the good Lord) had been unusually brisk, not only tonight, but for the last couple months. Word about Antonio's had spread quickly. You could get a good meal there, reasonably portioned, and best of all, sensibly priced—a hard to find combination these days. Still, they both knew the real test would come when, and if, they got some competition. For now though, Antonio's was the only place in town with ambiance enough to make you feel like you had gone out for the evening. Julio, a very observant man, had noticed the steadily growing number of cars headed for the interstate each morning. Clearly, there was money in Hunt, and like a dedicated capitalist, he wanted a chunk of it. So Julio and Rosita had invested their life savings—taking stock in the American Dream and holding firm to the adage that it takes money to make money.

They walked hand in hand, their palms cupped lightly together, choosing not to talk, content with each other's company. Their home, about a mile from the Higgins' home and on the other side of Main Street, was just beyond an area recently ravaged by the worst fire in the town's history, or at least as far back as anyone could remember. Cal Simmons, the town historian, said that in 1893 half a block went up in smoke, but there was no proof of that, just Cal's say so, which, because Cal's memory had begun to play tricks on him, sorely lacked credibility.

This recent fire had pulled in trucks from as far away as Rochester. Four homes had been ravaged that night, one month ago. Three had been leveled to the foundations, but one, although gutted, had been given a last-minute stay of execution. "Brick," the fire chief had said, "takes a lickin'. . . ." Each night, as they walked past, Rosita found herself thinking about the three little pigs and the big bad wolf, once even envisioning a huge pig standing on his hind legs sneering at her from the blackened doorway, a long, lit wooden match held between its cloven hooves. The light played onto his pig face and revealed a very sinister, human quality. It was not a vision she cared to remember, but at the same time found difficult to forget.

At night the house projected a near normal appearance. Its gabled three stories rose defiantly toward the black, starlit sky while an enormous oak in the front yard acted as sentinel. But the morning sun always burned the lie away. Every window had been blown out by the heat, and the roof looked like a bum's blanket.

Of course, it had only been blind, dumb luck that no one had been killed that fateful night. Bart Parkins, the fire chief, had been overcome by smoke, but he was back on the job. All four families had been away that evening: one at the four corners Methodist church christening their newborn, one at Antonio's having supper, the last two in Rochester visiting relatives. What could have been an immense disaster had only been disastrous in the sense that four families lost their homes and possessions.

The yard was still littered with charred and uncharred wood thrown from the house next door as firemen had battled the blaze. The heavy smell, almost tangible, hadn't dissipated yet—some, like Bart Parkins, who had expertise in that area, said it never would. A red streamer slung across the front steps had the word "HAZARD" printed onto it every six inches or so. An assortment of litter had caught up in the hedges fronting the tall, deep porch which wrapped around the front and sides of the house. It had been a magnificent home before the fire, easily the largest on the street, if not the entire town. So the remorse that gripped Julio and Rosita as they walked past, remorse for the family and for the house, for the splendor and majesty that had succumbed to the fire, leaving only the cloying odor of rotting, wet wood that stung their nostrils, the stench of decay and death, was only a natural reaction. Julio's face assumed a wizened look as he contemplated the irony, that the dark of night could mask the truth about this house. He smiled. He was such a romantic.

Feeling the caress of the rising wind on his face, Julio squeezed his wife's long-fingered hand and said, "There's opportunity here, Rosita. Here, dreams can come true."

But she had been distracted by movement on the porch. She pointed loosely.

Julio looked up just in time to see what he thought was a boy disappear beyond the front door. He thought of their next door neighbor's son, how he had snuck inside only to break his ankle as his foot punched through the weakened floor. And it was a good thing the kid hadn't done worse, Julio thought. At least with a broken ankle you could yell for help. With a broken neck you were just bat bait. That HAZARD warning was there for a reason, a damn good reason. Why was it kids always did the opposite of what a sign said to do? Don't walk, they'd walk; don't talk, they'd talk. HAZARD—YOU COULD BREAK YOUR GODDAMN NECK! FUN-TIME AT THE BURNED-OUT HULK! He let go of Rosita's hand and, as a sense of civic duty swelled within him, rushed into the front yard, just a step away from the HAZARD warning, now snapping in the wind.

"All right, come on," he said. "What are you trying to do—kill yourself?" Well, he mused, that was brilliant. Kids love to almost kill themselves. The closer the better. He hopped over the streamer and stepped onto the porch, the odor here strong enough to stop him abruptly, as if someone had slammed a door in his face. He fanned his nose.

"Oh, Julio," Rosita pleaded, "come on. Let the kid alone."

Apathetic, alienated. This country had done that to her. But he didn't have to approve.

"For God's sake, Rosita, we can't let him stay in there. What—you wanta read about him in the paper tomorrow? You wanta read about some stupid kid who got squashed by a ceiling or broke his neck because the floor couldn't hold him? Is that what you want?"

She only stared. Sure, that was okay with her—as long as nothing happened to them. It happened all the time in America.

Julio waved with disgust and stuck his head inside the doorway.

"Be careful, Julio, please be careful." She glanced up and down the dark street, hoping to find someone who could convince her stubborn husband that what he was doing was not only illegal, but stupid, too. But the street, save for a skinny mongrel dog slinking across the road fifty or so feet away, was empty. "Oh, Julio," she said somewhat frantically, shivering now despite the warm wind.

Julio squinted. "Where are you, boy?" he said only moderately loud, but still raising echoes. Because the windows were bare, moonlight easily found his eyes. They adjusted rapidly. About twenty feet in front of him was the stairway; to the left of it and down a long, thin hallway, the kitchen. Moonlight glinted dully off a dirty white stove and the back door just to the right. Tall floor-to-ceiling windows, popular when the house was built, rose from both sides of what Julio thought was probably the living room. Most of the ceiling and roof were gone, the jeweled night sky framed by a yawning, jagged hole. He felt a strange anxiety because of it. People couldn't live here now. Wild things, squirrels, skunks—he looked upward—birds, sure, birds. But not humans, not civilized humans, at least. And what about the obvious dangers? The floor, the fire-damaged, wind-weakened roof. The sooner he found that kid, the better off everyone would be. But then, maybe the kid had already left. Maybe he ran out the back door. As he stood very still and listened, he thought that was at least probable. He hadn't heard anything since he had walked in here; he hadn't seen anything.

"Come on, kid," he said, agitated now. "I'm a cop," he lied.

Still nothing, only the sound of the house screeching like a pain-filled old man against the buffeting wind. Julio shrugged lightly and glanced around one last time before he turned to leave. It was then he heard, "They're gone."

The voice, a boy's, came from his right. He wheeled. "How the hell?" he mumbled. The boy stood in front of a window, his small body outlined against it. Julio sucked in a deep, nerve-calming breath. The boy had frightened him, not a lot, but enough to raise his pulse rate.

"What do you mean, 'they're gone'? Of course, they're gone. No one lives here now. What's the matter with you?"

But even as he spoke, Julio assayed what the boy had said. Obviously the kid had lived here and for some ungodly reason still thought of it as home. Julio stepped toward him. "Come on," he said, hoping he sounded like an adult giving orders to a child. Something crunched underfoot. He stopped short, remembering the neighbor kid's broken ankle, and held his hand out to the boy, still about ten feet away.

"Come on," he said, forcing a calm demeanor, beckoning with his outstretched hand.

The boy only looked at him.

"Okay, okay—go out the window, then. Go out the window and I'll meet you on the porch. The porch is a hell of a lot safer. Go on!"

Julio waited, but the boy didn't budge. As Julio was about to try his command voice again, the boy said, "Take me to them."

"Well, now we're getting somewhere."

He took another step toward the boy, expecting another underfoot crunch. There was none. "Sure, whatever you say. Listen, I think they're back at my place waiting for you. Actually, they thought you might come back here, so they sent me to find you."

The boy cocked his head in bewilderment, then stepped toward him, stopping a foot or so away, his face more defined, his delicate features visible as well as his blue GIANTS jacket. But even over the odor of the house, a musty smell clouded about the boy. It saddened Julio to think the boy might be mistreated. He put a hand on the boy's shoulder and guided him out of the house and onto the porch. Even in the darkness he could see Rosita's shoulders droop.

"Oh, you found him," she said as Julio and the boy walked down the steps toward her.

"More like he found me," Julio said. "He worries me, though. I think we should take him home with us, at least for now."

Rosita's expression was a mixture of anger and confusion. "Home? Why, Julio? You got him out of there; you've done your duty."

Julio pointed at the boy. "Stay right here," he said and pulled Rosita out of earshot. "He's not real bright," he said like a ventriloquist.

"So? You're not too bright either, Julio. Anyone that would go inside a falling down house like that. . . ."

"I think he might be retarded, Rosita."

"Oh, you mean like my cousin, Carlotta?"

Julio nodded.

Rosita looked worriedly at the boy then back at her husband. "So, what do we do?"

"He thinks he lives here."

"You're kidding! Oh, I see, that's how. . . ."

"Exactly. Only someone like Carlotta, you know, retarded, would think like that. I told him his parents were at our house, that they sent me out to look for him. That's why we've got to take him home. At any rate, Sheriff Lucas will know what to do. I'll call him first thing."

"But it's late, Julio. What can the sheriff do now?"

Julio shrugged. "You're right. Well, if he has to—"

Rosita stopped him in mid-sentence. "Spend the night?"

"Just tonight."

"He smells!"

"We'll give him a bath."

Rosita spent an inordinate amount of time cleaning her small house. Letting this foul-smelling boy spend the night was not something she cared to do. But Julio, she knew, was probably right.

"Let's at least try the sheriff. Okay?"

Julio smiled lightly.

Stoically the boy went where he was led, Julio and Rosita flanking him, one small—very cold—hand held by each. Arriving at their house, a brown, fifty-year-old colonial with white trim and a tiny front yard, the boy stopped and slowly shook his head. Julio stepped in front of him, squatted and gripped his shoulders. "Don't be scared," he said. "This is our house."

The boy only stared.

Rosita bent at the waist and smiled an absurdly manufactured smile. "I'll make you a sandwich, how would that be?"

Confusion suddenly mapped the boy's face.

"A ham and cheese—on white bread," Rosita added. "I know boys don't like anything but white bread."

Julio sensed an inroad. "First a sandwich—ham and cheese on white—and then you can lie down and wait for your parents."

"In our new waterbed," Rosita said. "You can sleep in our waterbed. It's so comfortable. It's waveless—they're the best. Of course, you'll have to take a bath—"

"No!" the boy yelled, startling Rosita. "I won't lay down; I won't lay down!"

Julio felt a pin prick of anxiety, just another in a series he had felt since he had coaxed the boy out of the house. There was something alien about this kid, something Julio couldn't quite figure out. He smiled, hoping to counterbalance his anxiety.

"Well," he said, "we'll see. Maybe you're not tired right now, but later, after you've had something to eat—"

His eyes suddenly round with anger, the boy pushed Julio away. The strength in that shove startled Julio. "I won't lay down; I won't lay down!" he said again.

Porch lights began to flick on. "Julio," Rosita said, "maybe we should leave him out here. Maybe we should just go into the house and let him find his own way home."

Julio looked at the boy and actually gave that idea

some thought. Maybe Rosita was right; maybe he should be guided by her intuition. But he wasn't convinced. Had the boy not been, at least so he thought, retarded, he might have. But if he left the kid on the street, knowing that he would more than likely go back to that burned-out house . . . well, if something happened, he would never be able to forgive himself.

"Television," he said. "You like TV? We've got cable. Just had it installed. You got cable?"

The boy only stared, which, Julio concluded, was a vast improvement, prompting him to drape a hand onto the boy's shoulder. Surprisingly, the boy allowed it. Julio guided him toward the front steps. As they walked, the boy muttered, "I will not lay down; I will not lay down," almost as if he were repeating prayers.

Once inside, Rosita went into the kichen to prepare the sandwich she had promised while Julio flicked on the TV set. The boy stood in front of it and stared wildly, as if seeing television for the first time. The Red Sox and Yankees were in the eighth inning of a tie game. "Don't tell me you like them guys," Julio said.

Nothing, just the same wildly fascinated look.

"I guess it doesn't matter, although I usually don't let Yankee fans into the house." He patted the cushion next to him. "Come on, sit down."

To his surprise, the boy did as asked.

Well, Julio thought, *at least he's more open to suggestion now. He let me bring him into the house; he's watching the game. A little food, a little sleep and he'll be right as rain.* Julio smiled—he had never liked naps either. Kids were pretty much the same everywhere.

Rosita came around the couch, the promised ham and cheese on white on a plate. She attempted to hand it to the boy, but he only glanced at it and turned away.

"Here, you wanted him, you feed him," she said to Julio as she shoved the plate toward him.

"He's only distracted by the game, that's all," Julio said as he took the plate, a sheepish smile on his face, a smile Rosita didn't even begin to return.

Julio pushed the plate under the boy's chin. "Go on," he coaxed, then to Rosita, "He's really pale, isn't he?"

"And he still smells, Julio," Rosita said, which struck Julio as a little uncaring—the boy was sitting right there. Julio grimaced sourly and waved angrily at the screen as Ricky Henderson stole second.

Rosita curled up on the rocking chair, kitty corner to the couch. Suddenly the boy took the plate and set it on his lap.

"Go ahead," Julio prompted.

The boy looked at him and then picked up the sandwich and studied it as if through a microscope.

"It's only a sandwich. It's not going to bite!"

Like a curious animal, the boy sniffed at the sandwich.

"That's it," Julio said, "go ahead."

Carefully, the boy bit off a quarter-size piece, but he didn't chew; it simply sat in his half-open mouth. Julio glanced at his wife then back at the boy, who turned and looked at him, his eyes suggesting that he needed a little advice about what to do with the lump of dead animal meat on his tongue. Julio could only stare at the boy and at the chunk of ham and cheese on white until he had a thought. Mimicry. Maybe all this kid needed was for someone to show him . . . but, dear God, this was really strange! Why in the world should he need to show some eight-year-old how to eat? Obviously the kid hadn't fasted for the past eight years! But still, what else could he do? Everything indicated that this kid needed a teacher. Not really believing what he was doing, Julio began a proper chewing motion. The boy immediately parroted him. It had worked. But as Julio watched, he saw that it hadn't worked to perfection. He was chewing, sure, but like a machine. The food was still pretty much in one piece.

"Harder," Julio prompted. "No, no, bite the food. What's your name? No, no, don't answer that, just chew."

Rosita leaned forward. "Julio, what's wrong with him? What in the world is wrong with him?" she asked, anxiety drawn across her face.

Julio could only shrug. Eating was not something that required a Ph.D. He reached out and put a hand on the boy's chin. "Harder, you'll never get the job done that way!"

The boy's chewing motion suddenly became more natural, as if he had somehow only been out of practice.

"That's it, that's it," Julio said, wondering if he sounded too much like a cheerleader. "Now swallow."

So the boy did—but it was a loud, exaggerated effort. Julio smiled and rubbed his hands along his pant legs, then glanced for approval from Rosita.

"Okay, okay, now take another bite," he said to the boy.

The boy looked at the sandwich, then back at Julio, and as he did, a nauseous look fixed onto his small face. Seconds later his thin chest heaved spasmodically and the ham and cheese he had just swallowed came back up, furiously jettisoned to the carpeted floor.

Mumbling, Rosita pushed herself up and ran to the kitchen for paper towels while Julio attended to the boy, who was once again staring at the TV as Wade Boggs took a high slider for ball four and trotted down to first. "Call Sheriff Lucas," Julio yelled into the kitchen.

Rosita didn't answer, but he heard her lift the receiver, swearing as her haste caused her to misdial.

He leaned toward the boy. "You okay?" he asked.

The boy only watched as Boggs galloped to second after a wild pitch.

Seconds later Rosita returned armed with the paper towels.

As she picked up the food, she said, "The sheriff's not there, but the lady said that maybe we should take him to the hospital."

Julio looked at the boy. "He just needs some rest, that's all. Maybe he should lie down on the couch—"

The boy's eyes suddenly grew large, red saucers with pale blue, dime-sized centers. He turned toward Julio. "No! I won't lay down, I won't!" he screamed suddenly, just as suddenly returning his attention to the ballgame, or so it seemed.

Julio pushed himself up. "I'm calling the sheriff again," he said with conviction. "Let them handle this," he added as he walked toward the kitchen.

"Wait, I'm going with you," Rosita said with a sideways glance at the boy.

Julio stopped, regarding his wife. "What for? I'm just going into the kitchen. Rosita, you're not afraid. . . ."

"No, no. Of course not."

"Then, why . . . ?"

"Please, just go call. Please, Julio."

Julio and Rosita went into the kitchen, Rosita right behind him as he dialed.

The other end picked up after the third ring. "Sheriff's office. Ann Schaffer."

"This is Julio Vasquez—"

"Mr. Vasquez? Your wife just called."

"Yes, yes, I know. Listen, is the sheriff there?"

"No, not at this hour. And I really don't want to disturb him right now. He's had a very difficult week, what with his brother dying. . . ."

"Can you send someone over?"

"Is this an emergency, Mr. Vasquez."

Julio looked at Rosita, into her wide, anxious eyes. To her, this was most definitely an emergency, but to someone else. . . .

"No. No, I guess not."

"Is it about the boy? Are you going to take him to the hospital?"

"Well, I guess we'll have to now, won't we?"

He hung up and sighed.

"What'd she say?" Rosita said quickly.

"That the sheriff can't be disturbed. I guess we'll have to take him to the hospital ourselves."

"And who will pay the bill, Julio?"

He hadn't thought about that. "I guess he'll just have to stay the night, then. In the morning—"

"Damn!" Rosita said venomously, confusing Julio. She never swore; now she had sworn twice within five minutes.

"Look, maybe I should just put him into the car and drive him to the sheriff's office," Julio suggested, convinced now that they would probably have been better off if they had left him in the gutted eyesore where they had found him.

Rosita quickly agreed, saying, "Great, you take him; I'll put on some tea or something."

"I don't drink tea," Julio evenly reminded her.

"I said 'or something.' Just do it, Julio."

O thank you, God, thank you!

They went back into the living room, but the boy, inexplicably, was gone.

Julio glanced at the stairs. "Probably just went to the bathroom," he said.

But Rosita wasn't sure. She half expected him to spring from some dark corner of the living room and spray her with whatever hadn't taken the last ride out of his stomach.

Agitated by his wife's paranoiac display—her eyes were like those of a cornered rat—Julio said, "C'mon, Rosita, he's just a kid, a small boy."

Suddenly they heard a noise in their bedroom, directly above them. They looked upward at the shadow-dappled ceiling. "See," Julio said with a small measure of relief, a knowing smile on his face, "he's decided to take a nap. Well, I'm going up there and tuck him in. You can stay here if you want, but I'm going to tuck that boy in."

As Roger Clemens hummed a fastball on the outside corner for strike three, Rosita, as undecided as she had ever been, simply followed her husband up the stairs.

CHAPTER FOUR

Judd Lucas put the ax down and toweled a thick accumulation of sweat from his broad forehead. It was as he walked in to answer the phone that he realized he was only dreaming. He forced himself to open his eyes, understanding then that the phone was indeed ringing—in both worlds. He washed his hands over his face, sat up and picked up the receiver.

"Yeah?" The scratchiness in his throat was obvious. He cleared, then tried again. "Sheriff Lucas."

"Ann, Sheriff."

Judd glanced at his watch on the coffee table beside him: 8:15. "Kinda early, Ann."

"Late night, Sheriff?" she asked, her tone vaguely inquisitive. She had never given up hope that one day they would be the subject of town gossip. Her interest in him was well-known—she made little effort to hide it—even though he obviously still carried a torch for his wife, wherever the hell she was. And from time to time, Judd had to admit, he too had fantasies of the two of them passionately entwined, mostly in the storage room while she took her break. Hell, she was attractive, and he was still a man, with wants, desires. Still, each time he thought about making the transition from fantasy to reality, he'd give his wedding ring a twirl and forget about it.

"No, I didn't have a late night, Ann. What's up?"

"Couple reports, that's all. I'd have Ed take care of them, but one concerns your in-laws. Neighbors been complainin' again."

"The usual?"

"'Fraid so. Listen, I know you said you wanted to take care of that stuff personally, but I can send Ed—"

"No, no. I'll handle it. I've been meaning to talk with them anyway."

"Still owe you that money, huh?"

Judd felt his body go limp. *Small towns,* he thought. *Might as well put a sign in the window. "Hey, guess what, Barb and Walt owe me a bundle. Come one, come all, see the debtors, see the debtee."* He cleared his throat. "You said, reports?"

"Yeah, couple kids broke into one of the new houses out at Hidden Valley. You wanta handle that, too?"

"Sure," Judd answered without hesitating. It was about time he went out there and had a look around, met some people.

After he hung up, he called up to the loft and asked Steven if he wanted to go into town or stay here. Steven came to the railing and peered down at his uncle, a low dread on his face. Normal, Judd thought. These woods could be scary sometimes. A variety of carnivorous animals made their homes here. Steven shrugged as if to say it didn't really matter, secretly hoping his Uncle Judd would read the look on his face and take him with him.

"Well," Judd offered, "why don't you come along. Give us time to get to know each other better anyway."

Steven tried to suppress a smile, with little success.

In the Jeep, Judd ran his fingers through his hair and flipped the channel to a local C&W station. As Gentleman Jim Reeves belted out a tune as smooth as fresh oil, he settled back and glanced toward Steven, who rolled his eyes. Judd hadn't always liked country and western, but it had managed to grow on him over the years. Lately, though, it seemed the rock and rollers were spending big bucks on huge transmitters—WCMF, out of Rochester, rocked into town with hurricane force.

As he drove, he thought about Walter and Barbara, how they were up to their old tricks—if there was one thing Walter and Barbara did well, it was create a nuisance. Walter would struggle home, barely conscious, and Barbara would holler at him because it was all his fault she had gotten so fat, which was actually partly true. If Walter could drink, Barbara rationalized, then she could damn well eat and pop a Valium now and then. Judd often wondered how Cynthia would look today if she were still alive—and with no evidence to the contrary, he could still hope. But her twin sister certainly hadn't aged gracefully.

Rolling past The Krohbar and The Settler's Post, he remembered—how could he forget?—the two grand he had lent Barbara and Walter to get the place fixed up: the roof needed patching, the plumbing pounded like a thunderstorm, the basement collected water. He had only given it to them because he hated to see the house fall apart like that. Sure, he had only lived there a couple of years, but he couldn't put a price tag on his memories. Letting Walter and Barbara run roughshod over the old house cheapened his memories just as surely as rust rots a car. He wasn't about to let an important part of his past die just because they couldn't give two shits.

He parked behind a black Camaro a house down from Walter and Barbara's and told Steven to stay put. As he got out, he checked for movement at the windows. *Oh, damn, it's Judd come for a payment.* He had called from the Jeep, but no one had answered, which was just part of the routine. Every time Walter and Barbara disturbed the peace, they didn't answer the phone. It was a game they played with him, a big, stupid game, and that, Judd thought, was too bad because Walter could be okay at times—when he was sober, which wasn't too often. He didn't at all envy them their lives, their day-to-day existence, just waiting for the last one. He walked up the front path and then veered off toward the side door.

He knocked with his fist, glad that they were quiet now and wondering what excuse they would have this time. He waited a few seconds, heard nothing, then knocked again, a little harder. Still nothing. He put his face against the glass, his hands blocking the glare. The kitchen was empty. *Maybe they're out,* he thought. *Maybe they walked to Breens or something.* They did that sometimes. Walter would make some crack about Barbara's weight and add that walking might take some of it off, so she'd say something about his drinking. Eventually they would agree to a walk to Breens, a mile and a half away, Barbara commenting along the way how many calories she had burned and how no one was going to look funny at her much longer. Usually she'd pick up a gallon of Flavor-Rite ice cream and maybe a Breens deep-dish apple pie—just to bolster the strength she had lost.

Judd knocked again, louder this time. But he wasn't as agitated as he probably should have been. He was experiencing a low-wattage electric dread, and as he looked into the kitchen, he felt empty, as if he were peering into a mausoleum. In the back of his mind a disturbingly loud voice told him that no one lived in this house now. Despite the warm, sleep-inducing wind and the teasing smell of baked goods wafting from the house next door, he knew that this house—a house he knew so well—could no longer be called a home. He prayed he was wrong, but inside, where the truth lay covered by a thin and quickly disintegrating blanket of denial, he knew he was right. Feeling a rush of frustration and anxiety, he elbowed in the window. The gunshot-like noise of glass breaking smashed through the quiet neighborhood, and Judd had a fleeting vision of aroused townfolk coming to the Higgins' aid armed with frying pans, shovels, and pitchforks. He waited a second, and when nothing happened he reached in, unlocked the door and stepped inside. The smell was hotly sour, as if the cat had used the stove as a litter box. But Judd knew the smell, and Carl wasn't to blame.

Judd proceeded cautiously. If Walter and Barbara

were dead, and had died by other than natural causes—and natural causes were highly unlikely—then their killer could still be in the house. It had happened before, nutcases who would sometimes masturbate over their victims in a lust-crazed baptism of death, and then seek out some far corner of the house in which to hide, to stoke their madness. It was rare, sure, but it happened—hopefully not here, in Hunt—but it happened.

As he turned the corner of the kitchen and looked into the living room, he sighed audibly. Walter was on the floor, obviously dead. His mouth was open, a huge circle of dried blood soaked into his shirt like some grotesque tie-dye design. Judd walked over and dropped to his right knee over the body. Through a puzzle of emotions, he noticed that Walter actually looked content, more so than he had looked in a long time.

Just to be sure, Judd called softly, "Walter? Walter?" Nothing. "C'mon, Walter, you can do it." Still nothing.

A low groan worked out of him. Walter didn't deserve this fate—no one did. In what was a purely mechanical motion, Judd pulled the blue slip cover off the sofa and let it flutter onto Walter's remains. Where was Barbara? Upstairs? In the basement, maybe? He started upstairs, and as he grabbed the railing and looked toward the landing, he envisioned her there, fussing with her hair, pulling down her tight-fitting static-charged skirt. This was how he would remember her—Barbara at her best.

He found her slumped in the chair in front of her mirror. Her huge chest was torn open; the room, mirror included, painted with blood suggesting that she may have thrashed about just before her heart stopped. Her dead eyes were like those of a half-awake doll. He reached over, hesitated briefly, and then applied the necessary pressure to close them. He glanced around. The window was open, but he didn't bother to close it. The scene had to remain essentially unchanged. But still, he couldn't bring himself to leave without covering Barbara, as he had Walter. He pulled the cream-colored spread off the rumpled bed, draped it over her, then left the room. He stopped just outside. Carl was sitting on the top stair looking at him. The cat uttered a feeble cry—as if he somehow knew—then walked slowly past and into the bedroom.

After he had searched the house and grounds thoroughly, Judd went to his car. And even though he knew Steven had to find out sometime, Judd hoped the look on his face wouldn't arouse suspicion.

"What were you looking for, Uncle Judd?" Steven asked with passing curiosity as Judd slid in behind the wheel and flipped on the two-way radio.

"What?"

Steven's brow tightened thoughtfully. "You looked like you were looking for something."

"Oh, that. Nothing. Listen, Steven . . . something's happened." Judd hesitated briefly, expecting a response. There was none. "So I'd really appreciate it if you'd be a pal and sit there until we get things straightened out—okay?"

Steven looked at the house then back at his uncle. Judd thought he wanted to say something, but he didn't. He simply nodded slightly.

He knows, dammit, he knows. He can smell it! Judd smiled, but it was forced, he knew that, and Steven, he thought, probably knew it, too. He radioed the town's three deputies, hoping they felt sharp today. They would need it. He would need it. For Ed Land and Ricky Smits, this would be their first door-to-door. *Hope you three got your sleep last night,* he mused, smiling another tight smile at Steven.

Somebody had to have seen something, anything, even though there was no sign of forced entry, no doors jimmied, no windows busted. And the front and side doors had been locked. The only thing even remotely suspicious was the open bedroom window, but in this weather, even that was normal. He had searched the area beneath the window for footprints and ladder impressions—not a one. The house, except for the open window, had been tightly closed. No one could have entered and then left without leaving some kind of sign. He remembered something he'd heard in a Charlie Chan mystery: Even a snail drags a trail. He shuddered—a snail wasn't responsible for what had happened inside.

His deputies, two men and a woman, sirens blaring, rolled onto Fitzhugh and skidded to a halt. They got out and hurried over. Their uniforms, gray with black trim, were badly wrinkled. They had been issued hats, but only Estelle Meath chose to wear one, her brown hair stuffed under it. Judd pulled them out of earshot and told them what had happened. Ricky Smits, a short, neat, bald man with a red face and light blue eyes, was the first to speak. "Did you find anything, chief?" he asked, trying very hard to mask his excitement—this was his first murder, as well as his first door-to-door.

Judd looked at them: Rick, Estelle Meath, Ed Land. Estelle, a tall, hard-looking woman with dark eyes and hawk-like features, was easily the most efficient of the three. Ed Land's only claim was his size—he was probably the thinnest man in town—but luckily he could take a joke—usually about his size—as well as anyone.

"I haven't got much," Judd began. "The bedroom window's been left open, but that's not real unusual. I want you three to go door-to-door. Someone must have seen something. Ben's been contacted. Listen . . . don't take 'No' for an answer. Like I said, someone must have seen or heard something. Find him—or her. Ed, take the other side. Estelle, you and Ricky take this side. Good luck."

Judd left Steven in the Jeep and went back into the house. Standing in the doorway of the living room, he forced himself to look at Walter's remains. Although he was not an overtly religious man, he said a silent prayer for Walter's soul, vaguely envisioning him stumbling into some heavenly bar and asking for credit. Perhaps passing Barbara on her way back from the heavenly Breens. He smiled faintly. Sure, Walter was a drunk, a bum, but what the hell, everybody had to be something.

The county M.E., Dr. Ben Weisanthal, arrived a few minutes later, parking his '85 Volvo a few houses down to make room for the ambulance. Pushing seventy now, Ben Weisanthal had the body of a man half his age, not because of genetics, but because he daily found the time to shove a tape into his VCR and body-synch Richard Simmons. His gray, November-sky eyes saw most, missed little. The disgust was powerfully evident on his long, smooth face.

"Judd," he said, "my condolences. Terrible, just terrible." He looked closely at his friend. "If you want, I'll stop at Temple later, say a few words. I know it's not your way, but you never know." He spoke with his hands cupped as if he were preparing to pray.

Judd appreciated the gesture. "Sure, thanks, Ben. You know, they weren't bad people, not really." *Business, Judd, disassociation.* "Listen, I didn't touch either body, except to close Barbara's eyes. Well, I covered her, too."

Nodding slightly, Weisanthal gingerly lifted the sofa spread covering Walter's remains. "Oughta be a law," he said softly as he slowly withdrew the covering, pulling it down to Walter's chest. "Any weapon?"

"Not that I can find. I didn't look closely at the wounds, but they don't appear to have been inflicted by a knife. Knife wounds aren't as wide or as jagged. I mean, if someone did this with a knife, they had to have been homicidal and drunk." Ben looked at him, he at Ben. They had both thought of Walter swaying back and forth, a butcher knife in his hand. "It's almost as though the skin has been somehow pulled apart."

Just then Ed Land strolled into the room and stood near the doorway, hands clasped together as he waited to be acknowledged, a habit that infuriated Judd.

"Okay, what is it, Ed?" he asked, the deputy displaying no sense of urgency.

"Sheriff, they . . . that is, the Martins, other side of the street? They found something in their backyard, thought you might wanta take a look."

"What, Ed?"

"Clothes, kid's clothes."

Judd felt faint as he envisioned Jeffrey the night he had disappeared: bunny slippers, bathrobe.

"Probably don't concern the case much, but I thought . . ." Land continued.

"No, that's okay, Ed. Lead on," Judd replied, a gang of emotions running through him.

His feet barely touched the ground as he followed Land across the street to the Martins. He floated on the wings of memory, his son more real now than he had been in a very long time. He almost expected him to pop up in front of him. He spied a blue Dodge. *Maybe he's in the front seat of that car, just waiting to scare me like he used to do. Maybe . . . maybe . . .* Judd thought. The locked-up Dodge was quickly behind him.

Abigail Martin, a short, matronly, middle-aged woman, had the articles of clothing spread out on her kitchen table. The morning sun shining through the patio doors fell onto them harshly, making them look less soiled than they really were. Judd immediately recognized them as Jeffrey's. His father's words came back to him; "Best not show 'em what's in ya, Judd, boy. Best to keep it there, keep 'em guessin'." It was something he had become proficient at over the years. With stoic detachment, he silently tried to ascertain just how the clothing his son had been wearing the night he disappeared could possibly find its way into the Martin backyard the morning after Walter and Barbara had been brutally murdered.

"They were near the clothesline, Sheriff," Abigail Martin cut in. "And the underwear—never seen such filthy underwear—they were inside the robe. Those slippers? They were down at the bottom, you know, like some poor child had just . . . stepped out of them."

Judd's first priority was Steven. He took him to the cabin, spent ten minutes looking for Sam—to no avail—and told Steven he'd be back later, that there was work to be done. Steven tried his best, but he obviously did not like staying alone. As he drove off, Judd cursed the dog for his sense of independence.

After he had tagged the clothing as evidence, he pretended to busy himself with paperwork. He was alone, except for Ann, whom he could not see from his glass-enclosed office. Eventually he put the folder he had been thumbing through on the table and mindlessly began rearranging the clutter on his desk: assorted snapshots, a pen holder, an empty in-and-out box. On the top right corner of his desk lay a puzzle similar to Rubick's Cube called the Brain Puzzler. He picked it up, fumbled with it, then put it down. *Yeah, sure,* he thought, *brain teasers in my state of mind!*

An hour later, as Judd splashed water onto his face, Fred Parsons, the primary developer of Hidden Valley, called. The impatience in his voice was aggravating.

"I assume, Sheriff, that you intend to talk with those two boys?"

"Why wouldn't I?"

Parsons ignored the question. "And I'll tell you something else—if I find anything out of the ordinary, I won't hesitate to press charges. Kids today have to learn more respect for property; that's all there is to it, Sheriff!"

Judd's list of things to do was a mile long, and last on it was chewing out a couple of kids because they had been kids, because they had explored some half-finished house in the dead of night. Hell, he had done worse—lots worse. But then, maybe it would take his mind off things: Jeffrey's clothing, Jeffrey's life. Cynthia.

"I'll get on it," he said tiredly, hoping Parson's noticed the disdain in his tone.

Parsons pressed the issue, not hearing the respectfulness he thought due him. "See that you do, Sheriff! It's because of me that this town is beginning to thrive. It was my insight and my ability to recognize the value of that property that has saved this town—you remember that!"

You made your point—butthole—can it! was what Judd really wanted to say, but responsibility took precedence. "With you to remind me, how could I ever forget?"

The sharp smack of the receiver spanked Judd on the ear. Heat began to build around his collar. He had little patience with people like Parsons.

A few minutes later he got into his Cherokee and drove to Hidden Valley, his mind about as focused as the view through a kaleidoscope.

Brian Ferguson and Andy Swartz were sitting in the Ferguson living room with their parents. The boys and their mothers stayed on the couch while Ben Ferguson and Lenny Swartz, Andy's father, answered the door.

As Ben Ferguson opened the door, Judd couldn't help but notice how large a man Lenny Swartz was, easily six and a half feet tall and close to two hundred and fifty pounds. The dark face and carpeting body hair made him look like a caveman who shopped all the right stores. Guided into the living room, Judd was introduced to Carol Ferguson. Attractive, in a girl next door kind of way, he thought: freshly scrubbed, pale blue eyes, pretty, yet not pretty enough to puzzle your thoughts. Linda Swartz, on the other hand, was plain. Her medium-length brown hair was straight, and her nose and mouth were overly large, as was the wart on the side of her neck. The boys needed no introduction. The dark-haired one was Andy; the other, shorter and with blond hair, Brian. A quick perusal of the living room left him impressed by only one thing—a vase, a three-foot-tall gaily-colored Chinese vase that Judd knew had not been bought in Hunt. Vases like this one were bought only in ultra-exclusive stores. The most exclusive store in Hunt was a high-class men's store that sold Italian shirts for sixty-five bucks each. The vase was at the foot of the stairs on a tall, white pedestal, which was, Judd thought, a stupid place to put it.

As he looked at the boys, he knew this wouldn't be easy. But he *was* the law this side of town, and he had a duty to perform.

The boys didn't fidget, even when he tried to raise his voice, which, he thought, made him sound like Rod Steiger on a bad day. When he was done, Andy looked at Brian then back at Judd. "We weren't the only ones there, Sheriff," he said.

Judd raised an eyebrow. *Spread the guilt a little, huh, kid?* He really didn't want this boy to squeal.

"Yeah, there was some kid there before us—probably did that stuff in the basement."

Judd's curiosity was mildly piqued. "Stuff in the basement? What stuff in the basement?"

"A dead rabbit—I didn't do it, honest! Brian saw him. He thought I was playing a joke on him, but I wasn't—honest!"

Dead rabbit in the basement—rain on the roof. Rabbits died as quickly as they multiplied. "Did you damage the house at all, boys?"

"No—that window was already . . . busted!" Andy said, realizing by the time he had started that he would have to finish. He shrunk slightly in his seat.

"He's right, he's right," Brian blurted, glad to have this slender thread of truth to hold on to. He wasn't at all sure that Andy wasn't lying about the other boy. And the rabbit—this was the first he'd heard about that.

Judd studied the boys, who had nudged closer together on the flowered sofa. "Listen, boys, I'm going to have to check this out. Now, a dead rabbit in the basement—well, I'm not worried about that. But I hope that's all I find." He looked at Ben. "Mr. Ferguson, you mind if I use your phone?"

Ferguson nodded.

Before he left the room, he called the two men

aside. "You folks are new around here. Usually Hunt's a sleepy little town. But we had a tragedy in town, either last night or today. A couple were—" he groped for the right word—"guess there's no way to be gentle about this. We had a double homicide. . . ."

"Who—where?" Lenny Swartz asked disbelievingly. He had moved out here for the solitude, for the peace—hell, if he'd wanted murder, he would have stayed in the city.

Calmly, Judd said, "Like I told you, in town, man and his wife." He toyed with the idea of telling them the victims were his relations, but decided against it. No reason for them to know that. "Let me set your mind at ease. I've been the sheriff here for nine years now. We've had some missing persons, but this, this is only our second homicide. The first one took place at a pizza parlor, armed robbery where a clerk tried to be a hero. That happened eight years ago, and it'll most likely be a lot longer than that before it happens again."

He had tried to be authoritative, like he had some secret information regarding the inner workings of killers' minds. Looking into their faces, he knew it hadn't worked. He left the room and called Ann.

"No address, chief," she said. "It's the last house on the left on Hidden Pines Road. That Parsons fella wants you to look around real good. If there's any damage, he wants the parents to pay for it."

Judd hesitated, then said, "Takes money to make money, doesn't it, Ann? Call me if Ben calls."

"Chief?"

"Cause of death, Ann."

"Oh . . ."

A few minutes later, Judd turned into the driveway of the house the boys had allegedly broken into. Three workmen were standing by the garage.

"It's open, isn't it?" Judd asked as he got out of the Jeep.

A short black man wearing a Georgetown University T-shirt said it was, adding that they hadn't gone in yet because Mr. Parsons told them not to. Judd walked past them and into the house, leaving the front door open. He searched the first floor then the basement. The rabbit was near the furnace. The condition of the carcass disturbed him. It was as if all the air had been let out of the thing. Simon would want a look at it, he thought, if only because of the unusual condition of the remains. He went outside. The workmen hadn't moved. To the black man he said, "Listen, I need a bag or something. You got anything lying around?"

"What for?" the man asked nonchalantly.

"You got a dead rabbit in the basement. I'm going to take it with me."

The workman smiled. "A dead rabbit—in there?"

"In the basement."

"Wasn't there yesterday."

"It's there now. The bag?"

The man shrugged and went around to the rear of the house. "This oughta do," he said when he returned, an empty cement bag in his hand. "Lord knows what a man would want with a dead rabbit, though."

Judd thanked him and took the bag, adding that he would need a shovel.

The man gave him one, and Judd went back into

the basement and picked up the rabbit. After he had folded the bag over and put it into the backseat of the Cherokee, he went back into the house. It was from a second-floor bedroom window that he noticed the clothing lying in the hayfield about a quarter of a mile away.

When he got there, he found jeans, underwear, a faded red sweater and a pair of sneakers. Again as if a boy had just stepped out of them.

CHAPTER FIVE

1966
JUDD loves ROSEMARY.
ROBERT loves CYNTHIA.
MARTIN loves HIS AUNTY MAUDE.

The bleachers were packed with the hopeful, the faithful and the mildly curious: students, teachers, parents and a few people who had simply wandered in. At the edge of the arena, vivacious, tight-muscled, bouncing cheerleaders in peek-a-boo skirts and chest-hugging sweaters with the name Hunt Bull-dogs plastered in blue and red across the front, spurred the ballplayers on with spelling lessons, acrobatics, and an occasional shrill whistle from the ruby-red lips of Rosemary Hamilton. On the court, Rosemary's beau, Judd Lucas, shifted his feet with consummate skill and grace. The man he was guarding, Judd knew, was about ready to let go with his patented top-of-the-key jumper. As a matter of routine, Coach Myers gave Judd the assignment of shadowing the other team's best player; not only was Judd quick afoot, but he had an agile brain as well. The same could not be said for most of the other players. Judd's man stopped dribbling, drew the ball into his hands, flexed his legs and eyed the basket. With pickpocket-fast hands, Judd slapped the ball away, hustled after it, dribbled the length of the court and layed the ball in, sending the crowd into a crescendo of bleacher-rattling applause. And so it went for most of the game. Occasionally the opposition player dropped his jumper; but more often than not Judd made him hurry his shot or stole the ball cleanly, and by the end of the game the Hunt Bulldogs had chalked up their eighth win in a row.

In the now emptying bleachers, toward the top left, sat Cynthia Voorhees, one of the faithful, and Robert All, one of the mildly curious. They were, as a couple, the talk of the school, the mismatch of the century. Robert, big and tall and reputedly more than a little dumb, seemed to have gained her love purely by the power of suggestion. And that suggestion, if the scuttlebutt bandied about the girls' locker room was to be believed, had everything to do with his eyes, his mysterious, sea-blue eyes, eyes he had inherited from his dead father.

And as Cynthia knew, he was also remarkably possessive—all she had to do was glance in another boy's direction and those mesmerizing bedroom eyes would change dramatically, becoming what she could only term as homicidal. But tonight, right after the game, she told herself—having practiced her speech in front of her bedroom mirror—she'd tell it to him like it was. They were through. *Finis*. There was someone else, she would lie, although she did have romantic thoughts concerning that scrappy little ballplayer, Judd Lucas. She had even questioned Rosemary Hamilton about their relationship, how solid it was, whether she ever thought about going out with someone else, although her questions were not so blatantly asked, more couched in innuendo and supposition.

Sitting next to Robert was his best friend, Martin Crouper, a short, fat, not-very-nice-smelling man of forty-two with a cluster of acne on his forehead. Their May-December relationship was, on the surface, exceedingly strange. But although their physical differences were obvious, their emotional needs were pretty much the same, their relationship born out of the process of elimination. Bobby was overbearing, right most of the time, given to fits of violent temper and as impatient as a new groom, character flaws that the morose and brooding Martin had little trouble accepting. No one wanted to befriend Martin except Bobby, and no one wanted to befriend Bobby except Martin; a take-off on the last person on earth philosophy, hardly sound footing for a lasting relationship. But although their friendship got off to a sputtering start, it soon strengthened. Each was the other's crutch, someone with whom he could be himself and not worry about the outcome. They were salt and pepper, sure, but they were also the rose and its bouquet of thorns. Wrong for all the right reasons, and right for all the wrong reasons.

Rumor had it that Martin had never had a date, that his Aunty Maude, almost a hundred years old now, was his best girl, that a lot of the money he earned as custodian for the four corners churches went to buying her gifts. Martin, Cynthia thought, was just another reason to make a clean break, just one more straw.

Gruffly, Bobby All said, "I could play like that. I just don't wanta run around in front of all these people in my skivvies."

Martin laughed obscenely as Robert elbowed him.

But Cynthia had pretended not to hear. He knew damn well he couldn't play like that; he was just being superior in the only way he knew how. The bleachers almost empty, she looked at him, sucked in a deep breath, and let it out. "C'mon," she said, "we gotta talk."

"What about?" Bobby said, curious because topics of conversation were usually left up to him, and had been ever since they'd started dating a couple of weeks earlier.

She looked at him and at Martin, who quietly expressed just as much interest as Bobby. "Us," she said flatly, looking straight into Bobby All's hypnotizing eyes.

"Us? What do you mean, us?"

"Not here."

Bobby shrugged, stood and stretched his large, tight jeans and T-shirt-clad body. "Yeah, c'mon. Out in the hall," he said as though what she had to say would only be a distraction.

For what she had to say, Cynthia thought, it would probably be wise to have a few people milling about. She really had no way of knowing how he might react.

"Okay, out in the hall," she responded.

"C'mon, Martin," Bobby said as he hopped down to the next bleacher.

"No," Cynthia demanded with as much finality as she could summon. "Martin's got nothing to do with this." She looked at Martin. "Do you, Martin?"

Martin looked hopefully at Bobby, who said, "Be back in a flash. Why don't you go on out to the car and pop us a cold one."

Martin didn't answer; he simply got up, walked across the gym floor through a milling, happy crowd, and disappeared out the double swinging doors.

Cynthia walked in front of Bobby purposely, showing him only her back and not the look on her face, a look he was certain to read. She had always thought that despite his lousy grades and his misunderstood-rebel image, there was a smoldering intelligence behind those eyes. There had to be. With eyes like that. . . .

"Whoa, wait up," Bobby said, grabbing her by the elbow. "You got me out in the hall. Say what you gotta say."

Saying what she had to say, she knew, would take all the courage she had. And as she looked dead into those eyes, the brows coming together above his nose, little arrows of blood drifting in a field of blue, she knew that he knew exactly what was coming next.

And just as she was ready to tell him it was over, he smiled benignly, and said, "You'll never be shed of me, Cynthia, never." He pulled his class ring off his finger, letting it rest on his palm. "I was gonna give this to you tonight, let the world know." He fisted the ring tightly. "But you go ahead, run off to that ballplayer. Yeah, I saw that look in your eyes. Christ, you jumped around like a cat every time he did something! Well, you go on, do what you gotta do. But just know this. What we got is forever. What we got no man can take away. Ever!"

And with that said, he stroked her cheek with grandfatherly gentleness, turned and walked away, the crowd stepping aside, Bobby All allowing no quarter, as if the hall were empty of everyone but him.

Watching him, Cynthia's relief at being shed of him was diluted by not only what he had said, but how he had said it, as if it were actually true, as if there was absolutely nothing she could do to prevent it. As he took a left at an intersecting hallway and disappeared, she wondered if a slap across the face might not have been better. More final.

CHAPTER SIX

The Present

Wispy cirrus tickled the edge of space while the nestling sun turned the sky a soft, warm pink. Night would slip into town unnoticed. The phone rang in the sheriff's office. Ann Schaffer picked up the receiver.

"Hi," said a male voice on the other end of the line. "I'm the maitre d' down at Antonio's."

"Antonio's? Oh, sure, I know the place. Good T-bone. What's the problem, sir?"

"Probably nothin', but my bosses aren't here yet."

"Is that unusual, Mr. . . . ?"

"Sharpe, Neil Sharpe. I guess it's not real unusual, but they're usually right on time. I tried to call them, but no one answered."

"They?"

"Julio and Rosita Vasquez, that's V-a-s—"

"That's okay, I got it."

"They live on Bellows Ave. Two-twelve. I thought

they'd at least have called in by now. They're always here at opening time, you know, greet the customers, that kind of thing?"

"I'm sure there's a logical explanation, Mr. Sharpe, but we'll send a deputy out to the house anyway."

"Thanks. They're probably just out somewhere, or their phone's out of order, you know, not ringin' on their end."

"One or the other. We'll look into it."

She hung up. While she had been on the phone, Ed Land had returned to the office. She waved him over.

"What's up?" Ed said.

"I know you're busy, Ed, but you think you could go to this address and just make sure everything's okay? Their maitre d' is worried."

"Maitre d'?"

"Yeah, they own Antonio's, you know, the new place?"

"Oh, yeah, I've eaten there." He paused.

"Well?" she finally said.

"Jeez, Ann, I am pretty busy."

"C'mon, won't take long." She smiled like a vixen. "You can call Gloria when you get back."

"Shit, Ann, you never are gonna let me live that down, are you?"

She shook her head slowly, the vixen smile still evident.

Ed Land left the office and slid in behind the wheel of his cruiser. Given a preference, he would have chosen to follow up on the leads they had gotten from

Walt and Barb Higgins' neighbors—almost everyone had seen something, from shadows to a group of armed men. Sure, most of the reports were probably dead ends, but there was the off chance that he might luck onto the one clue that could lead them to the killer. And that would be a real career maker. He'd get the sheriff's job when Judd Lucas called it quits. But Judd Lucas was still the sheriff and, through the dispatcher, had given him a task, albeit a minor one. Hell, he'd probably find—what were their names? He looked at the report—Julio and Rosita Vasquez. Well, he'd probably find them doinking each other in the living room. Just because they didn't feel like going in to work didn't mean anything bad had happened to them for Christ sake!

It was a muggy evening, and Ed Land was having a hell of a time keeping his underarms dry. If there was anything he hated, it was wet pits. He stopped his cruiser in front of the Vasquez house and got out. *Not much of a house,* he thought, *'specially for restaurant owners . . . restaurateurs, yeah, restaurateurs. Think they'd own something a little bigger. Hell, I would.* As he walked up the steps and onto the porch, he listened for sounds of love-making. He thought he heard something, but he hadn't. He was just horny. The sounds he had heard were in his head, just a playback of the last time he and Gloria had done it, more than a week ago. (When she had come up from Elmira.) She was a strange one, that Gloria. Some women preferred muscled beach types, some liked them hairy; Gloria liked them skinny, the skinnier the better. She never told him why, but after he had given it a great deal of thought, he concluded, much to his satisfaction, that each part of him represented a penis: his toothpick arms and legs, even his sticking-out ribs. He was a goddamn walking, talking phallic symbol! A trip to Elmira, he thought, might be in order. Real soon.

Hitching his gun belt onto his thin hips, he looked for a doorbell; finding none, he rapped on the door. Nothing. He knocked again, louder—still nothing. *Shit,* he thought, and tried the door. It was unlocked. He opened it, stepped inside and closed it behind him.

He heard voices. They were home, he thought, and hadn't heard his knock. "Hello?" he said moderately loud while he waited for his eyes to adjust to the feeble light coming from the kitchen. "Anyone home?"

He stepped into the living room and realized that the voices he'd heard had come from the television. He walked in, watched about five seconds of the *Cosby Show* and then flicked off the set. He turned toward the kitchen, vaguely hearing the steady electric hum of the refrigerator, but nothing else.

"Damn!" he said, envisioning another scene like the one Sheriff Lucas had happened onto.

"This is Deputy Ed Land," he yelled. "Is there anyone home?"

The silence that followed, although only lasting a few seconds, sent a rattle of apprehension up his back. And when he heard a noise in the basement, the hairs on the back of his head stood at attention. He hesitated only briefly before he fumbled his gun out of its holster and stepped lightly toward the kitchen, supposing he would find the basement door there.

"Anyone home?" he said again, his voice a little higher and with a little more vibrato than usual. He thought of calling for a backup, but dismissed the idea; if nothing—untoward—had happened here, he'd be the laughing stock of the department.

He stepped into the semi-lighted kitchen. On the wood-look countertop, near the white porcelain sink, he saw a partially eaten ham and cheese sandwich. He picked up the plate, touched the sandwich, then put it back down. The bread felt like a shingle. Out the back window, some eighty feet or so away, he saw a light blue house with a white roof. There was an old woman in the window of what was probably the kitchen. She looked up and waved with just her hand, like a child. Ed Land waved back with his gun hand and noticed, as he did, that it was getting dark. Shadows had elongated and thickened, the sky a blue-gray now. He watched the woman disappear and secretly wished she hadn't. Company was two; company was good. Safe. *Where'd you go, lady? Come on back, give us another little wave.* The light went off in the blue house, and Ed drew in a quieting breath and turned away from the window, toward the cellar door. He gripped the gun, flipped off the safety, then pulled the door open and stuck his head into the opening. To his right was a light switch; below him about ten feet, the light. His muscles stalled a moment. At least in the dark he couldn't see what—*Christ, that's stupid,* he thought, chastising himself. He was a man with a big gun—safety off. *Stand up straight, Ed. Get this over with!* With a flourish he flicked on the light and immediately heard movement off to his right as the glow from the bulb at the bottom of the stairs spread throughout the cellar. "Hello?" he yelled, his tone friendlier than he had intended.

More movement, feet shuffling along the cement floor, something shattering.

Tensing, he yelled, "All right, who's down there?" *That's it, Ed,* he thought, *good command voice, get on top of this thing!*

Never having been tested, Ed Land wasn't sure whether he was brave or not. Gripping the gun hard enough to whiten his fingertips, he reasoned that the gun in his hand went a long way toward determining just how brave he was going to be. He stepped onto the first stair and concentrated on being as quiet as possible, but the stairs were old, tired. They groaned like worn-out knees. He took in a nerve-deadening breath and with crisp, sure steps walked down the stairs. Once down, gun raised, eyes working feverishly, he turned a slow circle. To his left was an octopus furnace, heat ducts fingering into the floorboards; to his right a stack of random-size boxes lay spaced a few feet away from the back wall. All the windows were boarded over in an obvious attempt to keep burglars out. There had been a number of burglaries over the last ten years or so, and many homeowners had done the same because basement windows offered easy access. He saw a pair of storm doors off to the right, toward the back of the house, and briefly wondered if they were as secure as the windows. His eyes fully adjusted now, Ed saw what had shattered. On the floor in front of the stack of boxes lay a broken lamp, the shade dented, pieces of the red base spread over the gray cement. Ed raised his eyes and squinted at what he thought was a shadow against the back wall. Obviously someone had knocked over the lamp in his haste to hide. Gun raised, Ed stooped under a heat duct and walked slowly toward the shadow, his focus concentrated on the burglar he fully expected to find hunkering down behind those boxes. "C'mon out!" he said in a conversational tone, his prey cornered. "I'm armed and prepared to defend myself!" *There,* he thought, *that oughta flush this joker.*

The shadow slowly grew in size, and seconds later Ed Land looked into the dark face of a young boy dressed in a blue jacket, the letters G-I-A-N-T-S vaguely outlined on it. Holstering his gun, Ed breathed a sigh of relief. "What the hell are you doing down here, kid?" he asked. "You live here?"

The boy said nothing.

"C'mon, answer me."

No response.

"Okay, we'll just have to go find your parents, then. They're gonna be plenty pissed, too." He stepped lightly toward the boy, arm extended, as the boy stepped toward him. Now Ed could see that his clothing was worn and soiled, although he did appear healthy, his cheeks ruddy, his gait strong. Ed squatted and cupped the boy's shoulders, looking into his clear, round eyes. It was then he saw a trace of blood at the side of the boy's mouth. Had he hurt himself trying to get away? Ed tugged out his handkerchief and dabbed at the spot, but the more he dabbed, the more blood appeared. *This kid's gonna need some stitches for sure,* Ed thought.

"What happened, kid?" he asked. "Your parents

do this?" Anger and revulsion swelled within him. How could anyone hurt a kid? There were agencies—see if this kid's parents didn't pay!

But Ed's silent commiserating did not last for very long. The boy curled back his upper lip, his eyes opening wider than Ed thought possible. And Ed could not believe what he was seeing. The boy had . . . fangs, long, white, pointed fangs. Utterly confused now, Ed fell backward and scuttled crablike across the floor. But the boy was amazingly fast and unbelievably strong. He rushed toward him and forced Ed's head to the cement, sending a shock wave of pain down his back. And while Ed lay dazed, the boy bent to him and sank his fangs deep into the deputy's neck. Semi-conscious, Ed Land did not realize that his mortal life was about to end, and as the blood siphoned out of him and his body pistoned up and down in a futile attempt to break free, his fingers groped for something—anything. Seconds before he died, Ed Land clutched a piece of broken ceramic, and as his muscles tensed in a death grip, it carved a jagged line into his palm.

It bled.

His last mortal thought was of his girl, Gloria.

CHAPTER SEVEN

Later

Harry Kroh thought, *I've seen this guy before.* Harry never forgot a face, especially one like the young man sitting at the bar in front of him had. Everything was so large. And the eyes—like a goddamn cat!

Harry, owner and bartender of The Krohbar, had been idly listening to a group of customers at the far end of the bar as they talked about Barb and Walt Higgins; the usual, how when it happens to people you know it drives home like a spike through the heart and, in so doing, makes you paranoid as hell. It had been, to Harry's way of thinking, a real shame (Harry often understated the obvious), Walt being a regular and a decent enough guy to boot. The town grapevine, as firmly rooted as any, had it that they had finally done each other in. But a more persistent, more nefarious rumor had it a little different: They had been murdered by some crazy, or a group of crazies. *Well, it doesn't matter much, I guess,* Harry mused. *They're dead. Conjecture about how they died ain't about to bring them back.*

Still half-thinking about just where he had seen this guy before, Harry toweled off the bar and asked him his preference.

The man's cold eyes brightened, and Harry thought he might smile; but he didn't. "I doubt you serve it here," he said.

Harry thought he had detected amusement in the man's voice. He shoved a towel into a glass and squeaked it clean. "Don't take no bets on that, pal," he said. "I learned to make just about anything at bartender school."

And Harry was abundantly proud of his prowess behind the bar, even though his knowledge was of little use. Most of his patrons drank beer, occasionally a margarita, but rarely did he have occasion to mix anything even remotely exotic. Actually, Harry was a little out of practice, so he hoped this guy wouldn't take his bet.

Harry was about to ask him again what he wanted when the man said, "You got any objections to my just sitting here for a while? I'm expecting someone."

The bar was fairly crowded this evening, to let him just sit wouldn't be at all profitable.

Harry was casual. "S'that right? So when's this friend of yours gonna show up?"

A smile parted the man's lips. "Oh, I see. I'm occupying a bar stool, and you, like everyone, has to make a buck."

Harry Kroh ground his palms hard into the bar

and locked his elbows. He liked to display his Popeye forearms, especially when the situation called for it. "Think of it, well, like, like you're a car and the seat's a parkin' meter—long as you feed it, you don't get ticketed. Now, you don't feed it, you don't park."

The man stared blankly at Harry, reached into his shirt pocket, took out a wad of bills and folded out a twenty. Laying it on the still-wet counter, he said, "That should buy this parkin' space for a while, shouldn't it?"

Harry picked up the twenty and pocketed it. "Man's gotta feed his family," he said, even though he wasn't married.

The formalities disposed of, Harry again tried to recall just where he had seen this guy before. Except for a brief stint in the Navy, he'd lived in Hunt his entire life. He knew just about everyone, past and present. He stared at the man, who had turned away to watch the crowd, and searched his memory banks. Big, dressed way out of style, tan cotton slacks and shirt to match, his brown hair cut long, about an inch past his collar—the stranger appeared to be watching four middle-aged women in the middle of the room. They, Harry thought, were too busy having a good time to notice him. Harry recognized them: Two worked at the paper factory, one was a secretary for a local lawyer and the fourth, Rosemary Hamilton, owned The Settler's Post flower shop two doors down. What was strange, however, was that one of the women was Teddy Dorsey's wife, and everyone knew that Teddy Dorsey and Rosemary Hamilton were getting it on. Harry was dumbfounded—what the hell did those two women have to get chummy over? Harry had asked Rosemary out, and she had politely, yet firmly, turned him down. Harry could appreciate this guy's interest—a lot of people snuck leerful glances at her. Suddenly it dawned on Harry just who this guy was.

"You're Bobby All—right?" he said to the back of the man's head.

The man turned, cocking his head slightly. "Excuse me?"

"Bobby All—you went to high school with my sister, Elaine. Yeah, sure, she used to talk about you all the time. Yeah, I remember her sayin' somethin' about you and the sheriff's wife just yesterday. Now, what was her name? Cynthia, that's it, sure, Cynthia . . . about what a strange couple—jeez, I'm sorry. I got a real big mouth sometimes."

Robert All smiled naturally, putting Harry more at ease.

"Well, you look, hell, you look great. Elaine's gotta be your age, forty or so, right? But she looks it. Hell, you look, shit, like you're still in your twenties."

"I've led a good life," he said.

"Yeah, it shows. Keep out of the sun I'll bet, too. That's the ticket, you know; you stay out of the sun and you'll live longer. A tan might look great now, but later on you'll pay for it."

"I avoid the sun at all costs."

Harry grinned and tapped his forehead. "Smart. Real smart. So, you live around here or what?"

"Just visiting, for now. Life has been . . . hectic. Maybe a few years in a small town like this would do me some good. What do you think?"

"Sure, why not? Everyone likes it here—no traffic jams, no crime. Well, I shouldn't say 'no' crime."

"Yeah, I heard about the murders."

"Walt Higgins came in here all the time. Good guy. Shame, real shame. Say, you sure you don't want something? Twenty bucks'll buy you a few cases of Genny."

Robert All looked at his watch. "No. I'm going to be leaving in a little while."

"Whatever you say. Really somethin', I mean, real coincidental Elaine just sayin' somethin' about you and you showin' up here."

A sage look fixed itself to Robert All's face. "If you wait long enough, Harry, coincidence kind of loses its meaning."

Harry Kroh thought a moment and then smiled an empty smile.

Either she was stupid or she just didn't give a shit. She had to know—hell, everyone knew! When her girlfriend, Sharon, called and asked her to meet her here, mentioning that she was bringing a couple of friends along, she had no idea Sue Dorsey was going to be one of them. Talk about your coincidences! But when Sharon introduced them, she saw no flicker of anger, no trace of the truth on her face. She had simply smiled like anyone meeting anyone, pleasantly, half-interested, not at all suspicious.

She was a big woman, easily six feet tall, and reasonably attractive, Rosemary thought. Her eyes were a pretty greenish-gray, her tanned skin flawless, her hair dark and long. Her features were a little large, but then, so was she. She'd probably look a little silly with a tiny nose and a tiny mouth, Rosemary thought.

Throughout the evening they had gotten to know each other better. She was okay, too, Rosemary decided; bright, witty. How the hell the truth had slipped by her, she didn't know. But then, maybe she knew the truth; maybe she was just setting her up. There was that possibility. Every now and then she would look at Rosemary and let her gaze linger for just the briefest of moments, almost as if she were reading her mind, which was remotely unsettling, but not enough so to cause her worry. Rosemary prided herself on being able to read people—this lady sitting across from her knew nothing about her and Teddy, not a damn thing. At that moment Susan Dorsey gave her "that look" again. This time, however, she spoke. "I used to dabble in floral arrangements, you know, simple things. I'll bet you've got some fabulous stuff, though. Tell me, do you do special orders, too? I mean, could you come over to the house sometime and take a look at my decor, you know, maybe recommend what kind of floral arrangements would be complementary?"

"Oh, sure, I do it all the time. Where do you live, Susan?"

Susan gestured to her left. "Right behind the high school. My husband teaches there. It's close enough so that he can walk to work."

"Just let me know when it's convenient, and I'll be happy to help you out."

"Oh, that'd be great. And I'll be sure to pick an evening when my husband's there—you'd like him.

He's very handsome. Some people say I was a little lucky to get him; I mean, I'm not exactly Miss America."

"Oh, you're too modest, Susan! I think you're very pretty. I wish I had skin like yours. You don't wear any makeup, do you?"

"Oh, absolutely not—it's bad for your skin. I was one of the lucky ones. Even as a teenager I never had one pimple, even when I was in cycle."

"Lucky you! When it came to pimples, I felt like Custer at Little Big Horn!"

Susan laughed politely. "You couldn't tell that now—no scars, nothing. And you do have a wonderful figure."

Again that look, but this time Rosemary attached little significance to it. Obviously envious, Susan Dorsey, like everyone, was just reacting to her voluptuousness in the only way she knew how—breathlessly and wordlessly.

Susan seemed to fidget. "Listen, Rosemary, I know this might sound a bit impulsive, but how about right now? My husband's not home, but well, that's okay. You see, we're seriously considering remodeling soon anyway, especially the bathroom, and I'd just love to have you take a look. How about it?" Her smile was like that of a very old friend.

Rosemary Hamilton thought a moment and finally considered that now just might be an opportune time to get this thing over with. She knew Teddy was out, and that meant she wouldn't have to worry about a face-to-face with him while his wife looked on in bewilderment. Teddy, dear one-track-mind Teddy, just might blurt out the truth, thinking his wife had brought her home to clear the air. Yes, now would be a good time—get it over with, suggest something to her and then leave. The next time she could warn Teddy beforehand—if there was a next time.

"Why not," she said. "Let's go. I've had one too many, anyway."

As Susan Dorsey got up and turned, she glanced toward the bar. The large man in tan she had noticed earlier was watching her, or at least he appeared to be watching her; she couldn't really tell. The lighting was terrible, and a circle of white-blue cigarette smoke had gathered around him. She felt a tightness in her chest. There was something strange about him, not simply the way he was dressed or the way he stared, but something else. When he looked at her, it was as though they shared a secret. She thought about Teddy and unsuccessfully tried to squelch a shudder; her attention was diverted as Rosemary Hamilton got up, smiled and said, "Ready whenever you are, Susan."

Once outside, they walked by Rosemary's flower shop and paused briefly to admire a few of the creations in the window. Susan pointed at a tall, wide grouping and said that peach and beige flowers, similar to the ones in the arrangement, were colors that would complement her decor—after they had remodeled. She turned toward Rosemary and smiled.

They took a left at the end of the block and left Main Street behind. A few hundred yards later, the shadow-scarred gray face of the three-story high school rose from its well-maintained lawns, a sprinkling of young, fragile evergreen trees in front. They walked quickly, their route taking them in front of the high school then around to the side. Sue Dorsey didn't exactly live behind the school; her home was on one of the side streets. Although there were no street lights here, the full moon behind them lit their way nicely. Almost grotesquely, their gray-black shadows exaggerated their size. Sue Dorsey was about a head taller, but their shadows on the sidewalk suggested that she was twice as large.

"Did you see that man at the bar?" Susan asked as they turned left.

"Which one? There were quite a few men at the bar."

"The tall, weird-looking guy all dressed in tan. Real strange-looking character!"

A mental picture looped through her brain. Although she did remember someone vaguely familiar at the bar dressed in tan, she didn't get a good look at him. "I saw someone, but not real well. Why?"

"I caught him staring at us."

"Well, The Krohbar is a bar, and men in bars do stare."

"I guess you're right."

A street sign indicated the corner of Elm and Scio streets.

"Right down here," Susan said. "Fifth house on the right. I hope you like it. Like I said, we've still got a lot of remodeling to do, but we've already done some. It's an older home, but then, there aren't many new homes in town, except for the new subdivisions, you know, like The Oaks or Hidden Valley. We talked about buying a house there, but I don't know, this is really convenient."

"Well, the school's only a stone's throw away. You said your husband—I'm sorry, what's his name?"

"Teddy."

"Teddy? I've got a cousin named Teddy. He's out?"

"Bowling. They got a summer league up at school. Teddy joined. Couple nights a week, but what the heck, gives me a chance to get out when I can, when I'm not working the B shift."

Rosemary remembered Teddy telling her about the bowling team, what a great excuse it was. It was only one night a week, not two, like he had told Susan. The other night was theirs. It seemed so weird to be listening to this. Sue Dorsey seemed so loving, so trusting.

"Do you have any children, Susan?"

Teddy had proudly displayed a walletful of snapshots: Ted Jr. riding a horse, Ted Jr. playing ball, Ted Jr. smiling. He was nine now, the blond hair his dad's, the large features, Susan's.

"One, a boy," Susan said. "He's visiting his grandparents for a couple of weeks. They live on a farm."

"I'll bet there's plenty to keep him busy there."

Sue Dorsey smiled slightly. "Oh, sure, there's always something to do on a farm. I grew up on a farm, the very same farm."

They turned right onto the sidewalk, then walked onto the porch. Susan stuck the key in the keyhole and pushed open the door. They were greeted by the soft light of the interior.

"Well?" Susan said.

"Thanks," Rosemary responded, stepping past her and into the hallway. To her right was the dining room, to her left, the living room, large-flowered wallpaper, leaded glass and dark wood moldings throughout. Straight ahead and to the right of the hall was the kitchen, and the stairway stood directly in front of them. Susan touched Rosemary lightly on the shoulder and stepped past her, stopping at the stairway. Holding on to the bannister and leaning forward, she hollered up the stairs. "Teddy? Are you home yet, dear? We have company."

God, Rosemary thought, *she sounds like a fifties sitcom!*

Susan turned and looked at Rosemary. "Oh, well, guess not. Sometimes he comes home early; sometimes he doesn't. I think it all depends on if they win or not." She spread her arms wide, palms out. "Well, what do you think?"

"I thought you said you'd already done some remodeling?"

"Upstairs. Most people start downstairs and work up—we decided to do the opposite. But we are keeping essentially the same concepts, you know, colors, paper, that kind of thing. Come on up and have a look, or would you like a cup of coffee first?"

"Maybe later."

"Sure. Let's look first, then we can chat."

Susan waved her forward and followed her up the L-shaped stairway and into the upstairs hall. Again she found flowered wallpaper and dark wood moldings. To her right was the bathroom; in front of her, a linen closet. There appeared to be three bedrooms, two to her left and one to her right, beyond the bathroom. The bedroom doors were all closed, but the bathroom door stood open, although the light was off. Rosemary stuck her head inside. The plain, white shower curtain, which looked light gray in the dark, had been drawn. To the left of the shower was a double sink and mirror. Suddenly she felt Susan's hand on her shoulder. For no conscious reason, she turned abruptly, fear beginning to bubble inside of her.

With a round-eyed smile that smacked of insanity, Susan Dorsey whispered, "Better not go in there—you might disturb Teddy—he's taking a bath."

Taking a bath—how can that be? Rosemary thought. *He's not home! Christ, he's bowling; that's what you said. . . .* Suddenly shit-scared, she felt Susan's hand tighten on her shoulder and saw her face harden once more. "And he certainly needs a bath—he's awfully dirty. He's got blood all over him, Rosemary!"

The only word she really heard was "blood." She pulled away and stumbled into the bathroom while Susan stayed in the doorway. She glanced to her left, at the shower curtain. It couldn't be true, it just couldn't, but Susan's face, which fairly screamed insanity now, said differently. Behind that shower curtain lay her lover, probably in a pool of bloodied water and Dial soap.

"Go ahead, have a look," Susan whispered, her eyes filled with childish glee.

"Why—why did you do it—why?" Rosemary cried.

The questioning look on Susan's face was genuine. "Why not? He took a vow. He said he'd be faithful, and he wasn't. He lied, and liars have to pay for their lies."

Rosemary could feel her left eye begin to twitch, as it often did when she was under stress. "Oh, God—what about me? Please, don't hurt me, Susan, don't hurt me!" she pleaded.

"Hurt you? Hurt you! . . . I've already killed Teddy; one more won't mean anything. And besides, Teddy's waiting for you . . . somewhere."

Susan stepped gracefully into the bathroom, only a few feet away now, the knife in her hand glinting dully. Rosemary stepped backward until she couldn't go any farther, then leaned against the dressing table, quite positive that her life was over.

But then, the doorbell rang.

"Shit!" Susan said, a fanatical resolve suddenly replacing the homicidal rage on her face.

"Help—help!" Rosemary yelled. "She's going to kill me—help!"

"Bitch!" Susan blurted, a dollop of spit gathering at the corner of her mouth. "Shut up or I'll kill you right now—do you understand?"

Susan held the knife in front of her, just a few feet away from Rosemary's belly. Rosemary froze.

"Come with me. And don't say anything because I'll have this knife at your back all the while. I'd kill you now, but I want you to say goodbye to your lover first."

Susan grabbed Rosemary by the arm, twisted, and followed her down the stairs, wondering all the while if the person at the door had heard Rosemary's blubbering cries.

The front door was covered by a white, full-length

curtain. Susan and Rosemary stopped a few feet away. As promised, Susan touched the blade to Rosemary's back.

"Yes?" she called, trying for nonchalance.

"My name is Robert; I saw you at the bar. May I come in?"

"You saw me at the bar?"

"Yes." A pause. "I know what you've done, Susan. If you let me in, maybe we can work something out."

How did he know?

After seeing *Psycho,* Teddy had harbored a secret fear of showers. Bashing him over the head with his fucking bowling ball while he washed the sweat off his ass had given her immense pleasure. But how did this guy know?

"What are you talking about. I haven't done anything."

"Sure you have. We both know that."

"What then—what have I done?"

That was stupid, she thought, she might as well tell the whole goddamn world!

"You've taken someone's life, haven't you? A precious, human life!" He seemed to be having fun with his phrasing.

Her mind raced. He knew—somehow, he knew! She had no choice. She'd let him in, kill him, take Rosemary upstairs, kill her, then. . . .

"I'm going to open the door," Susan Dorsey said.

"Good idea."

"Open the door," she said to Rosemary. "And remember, I'm right behind you."

Rosemary inched forward, grasped the knob, then pulled.

Robert All smiled at the two women. "You're not alone," he said.

"Brilliant. You wanted in, come on in."

"Thanks. I try not to enter where I'm not welcome."

He had a somewhat flat face and a barrel chest. And with a growing trepidation, Susan thought he looked a little stupid, like some big kid away from home for the first time, even though she guessed his age at around twenty-three or so. He carried himself with uncanny grace, however, a fact she further noticed as he stepped inside. And it was then she saw that each finger of his hand displayed a ring of precious stone encircled by glittering gold.

He looked at Rosemary and Susan. (At? No, not at—through maybe, into maybe—like some super mechanic checking out a new car, his eyes studying critically, but he certainly did not look merely at them.) This scrutiny did not go unnoticed by either woman; it revealed itself in the fact that they could actually hear themselves breathe now. And Rosemary was beginning to realize that she knew this man.

He turned slightly. "This is my friend, Cynthia," he continued.

From behind him there stepped a stunning woman with long, wavy, blond hair and an alabaster complexion. She was dressed in a white, long-sleeve blouse and Jordache jeans, the jeans fitting so snugly they revealed every inch of her perfect figure. Around her neck, weirdly enough, was a class ring, a man's. Rosemary knew her instantly. This was Judd's wife—Judd Lucas's wife. She was back! In the farthest depths of conscious thought, Rosemary pictured her own face and body, how the mirror had begun to reveal the laugh lines and crow's feet of approaching middle age, even though she was still a very attractive woman. How her body, although still firm and supple, had begun to feel the effect of forty years of gravity. Her breasts had more sag than Cynthia's; her thighs were fuller. And Cynthia's skin . . . so perfect, so white.

Finally Cynthia looked at Robert. "What do you want with these two?" she asked, a trace of amusement in her question.

"The one in back, the plain one, killed someone," he answered in a strangely soft voice. The words poured out of his chest like hailstones on tin. Susan was growing nervous; she didn't even mind being called plain. Were they cops? There was that possibility. She was almost beginning to wish—

"So, you killed someone, did you?" Cynthia said.

"Close the door," Susan ordered. It would be tough, but if she were fast enough. . . .

They stepped farther into the hallway and stopped about five feet away from the two women. Robert smiled, revealing a set of exceedingly bright, straight teeth. "Where's your victim?" he asked, that damnable amusement still evident.

Susan's face screwed up with confusion. Unable to control herself, she glanced quickly toward the ceiling, realizing instantly what she had done.

"Ahh," Robert said, smiling slightly. "Cynthia, go upstairs and bring the body down."

By now, Rosemary had come to her senses. "Bobby All, Cynthia—what the hell is going on here," she asked. "Where have you been, Cynthia? And what are you doing with him?" she continued, her words running nervously together.

Without a word in response, Cynthia stepped silently past Susan and Rosemary, then glided soundlessly up the stairs. Susan had briefly contemplated a quick stab at her as she whisked past, but thought better of it. Better to get them close together.

"How long ago did you do it?" Robert asked, as if he were asking directions.

"Jesus—how the hell. . . ."

"Couple hours—couple days? Oh, don't worry, atonement doesn't concern me."

"This evening, dammit! The son-of-a-bitch is in the tub for Christ sake!"

"Let me guess—you found out that Rosemary was having an affair with your husband; so you killed him, and you were about to kill her when Cynthia and I showed up."

Not knowing what to say—he had said enough—Sue Dorsey didn't say anything. Seconds later, Cynthia reappeared, and despite her slender build, she effortlessly carried the nude, dead body of Teddy Dorsey over her shoulder. Rosemary looked at her dead lover, his rear end pimpled and white, dime-sized droplets of blood falling to the carpet, then looked away. This insanity made her stomach churn acidly. She had a sudden urge to make a run for it. Despite the fact that she knew both All and Cynthia—or had—they weren't the people she remembered. The change was more than just physical, although that physical change expressed itself in the fact that they had barely changed at all. No longer was he the oafish braggart she remembered. He had a new confidence, an awareness, the ability to command a roomful of strangers by his mere presence. Cynthia looked at Robert, who nodded toward the living room and the dark green sofa against the far wall. She walked crisply to it and flopped Teddy down on his back while Robert extended his arm toward the living room and smiled. "Ladies," he said.

Susan and Rosemary did as they were told.

"Cynthia," Robert said, "I hope this is a fresh kill."

"The body's barely cold," Cynthia answered without hesitation.

"Then, watch these two."

After he'd said that, Susan saw an opening. Two women watched by one—a very large opening. As he stepped toward Teddy, Robert stopped and smiled. "Take my word for it, ladies—she stands guard as well as anyone." And with that said, Robert stepped toward Teddy Dorsey, dropped to one knee and, while Rosemary and Susan watched unbelievingly, sank his teeth into the corpse's neck and began to suck.

In reality, a flower-papered living room with a green sofa and assorted dark-wood tables surrounded Robert All. But when he fed, he was surrounded by desert sands, hot underfoot, and a blazing sun overhead. This was what he had always loved, the life he had wished to live. Immortality, although bringing with it certain advantages, could not rival white sands and hot, summer suns. There were no suns in immortality, just a blazing fever to reclaim mortal existence, if only for a little while. So whenever he fed, he closed his eyes and drifted while the blood coursed through him, strengthening and revitalizing. And as an immortal, he also discovered that his imagination was stronger, easier to call upon.

He heard the man's wife say something about "What the hell is he doing?" and thought, *Ignorant human, what the hell's it look like I'm doing?* He sometimes had little patience with mortals. He didn't like his pleasure disturbed by inanity.

He stayed over Teddy Dorsey for a long—and pleasurable—time. Rosemary wondered if these two were the ones who had killed Walt and Barb Higgins. If they had—what was going to happen to her and Susan? Mentally and physically drained, Rosemary Hamilton fainted. She fell limply to the floor, leaving Susan standing alone, the knife in her hand.

After he was finished, Robert All stood and wiped the blood away from his mouth with the back of his huge, bejeweled hand. *My God, his face,* Susan thought. *It's changed!* And it had. When he arrived, his face had been almost chalk white. It had a vibrant pinkish glow now, like a newborn's. Cynthia walked past him and, using the punctures created by Robert All, drank what was left. Immediately, her face changed, too. Susan Dorsey's belated response was to grip the knife as hard as she could and viciously utter, "Stay away from me—just stay the hell away! I don't know who you are—or what you are—but I'll kill you both, so help me God, I'll kill you dead!"

Robert All chuckled. "God, you are a dim bulb," he said. "What is it with you humans? I mean, you get all the proof you need, and still you don't believe!

The supernatural, Susan, is real, just as real as that knife you want to kill us with. Which, by the way, would do you about as much good as a rotten carrot!"

Suddenly, with uncanny speed, he dropped to one knee, gripped the back of Rosemary's slender neck firmly in one hand, and yanked. The snapping sound, like a whip striking hardwood, reverberated throughout the otherwise quiet house and raised a loud gasp from Susan. Robert, still bent over Rosemary, looked up at Cynthia, who turned away from Susan just long enough to allow her time to turn and run into the kitchen. Cynthia ran after her, catching her just as she opened the back door, freedom, or so she thought, only a few feet away. As she felt a hand on her shoulder, Susan turned, jamming the knife into Cynthia's stomach. But much to her confusion and horror, the knife simply slipped in and then slipped out, as if she had stuck it into fresh butter. Frantically, she clawed at her attacker, her nails finding Cynthia's face and throat, the chained ring tearing loose and falling unnoticed to the floor. But she may as well have been trying to draw blood from a stone. All she could do was stare incredulously as Cynthia emotionlessly reached out and, as Robert All had done to Rosemary Hamilton, wrapped a hand around her neck and snapped it as easily as if she were breaking twigs for a fire. Susan slumped dead to the floor; Cynthia left her there and rejoined Robert in the living room.

"Should we take them to the house?" she asked.

"Better than leaving them here," Robert answered. "Besides, Martin might like the company."

Her smile bordered on obscene. "You really

enjoyed that, didn't you?" she said.

"Killing her?"

Cynthia nodded.

Robert All smiled. "Immensely. Any friend of your husband's. . . ."

She nestled next to him. "And there's another boy now. His nephew, Steven."

CHAPTER EIGHT

The Next Morning

Judd snatched up his pencil and hurriedly wrote down the name and address, 18 St. Alben's Place, in an apartment complex called Chimney Ridge, and her name, Gloria Sternmyer. Only now did he learn her last name. Gloria Sternmyer from Elmira, where this call had originated from. Ed Land had been seen leaving the building very early that morning, in uniform. The body had been found by Delsa Luck, Gloria's ride to work.

"My deputy, any sign of him?"

"All we got's the patrol car, Sheriff. Found it parked around back, in the condo's lot. All the windows closed, locked up."

"The girl . . . ?"

"What about her?"

"Was she sexually molested in any way?"

"Can't tell that yet. She doesn't appear to have been, although you can't always go by first glance.

She is fully clothed, though. Well, a nighty and panties. We're going to forego the prelims until you arrive, out of courtesy, because your deputy may be involved. Of course, the patrol car's gonna have to be impounded as evidence in a possible homicide, you understand that."

"Yeah, sure, I understand. Those other things . . . ?"

The first thing Sheriff Crown had mentioned were a number of oddities, although he didn't detail them, only labeling them as oddities. Judd pressed him about those oddities, but Crown was vague. "Rather not discuss it just yet, you understand. See you in about an hour?"

Christ, Judd thought, *dangle a carrot!* "At the most," he said, a little irritated.

He had gotten the call at home, as he splashed some milk into a bowl of fork-stirred eggs, salt, pepper, nutmeg, and a dash of basil. He had planned to make an omelet—his very first, forsaking the help of a recipe book. A couple of days earlier he'd spent an hour at Breens stocking up on essentials, and even a few luxuries; the first step, he thought, toward putting some meat on Steven's bones. Of course, eating right wouldn't hurt Judd either. Steven sat patiently at the kitchen table, trusting his uncle, but only to a certain point. As he watched Judd shake spice after spice into the mix, he began to wonder about his uncle's culinary ability, which, Judd assured him, was at least adequate.

Judd pulled a sheet of Saran Wrap over the bowl, thwacked it with his finger to make sure it was tight, and shoved it into the refrigerator while Steven tied the laces on his sneakers.

"Is Elmira a long ways?" Steven asked.

"Forty miles maybe," Judd said.

"Are you gonna stay there all day?"

"That depends. I'll have to call. Listen, I'm going to leave you with my deputy, Estelle. She's a nice lady."

"What about Sam?"

The dog had left the house just as the top arc of the sun broke the cloudless horizon.

"We should be home in time to let him in. You all set?"

Steven nodded.

Elmira, about twice the size of Hunt, was just waking up as Judd's Cherokee rolled into town. To the left and right shopkeepers were preparing for the day while local DJ, Bert—your A.M. guy—Monroe, filled the airwaves with today's best bargains down at Gus's Auto Mart at the junctions of routes 5 and 20.

St. Alben's Place, in the Chimney Ridge Apartments, sat on the outskirts of town. Judd thought the boxlike, cement structures were probably the ugliest group of buildings he had ever seen; gray and square and looking for all the world like giant tombstones. The only thing differentiating one building from another were the street numbers. But, of course, the building in question was found easily enough. Cop cars, five of them, flashers on, had converged on 18 St. Alben's Place like vultures on desert carrion. Judd had decided to park in back, by the patrol car, so he could at least take a perfunctory look around—for what, he didn't know, just something the other investigators may have missed.

Sheriff Crown, who had seen him pull in, walked up to Judd while he looked over the patrol car. Judd stuck his hand out. Sheriff Crown was a short, fat man, whose face appeared to have been fixed with a perennial smile, laugh lines in abundance.

"We'll have her back as soon as possible," Crown said without looking at the car, as he casually pumped Judd's hand.

Judd, whose thoughts were still fixed on the oddities the portly little sheriff had spoken of, said, "Fill me in on the way," and started walking toward 18 St. Alben's Place.

Her color was one of the oddities. She didn't have the pallor of someone who was supposed to be dead. And the pupils did not respond like those of someone who was dead (although that, Judd knew, was not terribly unusual). But the real kicker, Crown said, were puncture wounds on the neck. Judd stopped short and turned, his face betraying a slowly growing horror.

"Puncture marks?" he said, trying to sound light and somewhat succeeding.

"Sure. Have a look for yourself."

Just then, a young woman, late twenties, Judd thought, with short blond hair and large-rimmed glasses entered the bedroom and smiled at him. "You must be Sheriff Lucas," she said. "I'm Doctor Grant, Suzanne Grant. County M.E."

She had enormous blue eyes, Judd noticed, eyes that a man could drown in. And, as the eyes of the mentally superior sometimes do, those enormous blue eyes seemed to reflect more light than was available. "Haunting" was the only word Judd could come up with, which he thought was a little trite but terribly accurate.

"A pleasure," Judd said as their hands came together. Firm, he noticed, but not dramatically so, not like a woman trying to prove she belonged in a man's world.

"I, uh, I've done a perfunctory exam." She looked at Sheriff Crown.

"Sure, sure," Crown said impatiently.

Judd tore his eyes away from Dr. Grant and took a look around.

The room, very much a woman's, a young woman's, was neat and populated with a hundred or more stuffed animals of all shapes, sizes and colors: giraffes, donkeys, the ever present teddys, a collection of stuffed mice on a shelf about halfway up the wall to the left of the bed. Over the twin bed was a framed, eight-by-ten color photograph of the deceased and Ed Land on a Harley, Ed at the controls, Gloria's head resting on the back of his neck, her arms around his waist. They were smiling. In a heap at the foot of the bed was a pink and white cotton bedspread. The bed itself was brass (or brass plated, Judd thought).

And then he asked himself—*Why the hell don't you look at her? The body's right there on the bed.* Until then he had busied himself with a perusal of the room, an over-long study. Now he knew he'd have to confront the deceased. He drew in a deep breath and stepped toward the head of the bed. The first thing he noticed was that the corpse, dressed in a light-blue nighty, did indeed look very much alive. She was actually radiant. Her skin glowed pink; her fingernails were still flushed. At first, he wondered if she were only sleeping.

"As you can see," Suzanne Grant said quietly, thereby somehow reaffirming that the body on the bed was, in fact, dead, "skin color is a problem here. If she were alive—which she is not—it wouldn't be, but this country girl look is . . . disturbing. And we do have pupil contraction. . . ."

"So I've heard."

Suzanne Grant took her glasses off, put them in her blouse pocket and pulled a penlight out of the same pocket. "Here, watch," she said. She rolled back one of the deceased's eyelids and trained the light onto the marble-like eye.

Judd watched the pupil contract. "My God," he said under his breath.

Suzanne Grant let the lid drop, then repocketed the penlight. "Unusual but not unheard of."

"Yes, I know."

"You've seen the reaction before?"

"No, I've read about it, though."

She seemed surprised. "Have you? Well, we were about to check the time of death. . . ."

"Through the, uh, through the rectum?"

"That's right." She spoke in an almost matter-of-fact tone. And coming from someone other than a scholarly, balding old man with crow's feet and a great bedside manner, Judd felt a little uncomfortable. "When the heart stops," she continued, sounding very much like an academician, "the blood tends to gather at the lowest point, like any liquid would. But then, you already knew that," she added with a smile.

Judd shrugged. "The wounds on the neck, what do you make of them?" he asked.

Suzanne Grant bent to the body and looked closely at the punctures, turning the head ever so carefully as she did. "Snake, maybe," she said, still studying. She looked at Judd. "You seem to have been well-versed here. What do you make of them?"

It was, although not very well masked, a plea for help. Snake bites were certainly a possibility, but he didn't think so. The condition of the body, the color, and the pupil contraction were not consistent with snake bite. "Wish to hell I knew," Judd said, although in the basement of his mind he had already begun to formulate an opinion, an opinion that if shared, would surely draw out gales of laughter, and questions about his sanity.

"Well, we'll find out," Grant said with practiced certainty.

What was pervasive in this young woman's room, with the eyes of a hundred cuddly manufactured beasts staring at him, was the sense of death. Or, more precisely, the paradox. Perhaps, Judd reasoned, if she only looked dead—if her throat had been slashed or her chest torn open like Barb's and Walt's had been—then it wouldn't be so bad. *But my God,* he thought, *she looks like she could jump out of bed at any second, pissed off because she was late for work.* And, he had observed immediately upon seeing the body, she was extraordinarily beautiful—even more beautiful than in the photograph over the bed: long, dark hair; perfect, clear skin; a well-muscled yet still-feminine body. And the demise of beauty was even more tragic because before long that beauty would be so dramatically altered. Death would stamp its hideous seal. She had died with her hands at her side and her heels together, the nighty precise, as if it had been placed on a mannequin. Everything was oh so perfect—they could lay her out right here and now, even forego the undertaker's bag of tricks. He turned away while she was turned over to check lividity. It was, he thought, almost sacrilege. With a last hurried glance at the body, he left the room, wondering, as he did, what part Ed Land had played in this.

Around noon Harry Kroh left his apartment over the Krohbar, intending to get a little fresh air; summer had turned up the heat on the town like a hot barbecue grill, and Harry's apartment air conditioner had gone on the fritz—again. He watched Judd Lucas drive by in his Cherokee and waved casually, noticing with a little confusion and a touch of annoyance that Lucas did not wave back. "Probably didn't see me," he mumbled to himself because Judd was customarily a friendly kind of guy, had a nice word for most folks. And wasn't it nice that he had taken his nephew in like he had. Harry watched the Cherokee pull in behind the jail and walked on toward the park, where he had intended to pull up to a nice shade tree and read a few chapters of *The Island,* a paperback horror novel he had picked up in the book section at Breens.

He went on into the park and walked listlessly toward a huge oak near the back; the tree large enough to block out every ray of sun this unusually warm and muggy day had to offer. From here he had a great view of Main Street as well as the four corners churches. Instead of reading he simply watched the goings on for a while, the book, open to chapter one, on his lap, his legs tucked under him Indian style as he leaned his back against the tree. Sandy Furness (the last syllable caught the accent, she insisted—she'd been called The Furnace far too many times) leaned out of her second-floor apartment and shook the dirt out of a small gaily-colored oriental rug onto the sidewalk below, a chore that Harry decided was best left to a cooler day. She seemed to look at him, although he didn't know if she could tell it was him from all the way over there. Still, he waved, and he was positive she acknowledged that wave with a slight smile and a nod. To him she was still The Furnace, still too hot to handle, although he never had. To her right, Jim Arnold rolled down the green and white awning on his store, a small, fashionable men's shop, catering to only the upper crust, although in Hunt, Harry thought, the upper crust was probably close to a slice only. He smiled. To the right of Arnold's Men's Store was The Settler's Post, Rosemary Hamilton's florist shop. It was as Harry started reading, not really seeing the words as yet, when he thought of Rosemary and the other woman, Susan—Susan Dorsey. And in the same thought Bobby All intruded. "Now, ain't that a strange one," Harry said, truly perplexed by the melding of the memories. He researched the problem, his brow tightening. *Sure, Rosemary and Susan left alone, then why—of course, All followed them. Not more than ten seconds behind. Ahh, so what?* his thought continued. Men followed women out of there regularly. It was expected. He raised his eyes to Main Street again and looked at The Settler's Post. "Vacation, maybe?" he thought aloud. "Probably. But there ain't no sign in the window. She usually leaves a sign." The sign, hand printed in black, said, "Thanks for stopping, but I'm on vacation. See you on . . ." and she'd have the date written in red. "Hmmm, why wouldn't she leave a sign? And hell, come to think of it, I ain't seen Teddy or Sue lately either. And that All fella—he was a strange bird. Anyone that'd lay down a twenty and not take a drink—ah, hell, it's only been a day. She probably slept late is all." He thought about that a moment and then caught sight of Sandy Furness, another rug flapping, dust motes rising in the still, hot air and reflecting the boiling sun like a million tiny diamonds. She pulled the rug in and then stuck her head out the window and waved toward Harry. Distracted now, Harry forgot about The Settler's Post and its AWOL owner and waved back.

CHAPTER NINE

The Next Day

Lines! Judd Lucas thought. *Everywhere you go there's a line. What's infinity? "Class, I want you to write a poem about infinity." What was her name? Mrs.—they hadn't invented Ms. yet—Mrs. Klemhamner? Infinity is . . . K-Mart checkouts, being the last table called to eat at a reception, getting plates at motor vehicle! Shit—forget about that other garbage, the edge of the universe, looking into a mirror with another behind you, all that stuff. Infinity is a line with an infinite number of people waiting in it and you're the last one!*

But Judd wasn't the last in line; he was the first, right behind Barb and Walt. So what was the gripe? Why had he invoked a poem from the distant past to help loosen the vise of impatience? Steven sat beside him, looking extremely uncomfortable in a light-gray J.C. Penney suit with a gray and blue tie.

Judd looked him over with a penetrating eye. Why

in the world did they make suits for little kids? To bury them in?

It seemed like the whole town had turned out for this one. The line stretched all the way behind Kardoff's white-pillared funeral home and came out the other side, then stretched down Bellows. And it was hot; heat waved and shimmered above the asphalt as idling cars belched noxious, invisible fumes. Already most of the men had loosened their ties. Judd looked into his rearview mirror at Harry Kroh sitting behind the wheel of his Mustang convertible, top down. Sweat oiled his forehead, but Harry wasn't about to put the top up, not until he was told to, in about two minutes. Out front Estelle Meath waited to direct traffic. Ed Land would have gotten the assignment, but Ed was missing. *Hell,* Judd thought, *he's more than missing. He's a goddamn murder suspect.* He thought about the girl again, as he had many times since he'd seen her. And the mysteries of the unknown crowded in on him.

The cemetery was about three miles away on the other side of the canal on a hill overlooking the town. The dead had the best view in town. Hunt Cemetery, as it was appropriately called, was a well-groomed, small cemetery with small monuments. It was difficult to find large ones—most people didn't have the money anyway. Small monuments, small people, small town, Judd thought. He felt his hands turn hard on the wheel, the knuckles white.

Judd could hear his father: "Why even bother, Judd, boy? Sooner or later that hill's gonna swallow you up! You'll be watchin' over this dead town with dead eyes!"

"You okay, Uncle Judd?" Steven asked, his gaze alternating between his uncle's sweating face and the large hands curling around the black, plastic wheel.

Judd glanced at his nephew, aware of how he must look; the hardened jaw, the steely-eyed glare. Christ, why the hell was he so impatient? He'd been to funerals before, in hotter weather, with more chugging cars surrounding him. Why now? He loosened his grip and tried to smile, failing miserably. "Sure, fine. Just hot, you know? Why don't you loosen that tie up?"

He suddenly felt alternating waves of grief and commiseration. Steven had not attended his own parents' funeral. He had been sick—diarrhea, vomiting—and now he was as calm as could be. Or was he? Why the hell had he brought the boy along anyway? What in the world had he been thinking about? All through the preliminaries, buying the suit, shining the shoes, washing the Jeep, he had only thought of the preliminaries, not how the boy felt. But why? Why had he been so . . . unfeeling? He wasn't like that. He had never been like that, ever! Maybe because his dad was up there, on that hill? Maybe because deep down inside, he knew that was where Cynthia and Jeffrey should be? He hadn't been up there since his father's death. There had been no reason.

"My mom and dad got buried side by side, you know," Steven said simply, without looking at his uncle.

Judd measured his thoughts, not wanting to spit out a hurried response, something catchy like "they're together in heaven now," or "they'll always be that way." The boy was too bright for that.

Steven continued before Judd could respond. "Why do people get buried like that, Uncle Judd? I mean, if you're dead. . . ."

Just then the hearse in front of him started to move. A small cloud of white-blue smoke ushered past, borne on the wings of a damp breeze. Judd felt like he had been saved by the proverbial bell.

Steven remained silent during the ride, as if he had guessed that was what his uncle wanted, silence, reverence; remember the dead without a word.

It was only now that Judd tried to determine just why he hadn't attended his brother's funeral. Bruce had been family, real family, blood kin. "Stay away from funerals, Judd, boy. They're catchy!" Wise old fart, his dad. Maybe he was attending Barb and Walt's funeral out of curiosity, just to see how his memory would stand up to a barrage of prayer and tears. Ten years though, that was a damn long time to grieve, to hold a torch. But Cynthia had been special, different. Damn well worth the wait. If she came back today—

"Look out, Uncle Judd!" Steven yelled.

The thought fog cleared, and Judd saw the white, sun-drenched back door of the hearse and a rainbow of flowers in the window come up fast, too fast. He jammed his foot on the brake and managed to grind to a stop only inches away. Hoyt Barber looked into his rearview mirror and raised a brow at Judd, who smiled feebly.

Steven just looked at him, then opened his door and stepped out. "You comin'?" he asked, as if they were going to a ballgame.

Judd stepped out and joined him. Together they mingled into the quiet crowd.

Off to their left was the canal bridge, rust inching like a cancer up the sides. Beyond it, a quarter mile or so, was Breens, where Walt and Barb used to shop. There was a crew of five wielding tar buckets on the flat roof. *Too goddamn hot for that,* Judd thought. *Might as well punch a time clock in hell.* The town was in front of them, trees and homes sandwiched toward the horizon. The three-story building that housed Mark's Pizzeria, among others, showed its top story to them. Behind and off to the left was Hidden Valley Subdivision. All they could see of it from here was a break in the trees. Judd thought of the rabbit as he glanced in that direction.

Cynthia had liked rabbits; Cynthia had liked animals. Cynthia had liked about anything likeable. Judd watched a fat ground hog waddle over the top of the hill, looking like an animated firelog. Obviously they had disturbed its slumber. *Well, move over, fella, we gotta plant somethin' here! Gotta feed the crawlies.* Christ, why was he thinking like that? He looked at Steven, who was busy people-watching, then at Father Sloan, still in the business of soul-saving. He was a short man with a full head of hair, although it was gray now. Barb and Walt had been semi-weekly attendees, offering what they could, and semi-weekly was better than not at all, according to Father Sloan, who was remembering them fondly, as evidenced by the half-smile on his face. His Dennis Day tenor, Judd noticed, sounded a little out of place. Tennessee Ernie Ford—now he, Judd thought, probably did a great eulogy.

"In this terrible tragedy, we still have something of Walter and Barbara, beacons that still light our mortal world—their smiles. Barbara and Walter Higgins always had a smile to give, to share."

Well, Judd mentally argued, *maybe Walter.*

"And behind those smiles were giving, caring hearts. And although they had little, they always gave to the church, gave to others less fortunate."

Always selling, huh, Father?

"They are with God now, as someday we will all be . . ."

Judd felt a tear tickle his cheek. He let it roll onto his white shirt. He wasn't thinking about Walt and Barb, not at all. He was thinking about Jeffrey and Cynthia at Roseland Amusement Park on the lake in Canandaigua before they tore the park down to make room for condos. Cynthia had ridden the roller coaster eight times straight, calling it a rush like she had never known before. Judd had dared it just once, and had closed his eyes the whole two minutes and four seconds. His butt hurt afterward. Cynthia had been the daredevil, the risk-taker, the type T personality. As had Jeffrey. Very little about Jeffrey had been his, only the gender. That was okay though, she was better than he was, smarter, wiser, better all the way around. Jeffrey was just like her.

Dead?

Father Sloan ran his finger down the page of his open Bible. "In Psalm 139 we find words of comfort. 'Whither shall I go from thy spirit? Or whither shall I flee from thy presence? If I ascend up into heaven, thou art there; if I make my bed in hell, behold, thou art there. If I say, Surely the darkness shall cover me;

even the night shall be light about me. Yea, the darkness hideth not from thee; but the night shineth as the day; the darkness and the light are both alike to thee.' Please join me in the Lord's Prayer."

With all the preparatory work now completed, the finality was overwhelming. Walter and Barbara had lived basically wasted lives, armoring themselves in booze and self-pity, waiting for fate to deal them a hand they could stick with. Judd remembered the wake, the open caskets. Thankfully no one had been stupid enough to say anything about how good they looked, that they hadn't looked that good in years. Judd had thought it, mainly because it was true, but the foolishness of actually saying such a thing made him keep his thoughts to himself. Others thought it, too, he was sure of that, but nobody said anything. Being butchered like a suckling pig was not supposed to improve your looks. But it had. Well, he thought, a few days of cavorting with a mindless army of insects would put an end to that! Give them suckers half a chance and they'd systematically erase any life unwittingly bestowed upon the deceased by a talented undertaker. That was why they stuck you in the ground quick, according to the law of the land. It wouldn't take long. Not at all. Barb and Walt would resemble nothing human in no time.

Another tear, then more.

A large, black, keeled cloud slid over the sun and threw the crowd into shadow.

"Looks like rain," Judd heard a woman whisper.

"Could be" came a baritone response.

Even Father Sloan, Judd saw, chanced a glance skyward. *What are you thinking, Father? Get it over with, stick them in the ground and head for cover? No, he wouldn't think that—would he?*

Steven was crying, too. But his tears were for obvious reasons.

God, Judd thought, it was stupid to bring him here.

Steven looked at his uncle, who returned his gaze, their eyes red, the tears streaming steadily. It felt good. Right. But Cynthia and Jeffrey weren't dead. Not yet. And it wasn't true after all. Funerals weren't catchy, just the grief.

CHAPTER TEN

Martin
"I want it all, I want it all, and I want it now!"
(With feeling)
Queen

There were rules. Surely there were rules. Everything had rules. Everybody had to follow them. Then, Martin had asked himself the next morning, why hadn't he been told?

Lying here, alone,

Shit, is that how I'm going to go? Alone? But then, immortals don't go; they just kind of . . . continue . . . like some hideous perpetual motion thing with limbs.

he remembered how it all got going. He and Robert and, for a while, a woman, who was gone now. Well, she hadn't really been a woman, not really; there really wasn't a sex thing anymore. Immortals weren't called he or she, not in the literal sense. They were called . . . immortal. And not many called them that, just the ones that believed, and there weren't many of those around, just a few who made a career out of preternatural studies.

1979—they had crossed over . . . good phrase; Robert used it a lot, some ten years ago.

He shuffled a little and looked around with those superman eyes. A little lantern with a little flame in it sat across the room. He was thankful for it.

He lay back and put his arm over his forehead. He visualized a movie screen on the ceiling. It was something he did often because there was little else to do. Eventually Robert would supply him with "companions," but they would prove to be rather useless. So he became producer, director and star, at least one of the stars, and the ceiling became the stage. Like his friends—the word sounded strange since he'd crossed over—he, too, had acquired a boundless imagination, one of the "bennies" of immortality.

He thought of Hollywood, of Bela Lugosi and Peter Cushing and others assigned the formidable task of portraying vampires. He preferred to call them immortals. It smacked of longevity. He smiled; he couldn't help it. "What foods these mortals be," he said aloud. Well, that *was* smileable, after all. Their portrayals were so farfetched, so removed from the truth. Nosferatu, now there was a vampire. Nosferatu, the pointy-eared, white-skinned, egg-eyed vampire appeared on the ceiling. Nosferatu was easily the most evil of them all. And the most ugly. But that was close to the truth. A couple of weeks without eating and they all took on a striking deathbed pallor. Which was exactly what he was trying to avoid the night he slipped out to dine. Rules—the goddamn rules. Next time he'd know better.

Nosferatu.

Am I going to look like that? he thought.

He closed his eyes, wiping the movie screen clean. Nosferatu sneered and was gone.

"Obviously," he said, "I'll be here awhile, at least until they can find a cure for this . . . disease. So if I start from the beginning—well, what better place than the beginning."

Aunty Maude. When he thought about her, lying there in her twin-size bed on Carter St., just down the street from the Kardoff house (later to become the Kardoff Funeral Home), the world outside her window parading by, oblivious to her and she probably to it, he could think of no better reason to give immortality a tumble. Whenever he looked into her blank, dying eyes, he could only wonder at what might be passing through her numbed brain. Memories, probably, all running together like alphabet soup. And at one hundred and one years old, she had a library full of memories. But what else went on in there? Did she ponder the political climate? Did she even go to church anymore and call upon her vengeful God? He had to be vengeful to have let her live that long. Oh, the quality of that woman's life. Time scarred her gray, withered skin like a dry riverbed. The quality of it. What the hell good did it do to live, what the hell good . . . ?

He recalled with awesome clarity the last time they "talked."

* * *

Simply walking up the wooden steps to the falling-down, two-bedroom ranch house, he was taking his life in his hands. Everything in the place needed repairs: the roof, the siding, the stairs themselves. And the cats, the goddamn cats: in the frying pan, on top of the fridge, under anything that had a top. Thirty-goddamn-two of them. Stinking, filthy, flea-ridden cats. How the hell did the old woman get to be an old woman with all those goddamn cats? Certainly over the years they had to have transmitted something to her. Sure, longevity. Take on a few lives here and there and suddenly you're a hundred and one years old.

Smiling, he knocked on the screen door—there was no bell—and waited. Within seconds the door was pushed outward. Martin stepped down to make room.

"She's sleeping," Naomi Aubin said. Naomi was Maude's daughter. She was over seventy now, but still cut a handsome figure. Only recently had she begun to show her age. She had been taking care of Aunty Maude for most of her adult life, forsaking any life of her own. Disgusted, Martin looked at her. Naomi always seemed to be smiling. Martin hated that. She should have been as miserable as dirt, locked up with that old woman day in and day out, never a chance to do anything but change bed pans and make sure Maude's motor was still running. She should have been miserable. He would have been.

"Oh, well . . ." he said, turning to go, knowing that Naomi would no sooner let him leave than she would get rid of one of the cats. He was company.

"No, she'll be up soon. C'mon in. Have a cold Pepsi."

Martin trembled at the thought. The Pepsi was kept cold, sure, but for some inexplicable reason it always smelled vaguely of piss. He declined the Pepsi but went on in anyway, opting for tap water.

"There you go," she said, handing the glass to him as she sat down across from him, pushing aside two large, slumbering cats to make room. The smell here was not merely a cat smell. It was a cat-kennel smell. Martin could imagine a real estate man coming in and pulling in a lungful. "Well, Mrs. Aubin, it is a lovely home, and I do think we can sell it; but there is a slight odor. Do you have any pets?" *Does she have any pets? Does a fart stink?*

He took the water, sipped, and set it down on the coffee table, the veneer edging up at the corners. "How's she doin'?" he asked.

Naomi took in a full breath, deep in thought. "Well, better? Yes, I think so. She smiled at me yesterday. I said to her, 'Ma, do you like the birthday cards everybody sent?' and she looked at me and smiled."

"Golly, that's—so, she's sleeping?"

Naomi fussed for a moment. Sleeping, as it concerned her mother, was a nebulous term. She actually slept in one form or another most of the time.

"I don't think she'd mind the company. You go on in; I'll, uh, do the dishes."

She got up and went into the kitchen. Martin started for the bedroom.

Walking into the old woman's room was strangely like walking into a mausoleum that stank of medicine. The combination attacked the senses, and visitors had to fight themselves to keep from running off. Martin edged beyond the door. There, her mouth open, one eye two-thirds shut, a dollop of drool on her chin, was Aunty Maude, looking every bit her age. And she was, in fact, asleep. Martin's knees went weak. He fought for balance, found it, then stepped forward. An old wooden chair that had seen many a cat claw sat at the head of the bed, just inches away from Maude's face. It was always easier to talk to her that way. To Maude's left was a grimy picture window, not a large one, just big enough for her to look out onto the tree-lined street if she wanted to. On the desk to the right of the chair were greeting cards from dignitaries, local, state and national, congratulating her on the occasion of her one hundredth birthday the year before. On her lap were several cards. One was gripped in her right hand; her clawlike fingers had punched fingernailed arches into the middle. As sometimes happens with the aged, Maude's skin and hair were almost the same color, her hair lying around her head like old, gray straw. She was skinny, not emaciated like old people sometimes get, but skinny, like a waiting-for-puberty teenager. Today she had on a white, blue-fringed nightgown given to her for her birthday by her son, Michael. It looked strange, all new and pressed. The price tag ($3.50 at Woolworths) was still pinned to the sleeve. Martin pictured her, as is, on display at Woolworths, on sale this week for only $3.50, and smiled despite himself. He also made a mental note to remove the tag before he left. She still had small circles of pink rouge on her cheeks. Martin wondered if Naomi had forgotten to remove it after the birthday party. *Gotta look your best, Ma. Never know when a handsome stranger might wander in.* She could, just by looking at her, Martin thought, make a person feel depressed. But he always came back to see her, always hoping beyond hope that someday the process would reverse, that his dear, sweet Aunty, who had loved him so in more lucid times, would someday sit up and say, "Martin—how about a game of Password?"

Well, how about a game of Pass Away, Aunty. How about that? Then I won't keep coming here all the time. Then I won't keep picturing years past, when we laughed and had fun, and sometimes even cried. Like when Uncle Homer died. Sure, a nice, quick game of Pass Away or Pass On, or Death Be My Next Door Neighbor.

Of course, Martin still remembered the good times; that's what made it so hard: those five-cent ice creams she sprang for, those boxes of birthday presents she used to send, always making him wonder where in the world she ever got the money. And so it was today. In this stiflingly hot room, with old Aunty Maude degenerating right before his loving eyes, she transformed into the woman he wanted to remember. And that made looking at her stroke-deformed face almost bearable.

It was the turn of her head that Martin noticed first. She was usually even too weak for that. Therefore something so profoundly physical caught his attention immediately. She was looking at him—with both eyes. Clear, round, crisply green eyes. As if an intelligence had suddenly grown behind them, as if some invisible healing hand had passed over her. Martin looked toward the door, half wondering if he should call Naomi in. But before he could do anything, Maude reached out and placed a gnarled, arthritic-clawed hand on his arm. He pulled back, then realized how foolish that had been. She smiled as she replaced the hand.

"It comes, it goes," she said, her voice stronger than it should have been, and thereby strangely malefic. But suddenly she lost her smile, and her fingers gripped his arm with a force he didn't believe possible. And she added, although he didn't know how because her mouth remained tightly closed, "Martin—I am in hell. Fetch me away, Martin! You were always such a good boy. Fetch me out of here—please! For Aunty?"

Then, as quickly as she had changed, she went back to being the old woman Martin knew. Her eyes became lusterless again, and her fingernails absently punched more holes into the birthday card with bunnies on it. She had returned to wherever she had briefly left, but Martin recognized his mission. A request from his aunty Maude. Obviously she *wanted* to die. Obviously she no longer considered life worthwhile. Obviously he would have to end that life. So he did. And she went without a peep. Her skinny little body just went limp. And the sound that came out of her at the end strangely resembled the words "Thank you."

On the way out he handed the price sticker to Naomi and said, "I think she's gone now."

Naomi pocketed the price sticker, said, "Oh, dear," looked him straight in the eye and added, "You sure I can't get you a nice cold Pepsi, Martin?"

Looking back, Martin wasn't sure whether Aunty

Maude had spoken or not. But that wasn't important. If she could have, she would have said exactly what he thought he had heard—or did hear. Whatever. The important thing was that he had helped his aunty. What was even more important was that he would never be put into a hot, little room with a million stinking cats and a grimy picture window to look out and see the world passing by. Which was one of the reasons he decided to take a chance at immortality when it was offered.

And the reason he was here, now, in this equally depressing basement with no windows to look out of, had everything to do with that hunger for immortality.

CHAPTER ELEVEN

Judd and Steven went to the office after the funeral. While the sheriff busied himself with some of the mundane aspects of his job, Estelle entertained Steven. "Great kid, Judd," she told him. "Would you believe it—he likes ice cream." Steven seemed comfortable with her. His small face flashed smiles constantly. She didn't have any kids of her own, and probably never would, she said, what with the burdens of a career. Well, okay, that and the fact that she was already forty, plain-looking, and stuck in a town that counted its eligible bachelors by the spinning light of the drunk tank. For a brief period, she and Ed Land had exchanged something more than affable glances, but nothing had ever come of it. Her children were like Steven—borrowed, on loan—hers just long enough to take down to Carvel's. Pity, Judd thought, as he watched them stroll hand in hand out the front door.

Ed's disappearance—and possible involvement in a homicide—dominated Judd's thoughts. A year earlier Ed had taken his cruiser down to Elmira to see Gloria Sternmyer. His pleadings with Judd, that it wouldn't happen again, that his job meant everything to him, touched Judd enough that he spared him the complete wrath of the department. After two weeks without pay, Ed returned, a new man. The look on his face that day, when he knew he was about to lose his job, was like that of a man facing castration. The chances of Ed cruising off to some romantic rendezvous in an official vehicle were slim, almost nil. So, Judd wondered, why had he done it? What had made him do it? What force had been strong enough to make him risk a job so important to him?

Fifteen minutes after they left, Estelle and Steven returned, ice cream cones in hand, strawberry for Estelle and chocolate for Steven. Thanks to the heat, the napkins encircling the cones were soaked with melted ice cream. After they were done, Estelle set a flashlight on the table and began creating shadow characters on the wall with her hands.

Judd gave them ten minutes, then said, "Time to call it a night."

Steven's shoulders noticeably drooped as his passable rabbit fell from the gray wall.

"Learns quick," Estelle said, ruffling Steven's hair. But his face had assumed an almost fey look, a look Judd didn't at all like. Probably the funeral, he mused.

"Hey, someone's gotta feed Sam, you know," Judd said.

Magic in a word—the fey look vanished. Sam, in his own unwitting fashion, would be as big a help with Steven as a dozen Estelles. Steven got up and gave Estelle a quick hug. Slightly flustered, Estelle ruffled his hair again, not really knowing what else to do. She looked at Judd. "Surrogate's better than nothin' at all," she said, smiling pleasantly.

Steven looked at his uncle and was about to question him about the word "surrogate" when Judd said, "Later, we gotta get goin'." Steven left with his mouth open, the word dangling, ready to fall.

It was dark by the time they left, and a fog had begun to cling to the low areas. Out here, away from town, anything could jump in front of the Cherokee, Sam included. Judd's eyesight had been declining of late, but his ego had kept him from wearing his glasses. He should have had them on now, but he had left them at the office. He breathed a little easier as he turned onto the dirt road leading to his cabin. A glance at the dashboard clock: almost nine-thirty. Morning would arrive early.

There was an aura of warmth, even friendliness that surrounded his cabin. But that was understandable. The cabin was, after all, somewhat of a shrine to his family. He had even used a bit of reverse reasoning in its construction. His logic went something like this, *If I build a one-bedroom, a loft, then they'll come back. Murphy's Law. They'll come back and there'll be no place for Jeffrey to sleep.* He even envisioned Cynthia chastising him for his lack of foresight. "You always were a little scatterbrained, you know that, Judd Lucas? Where's Jeffrey going to sleep, tell me that; where is that boy going to sleep?" Judd smiled. Right now they could all curl up together in the loft. Later, he'd add on. *But Jeffrey would be . . . eighteen now. He wouldn't want to sleep with his parents. Not now. He's dead anyway . . . probably dead. There was the clothing.*

As he cut the engine and got out, Sam waddled up to him, then went around to the other side to greet Steven. On the surface, a rare display of affection, but Judd concluded he was only hungry.

"C'mon," Steven said, rubbing the dog's large head, much as Estelle had rubbed his.

By now the dense fog had settled below the tips of the tallest evergreens, cozying in like it wanted to spend the night. Hearing the chirrup of crickets and the bellow of bullfrogs from the pond fifty yards or so behind the house, Judd glanced around, then followed Sam and Steven into the house.

The first thing he did was build a small fire, not for warmth but for comfort. As he piled kindling into a pyramid, he heard Sam whimper as he scratched at the bottom cupboard.

"Patience is a virtue," he said, without turning. Sam cocked his head and pointed his ears, that queerly intriguing routine common to intelligent dogs.

"I can feed him," Steven offered.

Judd, squatting, a poker in his hand, turned and looked at his nephew. "Okay, tell you what, that'll be your chore henceforth. That means from now on. I give him the Gravy Train under there. His bowl's just right of where you're standing."

"How many scoops," Steven asked after he'd pulled the bag out. The yellow scooper lay on top.

"Four'll do it. I was gonna switch him over to dry—that stuff makes him fart like an old car—but he likes it so much I haven't got the heart. If he can put up with the smell, I guess we can, too."

Steven wrinkled the top of his nose in mock disgust.

Judd smiled. "Yeah, he can light up a room, that's for sure."

Sam again cocked his head, almost as if he knew they were talking about him and wanted an interpreter.

While Sam ate, Steven brushed his teeth and then climbed the stairs to the loft and the comfort of the bed, the only one in the house. Earlier Judd had told him of his decision, that because kids needed their sleep more than adults, he'd let him have the loft until he could arrange something. When that would be, he didn't know. For now though, the couch would be his bed. And that was okay. It was reasonably comfortable, at least for the time being.

After Sam finished eating, he curled up in front of the fireplace, his lids heavy, his belly full, and his digestive tract gathering a full head of aromatic steam.

By now, Judd thought, Steven had been asleep for awhile. Still fully clothed, Judd pulled a throw pillow under his head and felt a sigh work out of him. The fire had died considerably, but small fires were better for watching than the large crackling kind anyway.

Except for the dappled, lethargic shadows created by the dying embers, the cabin was dark. Above Sam and the fireplace, the painting of Cynthia and Jeffrey lay in deep shadow, the light obscured by the expansive oak mantel. Cynthia's eyes were visible, but almost nothing else. Jeffrey was only an outline, as if his likeness had been cut away. Judd stared at the painting, his thoughts irretrievably focused on his family, and drifted.

Cynthia had been a nature lover. Long walks through the woods, day or night, had been one of her favorite pastimes. She knew a lot about the woods: trees, foliage, what animal burrowed where. He thought of the time they had strayed from the path when they had first started dating, discovering a remarkably secluded clearing in the thick woods. Making love outdoors had been her idea, something she had always wanted to do, she had told him.

"What if we get caught?" he had asked weakly, feeling a vague moral duty to dissuade her.

Grinning, she had said nothing. But later, entwined in a passionate embrace on the forest floor, he had forgotten about getting caught. After they had finished, she kissed him tenderly and told him that she would always love him, no matter what, no matter where, no matter when.

It was while this memory faded that Judd thought he heard a knock. He looked at Sam. The dog's chest heaved slowly as his front paws twitched, captured as he was by his own dreams.

"Who's there?" Judd said loud enough to be heard, but not loud enough to wake Steven, or so he hoped.

No answer.

Strange, he thought, *I was positive. . . .* He got up, walked cautiously toward the door, hesitated briefly, then pulled it open. Almost everything was draped by a gray-white darkness. He stepped beyond the door, stopped, then took a few steps into the night, toward the Jeep. Listening, he heard nothing, just night sounds: the crickets and the occasional bullfrog, sounds he had heard earlier. It was clammy out here though, because of the fog, this low-hanging cloud that obscured the forest floor but not the treetops, like an old blanket. He turned and looked back at the cabin. The door was open. *What the hell am I doing out here?* he thought. *I've got to get some sleep, and Steven'll probably wake up now. C'mon, Judd, pack it in. There's nothing out here, just the damn fog and a million bugs.* A cricket in mid-parabola smacked into his thigh. He reflexively brushed at it and went back inside.

The fire had died considerably, leaving only walnut-sized, red embers and occasional flashes of orange and blue flame; death throes. Half-awake, Sam raised his head and followed Judd with his eyes as he walked to the couch and fumbled off his shirt and slacks, leaving them on a cane-seated chair to the right of the fireplace. In his boxers now, Judd washed his hands over his face, slipped onto the couch and pulled the blanket over him. *Seven minutes,* he thought remotely as he settled in, *that's all it takes, average. God, I hope so.*

But before those seven minutes were up, before sleep could overtake him, he heard, "Judd?"

His eyes snapped open, and he looked toward the still-closed door. Cynthia, he had heard Cynthia's voice—he was sure of it! How many times over the last ten years had that voice edged into his thoughts? How many times had he heard her speak softly to him, heard her mumbled cries, her joyous laughter? True, he had only heard the one word "Judd," and yes, he could have mistaken a thousand different sounds. And when you considered the fact that they had gone to a funeral—

"Judd?"

Christ—it is her! It has to be; it just has to be! He groped for the light and flicked it on. Hesitating only briefly, he threw the blanket off, ran to the door, stopped, then flung it open. "Cynthia—Cynthia?" he whispered. He scanned the scene quickly. To his amazement, he saw a woman near the Jeep, about forty feet away, glancing back at him as she walked. But through the fog he could only see that it was a woman; he couldn't swear that it was Cynthia. The woman turned and moved quietly toward the thick stand of evergreens that surrounded the cabin. Barefoot and clad only in his boxer shorts, Judd hurried after her. The pine needles stung his feet but not so painfully that he thought of stopping.

"Cynthia?" he yelled, as she disappeared into the fog beyond the tree line.

Nothing.

He ran in after her, groping, dead branches of evergreens tearing at his bare flesh. He covered his face with his arms and plunged in, the closeness of bare, stinging branches preventing him from moving any faster than he was. Every now and again he caught a fleeting glimpse of her, as if this were just some nocturnal game of tag—then nothing, just the promise of her presence, because as he hurried past the spots where she had been, he was positive that he could smell her, the finite, but so very compelling odor of her perfume. Yet as soon as he smelled it, it was gone again, just like her. How long he chased her apparition, he didn't know, but as he did, he began to feel an overpowering déjà vu. And as he stumbled tiredly into a clearing, he realized why. She had led him to the very spot where they had first made love, about a mile from the cabin. It was one of the reasons he had built the cabin where he had in the first place. He had come here often to reminisce, Sam at his side when he could spare the time. But tonight, darkness surrounding him as he chased her through the woods, he hadn't realized just where he was going. He glanced upward, and the forest canopy parted ever so slightly, allowing him a fog-shrouded glimpse of the moon. He listened intently, hoping to hear her footfalls crunching on the forest floor, maybe even his name again. But he heard nothing. And what was peculiar was the absolute silence—no crickets or frogs, nothing at all—an eerie and thoroughly disquieting silence that sapped his reason and fueled the idea that he just might be dreaming all this. Turning a full circle, he could not see the house any longer, only the trunks of the surrounding evergreens, rising from the forest floor like thick prison bars.

"God, how stupid—" he began. But before he could finish, Cynthia—yes, it was her, he saw—stepped out from behind a tree. Currents of fog running over her face obscured her features, leaving Judd with only an unfocused image dressed in jeans and a white blouse. "Cynthia," he said softly, reverently. He stepped toward her, and she reached out her hand to him, giggling shyly as she did, bringing the memory of the first time they had made love back to him with profound clarity. But then, just as their hands were about to touch, a strangely gleeful laugh replaced the shy giggle, and she stepped quickly backward. Judd felt a clammy coolness wash over him as he watched. This laugh, this almost maniacal laugh, was not the Cynthia he remembered. By now the fog had almost totally enveloped her, wrapping her in a gray-white cocoon that to him seemed somehow right. Then she was gone, swallowed up by the night. And silence reigned once more. Judd's thoughts were inchoate, but then he remembered Steven back at the cabin. And as Steven became the focus of his thoughts, the eerie silence was broken by a furious flapping sound, the flutter of tiny wings. He looked quickly skyward and caught an ever so fleeting glimpse of something, its path erratic and meandering, very unbirdlike. . . . With dawning horror, he ran blindly from the clearing and back toward the cabin—at least a million miles away. And with each step, that horror grew, his brain giving it sharper and sharper focus. So sure was he that he would find the cabin empty, that Steven would—for some reason—be gone, that he even began planning to gather the remnants of his police force to begin a search. He stumbled into the yard, his lungs aching, his breath coming in retching gasps. He almost fell through the front door. "Steven—Steven?" he yelled as he rammed into the couch in his haste to get to the stairs. "Steven, wake up. Steven!" He grabbed the railing and began his ascent. But then, fists buried into his sleep-encrusted eyes, Steven appeared at the top of the stairs. Judd rushed to him and pulled him into his arms. Totally confused and still in the clutches of sleep, Steven said, "What's wrong, Uncle Judd?"

The next morning, as he looked into the mirror, Judd wondered if what had happened the night before had been just an isolated incident brought on by the funeral, the murders; if everything had just come together and somehow created her. It was a possibility. He stared into his pale blue eyes, the razor lying on his lathered cheek. And a faint line of deep-red blood appeared.

CHAPTER TWELVE

Behind the wheel of the Cherokee, the day awakened by a refreshing, dry coolness, the sky dotted with cottony fair-weather clouds that looked about the size of half dollars from the ground, Judd mulled over the events of the last few days: Barb and Walt had been brutally murdered and then buried, Ed Land had disappeared, his cruiser found at the scene of an apparent homicide, Jeffrey's clothing, as well as that of another boy, had been found, and he had had a rendezvous with Cynthia, or so it had seemed.

He stopped for a red light at the end of Main Street and let his eyes wander. The town looked like a Rockwell painting. The symptoms of an underlying malaise had not yet surfaced. A thin, yet strong, veneer of normalcy still covered the town, and it would take more than the recent tragic events to cause that veneer to peel back and reveal the black horrors beneath.

He thought about Steven, and about how he seemed less fearful of the woods than before. Today he had even suggested that he be allowed to stay home alone. Judd had planned on leaving him at the office every day for the remainder of the summer, if only because of the murders. But leaving him at the office would certainly impinge upon someone—probably Estelle—and the routine completion of his or her duties. So Judd had positioned his toolbox over the dog's exit, telling Steven that if Sam had to go, then he was to leash him and tie him to the chain behind the cabin until he had. Sam, he knew, would be one pissed-off dog, but for now, he would rather see the dog pissed and Steven safe. And he was going to call him every couple of hours anyway, or have someone call, just to be on the safe side.

As he pulled into his parking spot behind the office, he remembered to check over the phone log. Ann sometimes sent his deputies on calls and forgot to tell him, but she always made a phone record: who called, the date, the problem, who had been dispatched to see into it. Everything pertinent. The record was a way for him to cover all bases. If an irate citizen called and asked him what he had done about this, or hadn't done about that, he could routinely question the deputy sent to investigate the complaint.

He picked up the log. "Morning, Ann," he said to his dispatcher.

"Mornin', Sheriff," she said, raising a full glass of steaming, aromatic tea to her mouth.

As he ran his finger down the mimeographed sheet of paper, he thought vaguely about lightning not striking twice, that his lectures on the subject of following through with an investigation, no matter how trivial the offense, had had an effect. He stopped reading when he saw Ed Land's name scribbled under the heading of Officer Dispatched. Beside it, under the heading of Violation, was a large question mark.

"Ann," he said, somewhat annoyed, "why didn't you tell me you sent Ed on a call?"

She picked up the log and thought a moment. "Oh, that. . . ."

"He's missing, Ann—and a possible suspect in a murder case!"

She only shrugged and raised her eyebrows. "You're right—I messed up. I'm sorry."

Judd looked at the log. "Vasquez—that name sounds familiar."

"They own the new restaurant."

Judd showed her the log. "A question mark?"

"Well, as I recall, their maitre d' called and said they were late, that they were rarely late. About then Ed came in, so I sent him. I thought the guy was probably just crying wolf."

Judd crossed the room, took out his key chain and undid a rack full of shotguns. He lifted one off, flipped it open, checked the bore and closed it up again with a metallic click. Pocketing a couple of slugs, he left. Behind him he barely heard Ann say, "Now, what's that for?"

Not certain what he'd find at the Vasquez home, he thought the shotgun might be a good idea. He parked the car directly in front of the house and walked up the steps to the porch, remembering as he did how he had walked up to the Higgins' home just three days earlier. Here, on the porch, the low sun was blocked by two large bushes, leaving the area in shadows. He pushed the doorbell, heard two distant chimes, and waited. As he waited, he heard a car screech to a halt behind him. He turned, saw the front end of a police cruiser sticking beyond the large bush on the left side of the porch and watched Ricky Smits come into view and wave to him.

"Ann called, said you might need some help. Said you had a shotgun." He saw the gun. "Guess you do. What's goin' on, Sheriff?"

"Maybe nothing, maybe not. Take a look around the exterior of the house—and keep your eyes open."

Ricky Smits drew his own gun, pointed it toward the sky and began a modified tippy toe to the left.

Judd rang the door bell again. As he waited, a call came from the other side of the house. "Sheriff? I think I found somethin'."

He ran down the steps to the back of the house. Ricky stood about five feet away from a pair of storm doors that led to the basement; the left side stood open. On the top step was a boy's worn jacket, face-down. On the steps below were a pair of jeans and some underwear. A sneaker lay on the fourth step, another on the step below. Judd went over and picked up the jacket. On the front, in a semi-circle, was the outline of the GIANTS logo. When he picked up the jeans, he noticed something. He reached into his pocket, pulled out his glasses, and fumbled them on. On the steps was a residue of gray ash.

"When we're done here, I want you to get that up,"

he said to Ricky without looking at him.

Ricky stepped closer. "Get what up, Sheriff?" he asked.

Judd squatted, then pointed. "There's a residue of some kind on the steps here."

Ricky looked more closely. "By golly, there sure is! You got good eyes, Sheriff."

"Come on, we better have a look inside."

Now, Judd thought, as the ambulance pulled away with the remains of Rosita and Julio Vasquez, *we got problems, real problems.*

Ben Weisanthal, also watching the ambulance pull away, said, "If I were a betting man, which I'm not, I'd bet the farm that they were killed by the same person—or persons—that killed your brother- and sister-in-law."

"Four people, Ben, four good people. And one in Elmira that might be linked."

Weisanthal looked interested. "Oh?"

"Haven't had a chance to fill you in on that one."

"Same M.O.?"

"No."

"Then, why'd you bring it up?"

"Because Ed's involved—somehow, Ed Land's involved."

"Your deputy—that Ed Land?"

"A girl was killed, his girlfriend. They found his cruiser nearby."

"But she wasn't . . ."

"Mutilated? No. Just the opposite. Maybe that's why I didn't mention it, I don't know. A lot's been happening lately, Ben."

Weisanthal grinned. "You got a real knack for understatement, you know that?"

"Listen, that rabbit. . . ."

"Oh, yeah—blooded. Wasn't a drop in him. Which could account for the collapsed condition of the carcass."

"I thought so."

Weisanthal studied his friend. "You know, I'm gonna get you in a poker game someday—and when I do, I'll be able to retire! What aren't you telling me, Judd? I know there's something—your face is a dead giveaway!"

He looked at Ben, his brain putting everything together in logical, easily understood terms. But the paradox, logic versus insanity, kept those words from getting any farther than the formulation stage. "Nothin', really. Nothing at all. You said you'd take care of that package?"

Weisanthal held up the cellophane bag, the dark ash vacuumed from the steps inside, an inch or so deep. "I'll put it under a microscope. If that doesn't tell me anything, then I'll take it to the lab at Rochester General. You know what this is though, don't you?"

"I've got an idea."

CHAPTER THIRTEEN

Brian Ferguson

Only snapshots would show it, time inexorably stamping the town with its seal of change. Along Main, what were only saplings twenty-five years ago now provided a hundred yards of shade for walkers and browsers, while cracks in the sidewalk caused by expanding root systems widened like dry, weaving rivers, here and there even sprouting a hearty weed or two. Such was nature's barter system. In Soldiers' and Sailors' Park a fresh, new crop of etchings, carved into the green paint of park benches and the black paint of the cannon, trumpeted a myriad of teenage entanglements and philosophies: Leslie loves Mitch, E.R. plus T.P. equals heaven, high school sucks! But, as human nature would have it, only the names had been changed. A little paint remover would clearly detail like philosophies and similar sentiments: Al loves Carol, Pete plus Charlene, fuck high school, gimme a cherry-red Ford! And so, in another thirty years, it would all come full circle. The sidewalk would have been fixed numerous times, the dead trees replaced by saplings, and the park benches given at least five more coats of thick green paint. So it was that the only change that took place in Hunt was merely cosmetic: patches in the cement, brushes full of paint run over obscenities, a couple of new beer signs in the gin mills. Some, like the sage octogenarians who gathered at the hardware store on rainy days to play checkers, would even say that what goes around comes around, that history, as they have noticed over the course of their many years on this earth, does so repeat itself. And one of those wise, old checker players, one inordinately blessed with vision and profound wisdom, might even say that the only constant in this world was the laughter of children, that a ball slapped against the sidewalk now has the same tone as a ball slapped against the sidewalk thirty years ago. That, hell, if you put an ear to the pavement and listened real hard, you might still hear an echo of that long-ago bounce.

And that was pretty much true.

The town did have an echo.

A second, maybe, not much more, that was all the time it took for Brian Ferguson, in the process of sneaking out of the house, to brush against the ultra-expensive vase with his sleeve and send it somersaulting to the floor, the resulting explosion of sound surely rivaling an atomic blast. But in that second or so, time did a quick freeze for him. There was so much to see in that second, so much beyond a vase smashing into a zillion unglueable pieces. As it began its death fall, he saw his dad, strap in hand, glowering down at him like Frankenstein, and at midpoint he saw the strap raised high overhead, the gleaming buckle exposed like a bullet in the hot sun. And when that vase shattered, he actually felt his backside begin to blister. He had really screwed up this time. Not only would he be caught sneaking out of the house, but in the process he had cost the family a bundle. "Seven hundred and ninety-eight dollars, boy! That's what that vase cost! You never seen that much money in your miserable little life!" True enough. He had never seen that much money, and he was miserable.

Brian thought of flight even before the jagged pieces of ceramic stopped spinning on the hardwood. His rationale had something to do with the lesser of two evils. Flight, at least a protracted flight, would cause heart flutters and excessive worry, thereby giving the vase a secondary status, although his thoughts were more on the line of, *the longer I'm gone, the more they'll worry—and maybe they'll forget about that goddamn vase!*

Upstairs, meanwhile, his brain fumbling with a sound that had stolen into a semi-erotic dream, lay Brian's dad, Ben Ferguson. Frankenstein and he were about as similar as salt and pepper. But there had been that one time, that one moment of painful decision when the boy had really pissed him off, pissed him off to the nth degree, the time when the strap—*oh, why the hell'd I do it, why?*—had been the only solution. And ever since, the boy had regarded him like he might a rabid dog. Many times in his mind he had put that strap back on and applied only a tongue lashing—many times—God knew that. If anyone knew how much pain he suffered because of that buckle laying on his son's blistering backside, He did. But now, there had come a sound wafting to his room, a sound vaguely reminiscent of a vase shattering all to kingdom come. A VASE. A seven hundred and ninety-eight dollar plus tax vase. A vase that would be passed down from son to son until time stopped. *Well,* he thought, *time may have just stopped.* He felt his wife jostle him.

"Honey?" she whispered, a hint of desperation in her voice, what with all the burglaries (not to mention the murders) of late. "Wake up, Ben. Someone's downstairs; I hear someone downstairs."

Ben Ferguson, because of his wife's whispered ravings, forgot about the vase and remembered fear, a subject he knew as well as any; the knot it made of his gut, the glaze it pasted onto his eyeballs, the God it clarified. Ben Ferguson was a vet, a returnee from the land that Nixon made famous. Vietnam. Fear over there was a daily routine, something you carried around with you like a coiled, caged snake. Here, it only tapped you on the shoulder every so often, while you crossed a busy street or punched the accelerator too hard—or while someone stole around your dark house for reasons only he knew. But because fear was not a stranger to him, Ben Ferguson was prepared with a proper response, a response that took the form of the twelve gauge shotgun he kept in the closet behind his golf bag. He rubbed as much of the sleep out of his eyes as he could and shuffled toward the closet, vaguely wondering how much noise his bare feet were making on the carpeted floor. He pushed open the closet door, fumbled inside a moment, and then pulled the weapon out by the barrel. The shot was in a box overhead. He fished out a couple slugs, cozied them into the chamber, and gripped the weapon firmly, nodding to his wife, who was now standing by the door to the master bathroom, hands at her mouth, expecting the worst.

"Don't you worry, hon. If there's someone down there, this'll chase him off," he said confidently.

"Be careful, Ben, oh, please, be careful!"

How many times had she heard of prowlers taking a gun away from someone and killing him with it? How many times? And Ben was a small man. A small, weak man, easily overpowered.

He stepped toward the closed bedroom door and slowly pulled it open.

At the same time, Brian Ferguson glanced toward the stairs, positive he had heard something. His fear, as he froze in the darkness, was just as real as any Vietnam could provide, just as life-threatening. At any moment his father would appear at the top of those stairs, flip on the light and be greeted by the demise of The Vase. And his young life would be about as worthless as one of those sharp little pieces of ceramic spread like popcorn over the living room floor.

"Ohhhh, hellll," he murmured, realizing as he spoke that flight was indeed his only alternative.

So as he gripped the doorknob, pulled and heard, "Who's there? I'm armed. I've got a twelve gauge here, and it'll blow a hole in you so large . . . ," Brian threw open the door and tore off down the back porch, leaping the steps. Behind him, Ben Ferguson gave chase. And as he got to the back door and squinted past his slumbering prize roses, he saw a form, a small form to be sure, but a thief was a thief was a thief, and this thief was about to get a backside—

The sound of a twelve gauge loosing its load slammed through the night air—and that load barely missed the target. Brian heard shot rattle through the bushes around him, his little heart grabbing at his throat now, his legs churning furiously.

Behind him he heard curses, loud at first and then more faint as he finally reached the security of the railroad tracks, a couple hundred yards behind his house. And in his mind he actually half-believed that his father had been firing at him, not at a thief, but at him, using any excuse to finally do him in. Only half-believed. There was a part of him that still loved his father, despite the beating, the part of him that knew parents had a rough job, that every now and again a spared rod did, indeed, spoil a child. But the frightened, paranoid half, in this case, ruled.

Eventually, after he'd walked in circles for a half hour or so, he calmed down enough to remember just why he had chosen to sneak out of the house. Andy Swartz, his new "friend," had established a club, a midnight-to-dawn club. And the dues were this: For three nights running, you had to sneak out of the house, hole up at the club (sleep if you want, party, anything—as long as you stayed at the club headquarters) and then return home by dawn. If your parents found you out, you were out of the club. Tonight was Brian's first night. And probably his last because once his dad found him. . . .

He was tired, though, and the club would certainly be the best choice. Later, there was the possibility that after a few days of torture, he'd have to reveal the whereabouts of the secret club and the members' names, but, well, that was okay. Truth was, he didn't much care for Andy Swartz. He was a bully, and he, Brian Ferguson, had been his first victim. The only reason he agreed to the rules was to keep Andy from polishing his knuckles on the back of his head each morning.

The club itself was located in a stand of trees a hundred yards or so on the other side of the tracks, about three hundred yards from town. Using nature's canopy, Andy and the other club members had used unneeded plywood, leftover shingling, and tar paper from the new addition Andy's dad had built. The floor was made of green, plastic grass, discarded from his dad's deck. Two-by-fours, for framing, had also come from his dad's new addition. Windows were deemed a luxury. (Greg Munro suggested that whatever was out there they didn't want to see anyway.) When done, the club was actually a fair piece of carpentry. Over the front door was the club's name, M.T.D. (Midnight Till Dawn). Initials were used to fool anyone who might happen upon the ramshackle structure, which wasn't at all likely, according to Andy. You had to go through hell just to get in there, the hut surrounded as it was by wiry bushes and a choke of evergreens. "The only thing's gonna come in here," Andy offered, "is us and a shitload of mosquitoes." About that he was right; even sunlight could barely penetrate the undergrowth. High noon here was like a half hour past sunset anywhere else.

Sleeping in that hut, Brian thought, wouldn't be all that bad. It was getting to it in the dark that he was worried about. He stood on the tracks, moonlight slivered like long strands of gold on the steel rails, and looked over at the stand of trees rising from the earth in one huge, black, solid-looking clump. The path, just down a ways, through a field of timothy and clover, was straight and true, intersecting at the tree line with the path the boys had managed to slash through the thickets. Once Brian entered those woods, the moon would disappear, and his way would be guided only by clear footing. And it would be as dark in there as in a nightmare. He turned, looked back toward Hidden Valley, toward his own house, a tiny square of yellow light in the blackness. Back there was a beating the likes of which he could only guess. Ahead, down the path, were a few moments of anxiety, maybe a few mosquito bites, then a night's sleep while his mom and dad worried themselves sick. Sick enough, hopefully, to sweep up the remains of The Vase and put only love in their hearts. His choice was easy.

He hurried along the well-worn path, not running but walking fast, tall weeds slapping his arms as he occasionally tilted clumsily left or right, depending on the undulations of the ground. As he drew nearer the tree line, details began to emerge: the wings of an evergreen, the angled, dead wood of a long-forgotten fence. But most of all, his ears strained for sound, for here, near the entrance to the woods, he heard absolutely nothing except for the gentle moan of the wind through the trees. He turned and looked toward town again, all but invisible except for an occasional gasp of weak light whenever the wind parted the leaves, looking for all the world to Brian like someone signaling. *C'mon, boy! You really don't wanta go in there. What the hell's in there anyway? Darkness. A ramshackle hut that'd probably squash you like a bug if the wind rose up and somehow found a way in. That's all. And Andy Swartz.* He and the others were probably holed up at the club waiting for him, passing around a quart of warm beer and laughing at him between snorts. So, he had a choice, again a choice. Standing on the tracks that choice had been simple. Standing here with a stand of dark, obscenely quiet woods stretched before him, it wasn't so simple. But he made it.

Years later, had he lived, he would probably have looked back at this night as the night when he finally stretched out and touched manhood, could actually feel it warm in his hands. He would go home, he decided, face the music, and think of very clever ways to tell Andy Swartz just where he could put the Midnight Till Dawn club. Eventually Andy would even forget about using Brian's head as a knuckle polisher, and eventually his father would even forget about The Vase. He was as happy with his decision as he could be, given the spectre of his father's belt and the welts on his backside. And maybe, just maybe, his mom would bring him up a plate full of blueberry pancakes after his father was done with him, just like she had done the time before.

Lazily, a whistle on his lips, Brian retraced his steps, emerging onto the railroad tracks just before midnight. He squinted up the tracks and then to his left, his field of vision taking in the few squares of light from town and a squadron of fireflies switching on and off like far-off ships in a hit and miss fog. Alone, he thought somewhat desultorily. But as he turned his attention toward the tracks again, he saw something. He squinted. There was—a man?—standing on the tracks, a very large and tall man about fifty yards away. (Standing right there between the rails like a black statue, as though all he wanted was to have a quiet chat with the Amtrak, due shortly.) Brian felt a little hitch of fear as he studied the figure, mostly because he wondered if that could be his father up there, even though this man made his old man look small, even smaller than he was. But because his father had been so deeply entrenched in his thoughts, and because the night played weird tricks on the eyes, Brian concluded that the man up there could very well be his father. After all, what scared you always looked bigger. Always. *Look for a belt; see if you can catch a little light off the buckle.* Brian took a halting step forward, his confession playing through his mind lickity split, so it would come out right, so the belt buckle wouldn't dig too deeply into his backside. He took a few more steps, and as he did, so did the man; graceful, slow-motion steps, his arms swinging in a large arc, which made it look like a cushion of air had somehow worked up under his feet. That little hitch of fear was suddenly fanned into a full-scale terror.

It was late, real late, and he was a skinny little kid alone on the railroad tracks, where, in fact, more than one kid had met his maker over the years. He'd heard the stories, old stories told by older farts down at the hardware store. Kids had been lost near these tracks, or around these tracks, something like that.

The man seemed to speed up—but noiselessly, which was oh, so odd—and Brian started walking backward.

Sure, he'd heard those stories—and believed them. Those kids hadn't just run away from home; they'd been kidnapped and probably murdered.

He picked up his step because the man had broken into a trot.

And their bodies were probably somewhere close, maybe even in the woods where the M.T.D. club was meeting right now! Christ, if they went looking—

"Wait a minute, kid, wait a minute!"

Brian's fear lolled over and napped momentarily. This man had a light, even friendly voice. Probably just someone his mom sent to look for him, he thought. He sure was big, though. Brian slowed down and let the man draw closer.

"My mom send you?" Brian yelled at the man, who was now only sixty feet or so away.

"Your mom?"

"Yeah . . ."

"She sure did. She's worried about you, son."

"Thought so."

The man stopped within five feet of Brian and smiled down at him. "Maybe you better come with me, son. Like I said, your mom's real worried."

Brian studied the man. Yeah, he looked like someone who'd get sent out to look for some kid who had run off; big and kind of stupid-looking, someone who didn't have nothin' better to do. He searched his memory to see if he knew the man, to see if maybe he had met him on some holiday or something.

"My dad," Brian said haltingly, "is he real pissed?"

The man seemed to think a moment. "Now, why would your father be mad at you? He loves you, son, loves you a lot."

Apprehension began a slow boil. He thought a moment, images of long-dead kids, their bug-picked skeletons rising from the ground around M.T.D. headquarters. . . .

He took a step backward, wondering if the man saw him do it. "My brother, Greg, he there, too?"

"Greg? Sure, Greg's there," the man answered, taking a compensatory step forward.

Sonofabitch. Brian turned and ran, his skinny legs carrying him along those tracks as fast as they ever had, the bug-picked skeletons pursuing him now too, the stranger leading them; a hideous, supernatural posse that would do far more than simply string him up. "Oh, God, Oh, God, Oh, God!" he said to himself as he ran, hoping with everything in him that God did, in fact, know about this, that—as he turned and looked behind him—God knew that some big, stupid-looking killer was after him. "Oh, God, Oh, God, Oh, God!"

The stranger loped after him effortlessly. Brian's legs did three times the RPM, but still he was losing ground—still losing ground—he knew that because each time he turned, the man had drawn just a little closer. All he could think of was the dream where, no matter what, no matter how fast he thought he was moving, he was standing still. The fireflies, flickering all around him, got in the way, diving at his cheeks and forehead. Unconsciously he slapped them away, only remotely understanding that his face had become a burial ground. But then, inexplicably, when the man was within ten feet, arms outstretched, and when Brian was absolutely positive that at any second he would feel a huge hand on his shoulder, that turning would only reveal a huge head with maniac's eyes slammed into it, he turned to see only the moonlit tracks stretching into nothingness. He slowed down and let go with a giant sigh of relief. And after he'd scoured the area thoroughly, he actually took a few steps in the opposite direction, back from where he had come. He looked left then right, then down the tracks again. Nothing, just the weeds waving at him, just the winking fireflies. The man had disappeared—just like in a dream.

He thought of home. He was, at least, now pointed in the right direction, and in his mind he saw his dad and mom and his brother, *Hank,* not Greg. He had only used that to trick the stranger. And pretty quick thinking it was, too. Right now he even thought warmly of his dad's belt, and even more warmly of his mom's blueberry pancakes, her little peace offerings. So he walked faster, glancing to his right now as he passed the path he had taken earlier, wondering what Andy and the others were up to, whether they missed him or—

Suddenly he was thrown nine feet into the air, and out of him came only a ululating, reflexive sound, "Aaaagh," just a blending of many words and random, frightened thoughts, the only thing his brain would allow under the circumstances. "Aaaagh," he cried again as the large man pulled him down and cradled him in his arms and swung him back and forth like he might a baby, chuckling thinly to himself all the while and saying with crazy indifference, "Sure, Martin'll like you—you'll do just fine."

Brian saw only those eyes that burned bright like controlled fires against a large, dark head. The arms were clamped around him firmly but not so firmly that he didn't try to get away, screaming, "Lemme go, lemme go," his flailing fists firing into the man's chest and only provoking more papery-thin chuckles. "Lemme go, lemme go. I'll tell my dad; he's got a gun! A shotgun!" But then, as he realized how futile it was to hit this large, powerful man, Brian resorted to tears, natural, fear-induced tears. "Please, please, mister. Let me go! Please, I wanna go home, I wanna go home."

The man just looked at him as if he didn't understand. Then he smiled a friendly, Uncle Jim smile and said, "Home? Why would you wanna go there? There's better places than home. There are much better places than home. Let me take you there," and the passing Amtrak drowned out Brian's scream.

With consciousness came the smell of rotten flesh and from across the room the flicker of a small lantern. The smell was so powerful that Brian closed his eyes again and prayed that this place was only a dream place, that when he opened his eyes again, he would be in his own bed and that it would be morning and the cat would be licking his feet, as she always did. When he thought about it strongly enough, he could almost feel her raspy tongue pull along his heel, could almost feel the silky fur against his bare legs as she brushed against him while he shook some food into her bowl. But the smell could not be denied. Slowly yet surely, his eyes still closed, that smell made the image of Cleo the cat change. Her fur became matted and coarse, like threads of muddy steel, and her green eyes snapped with points of dark red blood, her fangs dripping with gleaming little droplets of spit. Then she hissed at him and raised her right foot to reveal her claws, long and razor sharp. "Oh, Cleo, no, Cleo, no. . . ."

Now, while Brian's eyes remained closed, thoughts of Cleo gave way to footsteps, heavy and shuffling. Dare he open his eyes to see? Dare he stare into the flickering dimness to see some hulkish thing bearing down on him? "No!" he whispered. "No, God, no, I won't, I won't!"

Muttering unintelligible offerings to whatever was out there, Brian pulled his arms over his face and curled into a fetal position. The footsteps grew closer, and now he heard a grunting sound. Still he preferred the darkness. He remembered how he would look out the back window of the station wagon at the reflected horrors of a drive-in movie, somehow believing that reflections were less evil, less able to harm.

The shuffling footsteps stopped, and he felt

something draw lightly along his leg, heard little squeals of grunted delight. And he knew that he would have to look sometime. He couldn't stay blind forever. Just because he couldn't see the monster, didn't mean it wasn't there. It had touched him—it had . . . liked what it had touched. And it was studying him, something that shuffled instead of walked, something that grunted instead of spoke. It was studying him just as surely as a cannibal. . . . But yet, he reasoned with forced sanity, he hadn't been harmed. Maybe he'd been kidnapped . . . sure, kidnapped. But why? His parents were just working stiffs. . . . He felt fingers trace the hair on the back of his head. His only response was to close his eyes so tightly that spots rose in front of them. But the hand, he noticed with a sudden glimmer of hope, was gentle. He was being stroked as if he were an animal. *That's not something normal people do! Great-grandma used to do it, but she was senile and almost blind. She couldn't think right; she just looked at you and remembered things that happened a million years ago.*

"Mar . . . tin," he heard, the voice gravelly, the word barely recognizable, punching a hole in the dimness of his thoughts. The hand withdrew. As it did, Brian's muscles lost some of the tension that had built in them. "Mar . . . tin," he heard again, sounding very much like an introduction, as if the owner of that voice expected Brian to tell him his name.

Brian lowered his arms and, holding firm to a new hope, slowly opened his eyes.

Grinning at him vacuously was a squatting

"Mar . . . tin." His large, hairy arms lay on his thighs, thick-fingered hands draped over his knees. The light, coming from the left, shimmered yellow on Martin's left side while the right remained in deep shadow.

Martin was huge and hairy, and he stank miserably. And he was obviously an idiot. Brian felt the Lord's Prayer come from his mouth, and he hadn't even given it a thought. The Lord's Prayer because he was oh, so sure that at any second this huge, hairy old, old man would reach out and with some reservoir of strength take his life. There could be no other reason for him to be here. He, Brian, was some kind of sacrifice—a rollicking good time for this old, old man. Brian stood and braced himself against the slimy, wet wall behind him, feeling something with many legs crawl slowly across the back of his hand. At the same time, Martin stood as best he could. But he stopped two-thirds of the way up, his body hunched, and tilted his neck back to further appraise the young tow-haired boy he had been given.

Then something remarkable happened. Martin, still in a gravelly, almost unintelligible voice, said, "Don't fear me, boy. We're going to be fast friends, you and I, very fast friends." And with that said, Martin turned, shuffled to his bed, sat down and simply stared, the lantern light catching his eyes in a hit and miss pattern that made them look like little sputtering fires.

Brian, using what little light there was, ran to the door and pulled frantically. It didn't budge. Within seconds, he realized the futility of his efforts and turned back toward the ill-lit room. As he did, he stumbled over the decaying bodies of Rosemary Hamilton and Susan Dorsey. Running his fingers over the growing knot on his forehead, Brian sat up and saw what he had tripped over. Rosemary's dead, black eyes stared at him soullessly. And Brian immediately fainted.

CHAPTER FOURTEEN

The Past

And this, too, Martin saw on the grimy ceiling of his prison:

One of Martin's employers, Father Unu—everybody called him, "Oh, no!"—pushing seventy now, knelt at the altar in prayer, smack dab in the middle of a huge shaft of stained-glass-window-filtered sunlight. With a certain amount of awe, Martin thought that Father Unu looked like God himself.

Martin was the "custodial engineer" for this and the other four corners churches in Hunt, a menial job to be sure, but Father Unu and the other caretakers of the cross always told him tips were far better here than in a restaurant: "Make peace with your maker, Martin—now there's a tip." "A prayer a day keeps the devil away." "God in your heart is like a dollar in your pocket." They had a million of them. Martin would have preferred a few bucks here and there to divine counseling; he'd never really been a churchgoer anyway. As a human, Martin had never delved too deeply into philosophy, religious or otherwise. When he crossed over, he dabbled a little more, but only because knowledge was another bennie.

Father Unu, Martin thought, was a snob, and as a man of the cloth, snobbery didn't look good on him. That snobbishness revealed itself not only in the wit-filled "tips," but in the knowing smile that washed over his face whenever Martin had somehow managed to formulate a question concerning Father Unu's employer, God: his existence, his methods, his seeming lack of compassion. Of course, the fact that Father Unu was considerably brighter than Martin, a fact Martin could not deny, was part and parcel of Martin's dislike.

The truth be known, Father Unu was not at all snobbish. He was a kind, extremely devout man who went out of his way to answer all of Martin's questions as best he could. But Martin saw only the surety of his answers, the quotations from scripture that slipped off his tongue like little daggers; knowledge that Martin would never possess. But the heaviest weight of all was that damnable knowing smile, that wall of grinning skin that wrapped his answers in an impregnable cocoon. Father Unu was a snob, and someday he, Martin Crouper, would rustle up a proper response to the scriptures, something violently suitable.

After what Martin thought was an inordinately long time to be on your knees, Father Unu finally got up and left, leaving the church empty except for Martin and his cleaning cart, which he rolled to the front pew. To his front were Jesus and Mary, around him the stations of the cross.

"Forty-six," he whispered. That was his age. "Forty-fuckin'-six!" And so his thought continued: *In ten years I'll be fifty-six; in twenty years I'll be sixty-six. In thirty years . . . in thirty years I'll be fertilizing the grass in the boneyard.* His large body sagged as though a huge, invisible weight had descended slowly onto it. "Christ, I've already lived more than half my life! Christ, oh, Christ, oh, Christ!"

This routine, that of spying on Father "Oh, no!" and then sitting at the front pew to have a chat with himself, had been going on for quite a few years now. It never changed; the words were always the same, their timbre always the same. And there were always a few unavoidable—extremely unmanly—tears. In some miniscule way, Martin thought that by bringing the subject up daily, he could avoid it ultimately. It hadn't worked, though. His hair was going gray, and not fashionably either, not like an executive or a movie star, someone who could at the same time, afford to keep his skin from sagging and his belly from bulging. Martin was not growing old gracefully, as men supposedly did. He was simply growing old.

Just then Bobby All came in and sat down next to him. He didn't look at him; he looked toward the altar, his face expressionless and blank. A praying face, Martin thought. They were friends, the quintessential odd couple, Bobby only twenty-two, less than half his age. Martin knew that he had been part of the reason Cynthia Voorhees had broken up with Bobby, that it was more than a little strange for a high school kid—although he didn't look like one—to hang around with a grown man in his forties. And now Cynthia Voorhees was married to that Judd Lucas, just returned from the army with a ton of medals on his chest.

After ten minutes or so, Martin said, "What are you doin' here? I thought you didn't like church," his words echoing all the way into the choir loft.

"I'm goin' to the fair on Saturday, thought you might like to come along," Bobby said.

"That fair they got down to Geneva?"

"Over to Geneva," Bobby corrected. Geneva and Hunt were, on a New York State map, about directly across from each other. You went *down* to Elmira or Binghamton, but not to Geneva. You went *over* to Geneva.

Bobby, who corrected Martin every chance he got, smiled.

"God, you can be a real pain," Martin said, without looking at his friend. "What fair is it, anyway?"

"It's new. Petry Brothers Fair they call it. It's got rides and tents and freaks, you know, like great big cows and two-headed pigs, that kind of thing."

Martin was fascinated. From time to time a carnival stopped in Hunt, but they were ripoffs.

"Saturday, huh?" Martin said.

"Pick you up around six—in the evenin'," Bobby said. "Fairs are always better at night when they turn on all the lights, like on the ferris wheel and the Tilt-a-Whirl."

"And it always seems like you go faster at night," Martin added.

"That's because you've got no point of reference," Bobby said.

Martin mulled that over a moment, the logic whizzing past his brain at light speed, too fast to catch. "Yeah, makes sense, I guess. Six, you said? Okay. Six o'clock you come down and get me."

Whenever Martin thought of this prelude to immortality, he couldn't help but smile. Smarter now—by miles—than he had been then, he wondered whether his newly acquired intelligence would have prevented him from going to the Petry Brothers Fair. If he had known about THAT attraction in particular. . . . Probably not.

Bobby All drove his dad's '53 Ford, a two-door. By the time they arrived at the fair some forty-five minutes later, the pits of Martin's madras shirt were soaked, the stains bleeding out toward his elbows then down his ribs toward the small of his back. Even though he'd plastered many layers of deodorant on, he still sweat like a football lineman.

"I told you to put pads under your arms, Martin," Bobby said as they got out. "What happens if we meet some girls? You wanta tell me that? They're gonna take one look at you and puke! That's what."

Martin, as most everyone who knew him believed, had never had a date. Whenever a woman got close, physically or verbally, his brain turned to mashed potatoes. Bobby, although, on the surface at least, a little stupid, a little too large, and with no sense of style, had the eyes of Valentino. It was always the eyes, he told Martin. "I know most people think I'm a dumbshit. I know I'm too big, and I know I smell sometimes. But I got these eyes, these eyes that even scare me a little. So whenever I need it, I can get it. I take me a bath, put on my best clothes, the ones Ma picked out, go on down to the Soda Shoppe and just look at 'em. You, Martin, you probably still choke your chicken."

It was a semi-cloudy day, the horizon a tad darker than overhead, threatening to storm. As they parked the Ford in a cut hay field and walked toward the banner slung over the entrance, each felt a ripple of disappointment. The fair itself, about a hundred yards from where they had parked, didn't even have the ferris wheel Bobby so wanted to see lit up at night. There were a few rides, the kid kind—ponies, tiny little fire engines on a circled track, go-karts, that kind of thing—but mostly the Petry Bros. Fair consisted of carnival barkers up and down the midway trying to haul in some suckers. A stand of old deciduous trees at the back, left and right of the fair, made it look even smaller. Beyond these, past a mile or so of hay fields, lay the interstate, cars and trucks whizzing along noiselessly like little electric models, in deference to the collection of sounds rising from the fair. The sweet, somewhat cloying smell of fair foods—cotton candy, candied apples, popcorn—filled the air and made the mouth water. Off to the right were a few fat, white trailers. As Martin watched, a large man puffing on a huge cigar and wearing a black bowler and a flowered vest walked out of one and stopped, his attention focused on a fistful of greenbacks.

"What's a carnival without a ferris wheel?" Bobby

asked no one in particular.

"Well, it's like a bull without balls, that's what," Martin said. Every now and then Martin tried a little off-color humor. Sometimes it worked, sometimes it didn't. Bobby smiled. This time it had worked.

They stopped under the banner, and after hemming and hawing for more than five minutes about whether they should go in or not, Martin made up his mind. "I didn't smell myself up for nothin'."

So they went in, side by side. By now, a few drops of rain had started to fall, and the horizon had darkened ominously.

As they walked, the sand collecting moisture quickly now, Martin remembered a rhythmic barker's plea his dad quoted from time to time: "Come one, come all, see JoJo the dog-faced boy; he walks, he talks, he crawls on his belly like a reptile." With barkers on either side, their ramblings sounding like Tower of Babel nonsense, Martin tried to cull out that particular phrase, really expecting to hear it—it was, after all, perfect for a carnival, a dog-faced boy who walks, who talks—

"Say there, you two look pretty healthy to me!"

Martin stopped when Bobby stopped, right in front of a tall pole with point totals indicated on the front and a large bell at the top. A muscular, hairy, half-bald man in a T-shirt advertising Petry Bros. Fair was beckoning to them with a curled finger and glimmering eyes. "Yeah, you two, you two fine examples of manhood." As if drawn by the sheer weight of suggestion, they stepped closer. "A dime, that's all it'll cost you, one thin dime. Ring the bell, win a prize, any prize on the shelf."

Bobby smiled confidently. "Those prizes," he said. "I'll bet they only cost you a nickel each."

The large man smiled so large a smile that it seemed he should have laughed. "Why, you're an astute gentleman, real astute. Tell you what, you give me a dollar—"

"A dollar—you said—"

"Hold on now, just hold on. You give me a dollar, I'll give you ten chances. You ring that bell just once, and I'll give you the whole shootin' match, every goddamn prize I got. That'd put me right out of business. Now, how's that suit you? You wanta give her a shot?"

"Just a dollar?"

"Eight bits. And I'll tell you what—I'll even let your friend take ten swings at it. How would that be? Twenty swings total."

Bobby pulled Martin aside. This was too easy, Bobby insisted. Something was wrong. This guy was gonna take their dollar, somehow, someway. While they waited, an average-sized man strolled up, gave the man his dime, picked up the war club and promptly rang the bell. He handed his prize—a stuffed bear—over to his blond, curvaceous, proud-as-peaches girlfriend, and together they strolled away.

"It's a set-up," Bobby immediately insisted to the proprietor. "You want a sucker, look somewhere else."

They left the muscular man speechless. Outwitted, outworded, Bobby had done him in with a flourish. By now it was raining lightly, and the ground gathered muddily around their shoes as they walked.

They strolled around the Petry Bros. Fair for the next couple of hours, stopping every now and then to throw darts at underinflated balloons that wouldn't break with anything short of a center hit, or try their hand in the shooting gallery, where Bobby proved to be the best shot. So by the time night had fallen, they were sure they had seen everything this close-to-being-bankrupt fair had to offer. And they were, for the most part, disappointed. Martin won a dribble glass; and Bobby, a plastic ring with a bolt of lightning on it, remarking, as he slipped it on, that someday he'd have a whole fistful of glittering stones, but that was the extent of their haul. Sure, they had seen a few girls, but Martin and his putrid pits had scared them off. And to top it all off, they were soaked to the bone by the light but steady rain.

"Whose idea was this anyway?" Bobby asked.

"Who cares," Martin said.

They were walking near the bell again now. The proprietor saw them and beckoned once more.

Bobby waved at him disdainfully. "What's the matter, not enough suckers around—you wanna try us again?"

The man threw his hands out to the side and smiled. Then, still smiling, he said, "No, not you two. Tell you what though, because you guys are such good sports, I'll let you in on a secret."

Bobby looked at Martin, Martin at Bobby. Secrets wouldn't cost much. They strolled over to the bell. "What secrets?" Bobby asked cautiously.

The man gestured, indicating the entire fair. "Now, boys, you and I both know this ain't much."

Bobby grinned. "You ain't tellin' us somethin' we

don't already know, mister."

"Well, it's true, there ain't much here now, but later, after it's all closed down, after everyone goes on home—there will be."

"What do you mean, after it's all closed down?" Bobby said.

"Just what I said. Boss comes around in a couple hours and closes the place up tight as a virgin's mousetrap. But after, we have us a hell of a time. Just thought you guys might want to join in the fun."

"Gamblin'?" Bobby asked.

"No, better than gamblin'. You'll know it when you see it."

"So what do we do till then?"

"Whatever you want. Go on out to your car and wait, stick around. Whatever you want."

Bobby regarded him suspiciously. "Why you tellin' us this anyway?"

The man smiled again. "Because you boys figured me right out and because I owe you. Sometimes I get to feelin' bad about takin' money from the likes of you, so sometimes I try to make peace with myself. You wouldn't want to deny a man his peace, now would you?"

Bobby agreed that his was a noble cause, and he and Martin did appreciate his honesty, and yes, they would be back later. With a new sense of purpose, they walked to their car to wait.

The last customer walked out around eleven-thirty. The fair was dark and quiet now, save for a gasp of weak light from within. Standing under the fair banner, hands on hips, legs spread, was the bald man. He was looking at them, Martin thought, although all they could see of him was a blackened outline. He raised an arm and waved them in.

Just before they got to the entrance, the man turned, still looking at them and pointed down the midway. Then he walked swiftly off, disappearing behind a baseball toss game.

A fair, at night, when no one was around, the rain splashing down, the wind picking up, was enough to give anyone a touch of goose-flesh. As he looked around, Martin saw the ghosts of all the suckers, of girls and guys, of little people and big. It gave him the willies.

Not knowing exactly where they were going, they walked down the midway, walked until they came to a small, gray tent set back about twenty feet or so, a tent they had not seen earlier. Along the top were small, triangular red-and-white pennants that looked like they'd been stolen from a used-car lot. The right side of the tent was flapped open enough to reveal the center pole. Beyond it, they saw a simple table with a folding chair behind it, apparently empty. Multi-colored, chasing lights had been strung along the front of the table. Shoved into the ground, as if the place were for sale, was a neat, hand-written sign that said simply, "ONE DOLLAR—IMMORTALITY." Their curiosity was piqued, if only because the reward was high and the price was right. Outside for a dollar, they could have had a truckload of stuffed animals and cheap shot glasses—here they could live forever, or so the sign promised. Of course, they didn't for a moment believe that sign. *Not entirely.* Immortality—for only a dollar! Bobby scoffed.

"What? They gonna carve your name in a rock or

something?" he said.

Martin laughed.

But Martin, who unlike Bobby, or so he thought, spent a great deal of time contemplating his empty future, the old age that was marching on him just as surely as that approaching thunderstorm, said, "I got a dollar, and I don't mind spending it. We been here most of the night, and we got nothing but trash to show! And we come a long ways. I say we go inside. I say we get immortal."

Bobby laughed out loud. "The only thing you're going to get in there, Martin, is fleeced! Instead of one dollar, they'll get two. Can't you see that?"

Sure he could, but he didn't mind. A dollar for immortality! The price was more than fair, even if that price didn't include a guarantee. And how would he feel in the morning, his cleaning cart beside him, the stations of the cross surrounding him like barred windows? How would he feel then if he didn't give this his best shot?

"I can see that, sure. But a dollar, Bobby. A dollar's nothin'."

With that said, he stepped past Bobby and into the tent, the sides of which had begun to inhale and exhale with the rising storm. Bobby followed, standing beside him as he stopped in front of the table. Seated behind the table was a dwarf—an old bald dwarf with a nose like a turkey vulture. He had on a short-sleeve white shirt and a black, butterfly-shaped bowtie that had been sprinkled with glitz. Their eyes betrayed them; Martin and Bobby were fascinated. The little man pushed himself up, and as he did, a clap of thunder crashed overhead, startling only the two of them. The dwarf looked as if he had expected it. *Maybe he's deaf,* Martin thought. But he wasn't deaf. He leaned back in the folding chair and appraised these fresh, new clients with tiny, sparkling eyes, eyes that looked as though they had gotten in the way when glitz was sprinkled onto his butterfly-shaped bowtie.

"A dollar, boys," he said in a crystalline tenor, "a dollar and she's yours. Now, I'm not sayin' it's that simple. I'm not sayin' that you give me a dollar and you're magically transformed. No, sir! I'm sayin' this: If you believe I can do it, if you believe in such stuff, then it'll happen. If you don't, well, if you don't. . . ."

He looked to his right. For the first time they saw that the tent had two rooms. The wind had worked underneath and curled the underside of the canvas doorway. It was totally dark beyond.

"That's where it happens, boys, after you give me your dollar. That's where time stops. Do you believe, boys? Tell me true, do you believe?"

No doubt they thought it was all just part of the act. But whether they believed or not, they were going to begin the trip to immortality that night, and nothing was going to stop them.

Martin watched Bobby, watched his face, how it took on a sinewy strength, a resolve. He had saved them a dollar already, and now he had a chance to save them two more. He fished a hand into his front pocket, pulled it out and waved a crumpled bill in front of the dwarf.

"Take this, little man, and step aside. I'll forfeit a dollar to uncover a ruse."

The dwarf swatted the bill out of Bobby's hand and stuffed it into his own pocket.

By now the tent walls were breathing in and out furiously—the center pole seemed ready to leap at the battered sky—while lightning strobed the canvas. Martin and Bobby glanced around nervously while the rain sheeted onto the tent, making it almost impossible to hear the little man.

"A ruse? A ruse? Hah. Go on then, go on and uncover this ruse," he said, somewhat agitated.

He seemed awfully sure of himself, and it was because of that bubbling confidence that Bobby hesitated.

The little man pulled the dollar out. "You wanta forget it? Here, take it back. Go on, take it back." Then he laughed. Cackled, actually, Martin thought. The truth be known, that little man cackled just as sure as a hen cackles. The cackle and the biblical storm rose the gooseflesh on his arms and almost sent him scurrying out into the rain. But Bobby ignored the little man, assumed that stony resolve and marched with alacrity into the adjoining room.

What happened from that point forward, until they awoke in their car—not really sure of what day it was—Martin still didn't know. Some minutes after Bobby went into that adjoining room, he reappeared. He was the same, everything about him, right down to his Valentino eyes, everything, that is, except that he had acquired a queerly mechanical way of speaking. Sure, he smiled, and he seemed awfully sure of himself, but still, that monotone was not Bobby.

"Well, give him a dollar, Martin. It's the truth," he said.

So he did, and the little man took his money willingly, then gestured toward the other room.

There were, Martin knew, few ways one could claim immortality. Well, only one that he really knew about, and that one was only fantasy. Vampires were misty, fictionalized beings who lived in some fantastical European netherworld. At least that was what Father Unu, who made it his business to know such things, had claimed.

What awaited him in that adjoining room, Martin theorized, was nothing more than what Bobby had said, some huge chunk of marble and some guy waiting to carve their initials into it for a dollar. A ripoff, just like Bobby said. But there hadn't been a huge chunk of marble in there, at least one he could see; there had only been darkness, a quick shuffling of feet, dark shadows and finally, a flash of remarkable pain. Then . . . then . . . he pushed his brain to its limits, trying to remember. But he couldn't. He had never been able to remember what happened next.

The immortality thing, he thought, didn't just leap on them afterward. They didn't walk out of that tent sneering and slobbering, their fangs glistening in the moonlight that had replaced the storm. Not at all. They woke up in the car the next morning, a lukewarm sun glaring at them from a cloudless horizon, a vague sense of knowing gnawing at their guts. Martin remembered thinking then that if they were immortal, they weren't vampires, thank goodness. They had become immortal some other way, some way even Father Unu didn't know about. But there were the telltale puncture marks on each of them, right there on their necks, right where legend said they'd be. And Bobby, who obviously knew just as much about the subject as Martin did, shot a wide-eyed look into the mirror of the '53 Ford, then breathed a sigh of relief as his reflection stared back at him.

"Weird" was all he could say, smiling.

They drove home immediately, keeping their conversation to a minimum.

After Bobby had dropped him off at his apartment about eight-thirty in the morning, Martin remembered thinking that it was going to be a hot day, as hot as any in memory, that the morning sun had seemed to double in size. He went upstairs, drew the curtains to hide that blazing sun, forgetting about work, and lay down on his unmade bed, as tired as he could ever remember being. And the dreams—oh, the dreams, just as real as an impacted wisdom tooth; hordes of slavering beasts that were both human and inhuman, darting in and out of caves, leaping from skyscrapers, attacking other slavering beasts. But during it all he didn't once push the panic button and force himself to wake up. Not once did he even consider it. The dreams seemed right, natural.

He didn't wake up until that evening, just as the sun nestled beyond the horizon, just as night shadows slithered into town.

And when he woke up, he knew, like a woman knows when she's pregnant, or like an elephant knows when to die, that he was now immortal. It wasn't simply the transparent image that looked back at him from the mirror, or the new-found reasoning power. It was a hunger, a thirst. A desire like none he had never known. A desire he satisfied that very evening.

Immortal, happy—and ignorant of the rules, the goddamned rules. Which was why he was here now, in this stinking, dank, rat-infested cellar.

The rules.

CHAPTER FIFTEEN

The Present

"Human skin," Ben Weisanthal said, as though that knowledge had only needed scientific verification.

The receiver in Judd's right hand dropped a few inches from his ear. He put it back. "You're sure?"

"Yes, quite sure."

"Thanks, Ben."

"Any time."

The county morgue in Elmira was as sterile as those rooms given over to the saving of the living. That irony never ceased to amaze Harvey Lipscomb. Leaning back in his wood chair, which rested against a stainless steel examining table, Harvey took a large bite out of his roast beef and lettuce sandwich and set his teeth to working, his mouth open. He swallowed noisily and smiled—roast beef and lettuce on white was his favorite. Extra lean beef, crisp, curly lettuce, gobs of mayo—a little slice of heaven.

The dead were stored with librarylike preciseness in numbered drawers inserted into the wall in front of him. Tonight, as mid-week often was, had been slow. In number three lay Chester Bathgate, age seventy-four, heart attack victim. In repose a couple of doors over lay Kyle Clery, age six, his skull crushed by his mother's LeSabre wagon as he played in the driveway. Gloria Sternmyer was the only other "guest" this evening. "What a waste, gorgeous broad like that," he thought aloud. "Wish I'd seen her before today." He took another bite, tearing off a quarter of the sandwich, his wet chewing sounds reverberating in the white tiled room.

As he swallowed, Harvey thought he detected a subtle change in the lighting, then, just as quick, a return to the normal washed-out glow. He felt uneasy enough to right his chair, put his sandwich on the examining table, and do a slow circle of the room, his eyes going to the closed drawers. He turned and saw the chart bearing the life-size rendering of the human body, its many parts labeled, little arrows pointing to each. Little balls of sweat began to form under his eyes, and the roof of his mouth grew as dry as cotton. Someone, he thought, was in here with him. Someone had come in through the double doors with all the quietness of thought. But then, he reasoned, there were explanations. His co-worker, Bill Triblehorn, played these kinds of tricks—and was really pretty good at them. ("One of these days, Harv, ole buddy, I'm gonna make your drawers a satchel for shit!") Harvey pushed a hand out in front of him and forced a smile. "Billy—God, Billy, you got me good that time, Billy, got me real good—"

Suddenly interrupting his flattery was a noise he thought sounded very much like one of the drawers opening; first the slight snick, then the whirr of rollers. He turned. Gloria Sternmyer, naked as Miss October, stood beside the now open drawer. Her mouth gaped open.

"Level-headed, thoughtful, not given to flights of fancy." Judd remembered those words well. They had been used by his guidance counselor to describe him as a boy. But if he really were those things, level-headed, thoughtful, not given to flights of fancy, what in the world was he doing here in the town library undertaking an examination of the occult? And more to the point, of vampires? For what purpose? He closed the card file, inhaled deeply, then let it out. "Why, indeed!" he said, the words, he thought, a prelude to reason. He looked toward the doors; a mother and her young son were leaving.

"That kid might believe what I'm thinking," he whispered. But who else? He was the sheriff—"just the facts, ma'am, just the facts"—a pillar of the community—*the* pillar of the community. If anyone went off the deep end and lent credence to other worldly ideas, it would most certainly *not* be the town sheriff.

Those denials aside, he tried another approach. After all, who was *better* equipped to acknowledge the supernatural? Who else had "all the facts, ma'am"? No one. No one but him. Fact one: four mutilated bodies—and in the case of Barb and Walt there had been no obvious method of entry. The storm door had been left open at the Vasquez home, but on the steps they'd found the clothing and, moreover, badly burned human skin. Fact number two: Gloria Sternmyer's so very alive-looking corpse. Fact number three: the shadowy, even mystical reappearance of his wife. These "facts" were as weighty as any "real, hard evidence." That's why he felt it imperative to research them just as thoroughly as any other lead; this thoroughness, of course, was why he was here. So why was he worried about the librarian watching him as he strolled over to the card catalogue?

He pulled the index file out and thumbed through the V's. "Vampires, vampires," he mumbled. What he found was a plethora of books on the subject. Some, like Cavanaugh's *Vampires—Myth or Reality,* had apparently been written as guides, like the many UFO books popular during the days of Operation Bluebook. Judd marked down the locations, closed the drawer, and proceeded to pull those books he thought might be helpful, all the while trying mightily to keep the open mind that had brought him here in the first place.

He thought he detected a smile on the librarian's face as he handed the books over. On his way to the desk, he had even thought of an excuse, that he was taking the books out for Steven, who had a fondness for monsters. But the librarian said nothing. She took the cards out, stamped them, and slid the books back across the desk, reminding him that they were due back in three weeks. *Three weeks,* Judd thought as he cradled the books under his arm, *that's an eternity.*

Judd pulled into his driveway a half hour before sunset. Reaching into the backseat, he picked up a Breens paper bag and put the books inside. Steven wouldn't question a grocery bag, but he would certainly question an armful of books about vampires.

As he got out of the Jeep, Sam ran up to him—sans leash.

"Hey, boy," Judd said, hefting the bag, "where's Steven."

"Back here," he heard. "Cleanin' up the dog crap."

Judd smiled and went inside, Sam right behind. He put the books behind closed doors in the bookcase and went out back to help.

Judd stood at the door staring into a far less foggy night, his thoughts centered on the feeling that he was somehow being compelled to leave the house. From the east he heard thunder roll, but the storm was moving away from Hunt. Northeastern storms tracked west to east, rarely the opposite. This particular storm had rumbled into town an hour earlier, but had mercifully spared his little corner of the universe. He turned and looked behind him, toward the loft where Steven was sleeping. Sam had taken up his customary position in front of the fireplace. There had been an unusually large cluster of burrs in his coat today, according to Steven, who had let the dog run free, although he had been told not to. Just how good a time the animal had had on any given day, Judd thought, could be determined by how burr-ridden he was by the time he finally dogged it home. Someday, maybe, the dog would hurt himself bad out there or catch something the vet couldn't cure. But the life he now lived, that of the four-legged vagabond, the finder of strange and wonderful things in a thickly treed, creature-filled forest, suited him far better than an apartment in the city and the occasional tethered walk with nothing to sniff and wonder at except sidewalks and previously discovered fire hydrants. Boredom, Judd thought, probably killed a dog as quickly as anything.

He stepped onto the porch, the events of the night before still very much with him. And it was then that he suddenly considered taking a walk in the woods. Even more precisely, to the clearing. He stepped off the porch, and a dark, consuming dread suddenly washed over him, dread of not only the strange compelling force he had experienced, but of what might be waiting for him out there in the clearing a mile or so away. Vampires, according to one of the books he had gotten from the library, were not simply confined to eastern Europe. The beliefs surrounding their legend would fill encyclopedias. And perhaps most vexing, most thought-provoking of all was the belief by the Greek Orthodox church that persons born on Christmas Day stood at special risk of becoming a vampire. Cynthia, he noted, a thread of cool fear tightening around his throat, was born at 12:01 A.M. Christmas morning. Coincidence, he calmly told himself. Hell, Mother Theresa was probably born on Halloween. But there was so much more to the legends than what was covered by Hollywood. The Ekimmu of Assyrian legend were said to devour their victims. And, of course, there were the succubus and incubus, sexually crazed female and male vampires. And one vampire no larger than a thumbnail. It seemed that each culture had manufactured its own vampire legend to accommodate its particular social, political and religious philosophies. Of course, there were academic theories offered for the vampire legend, one having to do with the similarity between the symptoms of rabies and vampire-like reactions. It seemed, based on everything Judd had read about them, that a person could get a Ph.D. in vampirology. There were even clubs headed by Ph.D.s, and very serious academicians who claimed that at least in theory, vampires could exist. How much he didn't know about vampires, what he didn't even begin to suspect, surprised him immensely. And those chapters given to how to kill a vampire, he read with vulpine eyes.

He stopped at the tree line and flicked on his flashlight, his eyes scanning the dark forest, a parade of evergreens appearing like prison bars before him. He turned and looked toward the house. One thing he had picked up from the movies and had now been verified in print—a vampire would not enter where he was not invited, which had always struck him as a little strange. Kind of like a mafia hit man coming to the door, violin case firmly clutched under his arm, and saying, "I certainly don't want to be rude, but might I come in? I've got this assignment, you see. . . ." It all seemed so nonsensical, so inconsistent with the rules of good and evil. But then the very idea that vampires roamed the earth was even more nonsensical, so the vagaries that attached themselves to their mythology would not be any less—or any more—nonsensical. He studied the house. If vampires existed—if that were true—then they would need an invitation. He would have to accept that much, because it held that the acceptance of part of an ideology would further mean acceptance of the whole. He smiled, stuck his hand into his pocket and pulled out the contents. "Hell," he said as he slipped the chain around his neck. "This thing's even got me believing in the power of the cross again." Then he realized something, something that if one was to believe the vampire lore, would also have to be believed. The words slid from his mouth with wonder and awakening fear, his unblinking, unfocused eyes scanning the night woods. "But if you really don't believe in its power . . . ," and the cross slipped from his fingers and lay cold and still against his chest.

CHAPTER SIXTEEN

At The Cabin

In his dream Steven was first surrounded by classmates, and then, in the blink of an eye, they were gone. A shudder ran through him and his eyes snapped open. On the vaulted ceiling overhead, shadows cast by a dying fire danced slowly.

He drew away the sheet and sat up. "Uncle Judd?" he said, rubbing his hands over his face.

No answer.

He got up and walked to the railing. Sam, head between his forepaws, opened his eyes and slanted his gaze up at him, the dying fire reflected from them suggesting the dog was only half-awake. The couch, Steven saw now that his eyes had adjusted, was empty. He looked up. The door was closed. He was alone.

Well, at least I'll be able to see something tonight,

Judd thought as he stepped into the clearing, the sky not obscured by fog as it had been the night before. He flicked the flashlight on and then off again. The moon tracked low on the horizon, barely visible through the trees and the dead branches littering the forest like giant cobwebs.

He was sure the trip had been his idea, his alone. Now, standing in the center of this clearing, with the sweet odor of pine needles in the air, the crunch of them underfoot as he slowly turned on the balls of his feet, he wasn't so sure. He flicked the flashlight on again and drew it slowly from left to right. The circle of white light trapped the brown bark of nearby trees, yet only the shadowy shapes of those farther away. But as the light circled, leaving its glowing trail mapped faintly on his eyes, he slowly began to realize that he was not alone. Someone was here, somewhere, behind one of those trees or hidden in the darkness beyond the light. Their presence was undeniable.

"Cynthia?" he said softly.

No answer.

He waited, doubt beginning to surface.

Finally, just when he was about to give up, he saw her. He did not catch her stepping from behind a tree or gliding casually toward him from the depths of the forest. Not at all. She simply appeared in the corner of his vision.

He stepped quickly backward, and she smiled, no less a smile than he remembered, still clothed in the jeans and white blouse she had worn the night before. But her features had somehow changed. Now they were harsh and sharply defined; except for her eyes, which were, from the ten feet that separated them, only dark circles. Whites, irises and pupils had all drawn together into dark, oval pools. Her hair was still long and shimmered in the moonlight like spun gold.

Again his thoughts became muddied, his focus unsure. And even though he'd had a hundred questions to ask her should he ever see her again, he forgot them now.

As she drew closer, he noticed that her breath was warm and sweet smelling. Sweet smelling, yes, but there was something, another odor, penetrating and rank . . . underlying. She bent forward and pulled her lips along his neck, a feathery, innocently provocative, intoxicating kiss. Despite himself, despite the fact that sex was the farthest thing from his mind, he was becoming aroused. He silently cursed his physiology, his Pavlovian responses. He thought of the succubus.

"Just hold me, Judd," she whispered, her fingers tracing lightly through his hair.

Her face was inches away. He looked at it closely. But he couldn't see what he thought should be there, not the gravity-drawn skin, not the laugh lines. The light flattered her, flashing in her beguiling eyes. Those eyes—they had always been like that. Otherworldly. And they were straw-dry tonight, not a hint of moisture in them. In his mind an image of a department store mannequin took shape. And now his sense of touch sparked another image, that of the slab that had dropped over Walt and Barb, the etched square of cold granite. He ran his hand along her cheek. It wasn't just cool to the touch, it was *deathly* cold, the skin smooth and hard, like the skin of a shark. A mental tug of war ensued. Had Cynthia, older, but as he remembered her, returned? Or had sleep overtaken him while he lay on the couch reading, producing the coal-eyed thing that seemed intent on making love to him here in the woods under the cover of darkness? He saw her smile again, but only with her mouth.

"Kiss me, Judd," she said.

Unable to do anything but what she asked, he closed his eyes and put his mouth tenderly on hers—and as he did, gooseflesh prickled coldly on his arms. Her lips were as dry and as cold as the rest of her. There was no distinction between cheek and mouth, just the same cold, hard skin. With their lips pressed together, he opened his eyes and looked at her, expecting . . . but she was also looking at him, the light twinkling off her eyes like the moon off that damnable Higgins slab. And he thought that if he raised a finger and pushed on those eyes, he'd find that they were just like the rest of her, just as cold, just as hard, mere stone masquerading as something remotely human. And she would stand there and laugh at his stupid little game.

His horror almost complete, Judd tried to break free. He couldn't. She wouldn't let him. He grabbed her viciously by the shoulders and pushed with all the strength he could summon. He felt her chest heave with building laughter and saw her mouth widen into a grin, her eyes slit with amusement. He might as well have been pushing against that granite slab. She didn't flinch. Her muscles didn't even twitch in response. Sweat beaded on him thickly; the blood raced through him. Suddenly, when he was quite sure that his heart would burst like a water balloon, images rose on the screen of his mind: treasured images of long ago, so realistic, so believable, that he put everything aside and simply watched.

Jeffrey—there you are, son, right in the middle catching a ride, one small hand for Mom and one for Pop. Upppp we go. Upppp we go. That laugh—God, how I love that laugh! If ever a laugh was infectious, it's yours, son.

Slamming the cupboards again, Jeffrey? You know, Steven's a lot like you. No, c'mon, don't give me that hateful look. I love you! I'm your dad!

Hours, certainly that was how long the images continued: their family history waltzing by like a quickly read novel; joy mixed with sorrow, good times and bad; and through it all, hulking in the recesses of thought, a snow-white face alive with the maggots of death. And that face was Cynthia's.

Tears welled up inside of Steven as he pushed the stinging branches aside, his thin chest rising and falling like a bellows. But, as yet, his tears hadn't pushed all the way up to his eyes. As yet he was still the fine young man his uncle Judd wanted him to be—the fine young man his mom and dad would have been proud of. He knew he should have stayed in the house, but waking up and finding Judd gone, he had felt more alone than he ever had, even when his parents had died. So he had taken blindly to the woods, but not so blindly that he didn't think to leash Sam to help in the search. Now, having been gone for about fifteen minutes, the woods surrounding him had begun to close in just as surely as though he'd been locked inside a small, dark closet. By now he was almost hoarse from yelling.

"Uncle Judd?" he implored. "Please, Uncle Judd! I'm scared, Uncle Judd, I'm real scared!"

Suddenly Sam stopped and growled lowly, threateningly, his head below his shoulders, his lips pulled back from his canines.

A glowing ball of hot fear swelled inside Steven. "Uncle Judd, Uncle Judd," he whispered hoarsely.

Sam, still growling, stepped backward.

Through the cluster of dead branches just in front of him, Steven saw exactly why Sam was growling. There was someone up ahead in the clearing, a flashlight sweeping the ground at his feet, the beam lighting the way for a thousand tiny insects. With all the inner strength that was his, Steven parted the branches. No, not someone—two people. Holding each other. And one was . . . Oh, God!

"Uncle Judd! Uncle Judd!"

As though Steven's cry had been his cue, Sam crashed past him and ran into the clearing. Within five feet of Cynthia, he lunged. And with almost incalculable speed, a long-fingered hand caught him on the side of the head and sent him sprawling, his body somersaulting to a stop against a tree, his leg badly broken, the bone sticking white through the skin. He lay on the ground whimpering with pain, dazed and afraid.

Cynthia, enraged, pulled Judd's lips hard against hers, breaking the skin and sending a stream of blood down his chin. Then she turned and walked quietly away, the woods swallowing her whole.

CHAPTER SEVENTEEN

The Past

The Parthenon, The Sphinx, Castles along the Rhine. He, Martin Crouper, would be there when each—just as mortal skin succumbed to the many-legged insects of the earth—crumbled to the mindless wrath of time. He was immortal, had been for a number of years now—and hadn't aged a millisecond. It was all true; everything Father Unu had told him about the undead was really true. He was smarter now, by degrees (he smiled, remembering the old joke). He would live forever, and his conscience, especially where it concerned the lives of humans, no longer existed. When he had died that stormy night at the Petry Brothers Fair, he had left his conscience behind. Killing for the sake of it, to satisfy his hunger, was as easily done as opening up the fridge and glad-handing a cold chicken leg. Of course, care had to be taken, you couldn't simply walk into a crowded disco and munch on the cutest girl there—

uh, uh. Most important, or so he was told by a thirteen-year-old vampire in Yugoslavia, was never give yourself away. Vampires were legend, nothing more—like UFOs. "We," he had said, "aren't real. We're just neat things to think about."

"Well," Martin had replied, "with so many of us, you'd think at least one would have slipped up by now."

The boy had smiled. "Not so," he said. "You see, Martin, vampires have existed almost as long as man has, and during that time, during a complex period of evolution, we have acquired certain traits. One of those traits is an inherent ability to know when not to kill, when others are watching. There is a warning, a physical thing: You lose interest, not entirely, but enough to remind you that what you're doing may destroy you. If necessary, a vampire can go for centuries without sustenance. I, myself, went thirty-two years without a drop of blood because I had inadvertently allowed myself to be caught in a French cave during a flood. I was buried for that period of time, buried until I was discovered by another vampire passing by.

"You see, Martin, a vampire knows when another vampire is near. In my case, this trait saved me from the prison of earth that had confined me. Of course, after thirty-two years without so much as rat blood, I went a little stir-crazy. But that happens."

From their vantage point on the hill in Hunt Cemetery, the night the rules had been broken, Martin and Robert could see just how peacefully night had settled onto the town; a cloudless sky alive with the glittering beacons of a million lonely worlds, the chirr of crickets amplified on the damp night air, the four corners churches jutting dark and reproachful above the tree line. They were here because Martin had wanted to visit his Aunty Maude's grave, a slab of granite three feet across and a couple of feet tall that said simply, "Our Aunty, Maude Aubin." Dates had been omitted because it had been agreed that Aunty Maude had died long before her heart had actually stopped beating. They sat on tombstones, looking very much like two mortal men who had stopped off at the cemetery on their way home from work to discuss the supernatural. A length of uncut grass arced from Robert's mouth, making him look very much like the proverbial "hayseed." Suddenly, for apparently no reason, he broke into a fit of deep-throated laughter.

Nothing had been said; no joke had passed between them. The laughter was simply a response to their situation, to their status, to the large joke they had managed to play on mankind. Martin knew this, and it didn't take long for him to join in. And for a very long time laughter roared from the hilltop cemetery like a runaway locomotive, laughter that to the few people outside at this late hour, sounded more like a rogue wind charging through the rooftops.

Some time after they had parted company, opting to hunt alone this first night back in town, Martin settled back into his chair in a deep-shadowed corner of Stan's Bar and Grill, a bar at the west end of Main Street, and watched the clientele. A pretty girl in faded, tight jeans walked up to the bar and slipped her hand around a man's waist. The man turned, ran his hand brazenly over her backside and smiled as if he had happened upon familiar territory.

Women like her were Martin's favorite. He didn't know why. Supposedly blood was blood and that was it. But he was positive that a woman's blood gave him a different sensation than a man's. Coming into immortality with his virginity still intact probably had something to do with it, he thought. But that, he found out, was probably a little silly. The thrill of the kill had replaced sex. "Why, in three hundred years or so your dick'll up and disappear," a very old English vampire had told him. "Comes from not usin' it," he had added with a smile. Every now and then Martin, out of curiosity, would look at his to see if it had begun its centuries-long retreat. He didn't think it had, although it didn't really matter.

Sitting there, a glass of cold Genny in front of him, a drink he ordered only to allay suspicion, he remembered his old job as janitor for the four corners churches, and wondered just how everyone was getting along. He grinned at the glass of Genny cupped in his hand, squeezed, and sent a shower of beer and broken glass over the table. Only a small, timid-looking man standing against the booth next to him noticed. He glanced a couple of times, saw that Martin was looking at him, then, pretending to see a friend at the bar, wandered off.

Martin felt a surge of emotion. He had thought of his old job on this first night back in town and had heated up like a car in summer traffic. That, he thought, was very interesting. He wiped his hands on his shirt, got up, and left.

Father Unu.

It was the hum of silence inside a church that Father Unu liked. As was always the case, he had been on his knees for much longer than was probably necessary. Daily prayer, giving thanks to the heavenly father, had become—to his colleagues—somewhat of a routine. And in routine there was danger, the danger of doubt. And doubt was not a word in Father Unu's vocabulary. Not any longer. There had been a time, many years earlier, when he, like most young priests, he thought, had experienced the shallow yet sharp pains associated with doubt: the admitted lapses of faith that sometimes followed extended Bible study or even a protracted argument with a scientifically-minded parishioner.

But as the years passed, he came to realize that the real test of faith lay not in questioning the scriptures to attain truth, but in the acceptance of the scriptures without proof—through blind and obedient faith. The less believable a passage, the stronger the faith had to be to accept it. The realization of this gave him great strength, and soon after this acceptance, he began to think of death and life as somehow intertwined; and this acceptance of the life hereafter gave him unfathomable comfort. Still there would come a day—of this he was positive—when his faith would again be tested, when there would arise a situation that would glean from him all the faith he had been storing over these so many years. He rose, kissed the cross around his neck, and left the altar to prepare himself for his nightly walk.

From the east edge of Main Street, Martin could

barely see the four corners churches. The street itself was pretty much deserted, the hour late, tomorrow a work day. Only a few businesses sent a canopy of weak electric light onto the sidewalk.

"Well," he said, "maybe a peek."

But there was that rule: Churches made immortals feel lousy. No, not just lousy. A vampire sitting on the running board of an old pickup had used that wording. Another vampire from New York City, a Wall Street tycoon, used more colorful language. "Should you venture into a sanctum of God, your pain will be ineffable. The skin on your body will seem to stretch on your bones like wet rawhide under a desert sun."

Martin figured he didn't have to go in; he could just stand outside. He had nothing better to do. Robert was off somewhere looking for food. He would just sit on the bench on the corner in front of Father Unu's church and reminisce.

For the first half hour he watched the stop light as it went through its cycle, red to green to orange to red to green to orange, occasionally slipping a glance at the occupants of waiting cars.

Hi there, my name's Martin. I'm immortal and looking for a good meal. How about parking that car. . . .

He often wondered if humans could tell just by looking at him. He used Robert and a thousand other vampires as references. A well-fed vampire looked almost human. A hungry vampire didn't. But then, hungry vampires, at least for the first few days, only gave the appearance of being anemic. The traffic light ran its cycle again, amusing him: Red—cheeks aglow, healthy as a kitten. Stay home. Orange—getting antsy. Start looking. Green—find someone—anyone. He was orange, burning green, but for reasons he didn't fully understand, he remained on the bench, even suppressing the desire to take a young woman who strolled quickly past, drawing her sweater tightly around her as she did, and barely glancing at Martin when he smiled. He did, however, note which direction she turned, for future reference.

Of course, he knew exactly why he had chosen to sit here on this bench, surrounded by churches. Father Unu, Martin knew, took a nightly stroll along this route around midnight, his routine as unwavering as a mailman's. Martin guessed it to be very near twelve now. But what if the good Father had altered his routine? What if he was dead? What if—

"Well, I don't believe it!"

Father Unu's cracking voice snuck into Martin's thoughts and delivered him from his memories. He looked up and saw the old man there, looking down at him, his face bearing an uncanny resemblance to Aunty Maude's; the gray-white skin, drawn and leathery, the light blue eyes looking like tiny bits of sky pulsing behind breaks in the clouds. He leaned against a gnarled cane, curled and knobbed and bony. Time had bent him. And he still wore that damnable knowing smile, although this time it seemed there was a touch of gaity in it. The light turned red, and his old skin reflected it. Martin could only think of a fragile container, blood being poured into it over capacity.

"Martin, Martin Crouper. My goodness, my goodness. Where have you been all these many years?"

Martin, whose arms were spread over the top of the bench, raised his hands in a kind of shrug. He could feel his temples throb. "Here and there," he said.

"Ten years it's been, hasn't it, Martin? Ten years! My, my!"

They just looked at each other then, and there passed between them a realization that neither had anything else to say to the other. After ten years, an exchange of amenities was it.

Pressing for something, anything, Father Unu said, "You look well, Martin." It was then he realized just how well. "I'd have to say you look very well, very well, indeed!"

Martin gestured at the night, indicating the lack of light. "The night flatters me, Father. I don't look as good during the day." He laughed.

Father Unu nodded. "Me, too, Martin, me, too. Well, it is very good to see you again. Tell me, are you still doing custodial work?"

By now Father Unu's skin had begun a slow crawl.

Martin looked up the street, as if he hadn't heard the question.

"I said—"

Martin turned quickly, eyes ablaze. "No," he said flatly. "Are you still saving souls?"

Father Unu cleared his throat and pushed his sleeve back from his wrist. "That late," he said, although the hands of his watch were hidden by darkness. "I hadn't realized. Well, Martin, good to see you. . . ."

Martin stood slowly and tented his fingers around Father Unu's elbow. "Wait, Father, not yet. We must talk. Perhaps you've come up with a few more adages? Maybe you've read a little more into the occult? So much, Father, so much."

Somewhere in the cluttered basement of his mind, Father Unu recalled the stories he had told Martin the custodian, the man who had trouble with words, the man who had trouble with most anything. This man standing in front of him was not the Martin he remembered.

Still, with blind, implacable faith, he stuck to his friendliness. "Yes, of course, of course. You were always such a good listener."

And so they walked away from the corner, out of the meager light, toward the high school. On the way Father Unu felt a tremendous tugging at his faith, felt it begin to tear apart, assaulted by a rising doubt. Instinctively, his fingers felt for the cross around his neck as Martin, still guiding him by the elbow, glanced at him. Father Unu looked at Martin, at how his mouth had turned under, and at how his eyes had rounded and glazed. Martin's words came from a feather-dry throat. "That—cross—has nothing to do with us, Father. Nothing at all. Is your faith so weak that you would use it to defend yourself?" Still, Father Unu fingered the cross, realizing its strength, its power. It was even warm to the touch, almost alive, as if somehow inherent in it was the ability to recognize evil. He smiled confidently. "The Lord is my shepherd, I shall not want; He maketh me to lie down—"

But Martin cut him off with another fit of laughter, laughter that startled Father Unu with its sharpness and disdain. His fingers traced the cross furiously now, the words of prayer pouring unintelligibly out of him. But then, in the depths of fear, the realization came to him. This was the test he had been waiting for for so very long; the cross around his neck only an obstacle. Surely his faith was strong enough, surely it was; he had nurtured it for so long, so very long. He fisted the cross, pulled it to his mouth, kissed it joyfully, then removed it, dropping it into his pants pocket.

Seconds later, Martin stopped and turned the muttering priest toward him face-to-face. Father Unu looked deep into his old custodian's eyes, eyes that were so very difficult to resist, the eyes of evil, evil that until now only lived in legend and old hidden books, eyes that burned with vengeful lust and grinned with homicidal rage just as surely as the mouth below grinned with the knowledge that this man cowering before him uttering foolishness was now totally defenseless.

The words trembled from Father Unu's lips. "The Lord is my shepherd, I shall not want; He maketh me to lie down in green pastures; He leadeth me beside the still waters . . ."

Martin bent to the wide-eyed priest.

"He restoreth my faith. Yea, verily, though I walk through the valley of the shadow of death . . ."

Martin drank.

Immediately, Martin Crouper, vampire, with Father Unu dead in his arms, noticed the undeniable, hushed, sweet stillness that follows a vampire's meal. What happened later, however, as he carried Father Unu's body off to the deep woods for burial, was a complete surprise. The fatigue, the aching joints and the sudden mental confusion were totally unexpected.

There was one thing Martin hadn't thought of. If simply visiting a church was painful, imagine what taking a man of the cloth could do? Why had he been so stupid? The answer, Robert told him, was simple. Revenge. Hunger. A combination of the two.

By the time Robert closed the cellar door behind him, Martin had already begun to age. And all he could think about for the first couple of days was what he might look like in a couple of years. But then, he needn't worry about that, Robert told him. It wouldn't take that long to find a cure. Surely it wouldn't take that long.

CHAPTER EIGHTEEN

M.T.D. Headquarters

Andy Swartz lay back against the wall of M.T.D. Headquarters, careful not to lean too heavily, and took a long pull on the half-finished quart of Old Milwaukee Light. His dad had switched brands to save a few bucks and a few pounds—much to Andy's chagrin—who preferred Lowenbrau Dark, the beer of choice until a few days ago. He propped the bottle between his thighs and looked toward the door. The others were late—or so he hoped. If they had chickened out, if they had said one thing and then did another . . . well, they'd pay and pay good. He turned the bottle between his fingers as if he were starting a fire, and glanced around the lantern-lit room. The somber yellow light gave the room an old attic patina, but he opted for the Coleman because flashlights left most of the room ominously dark.

On the back wall was a poster of Rowdy Roddy Piper playing the bagpipes. Another unnamed wrestler, somewhat less muscular, stood poised in the background, eyes huge with feigned hate, fingers flexed, ready to do grievous bodily harm to the unsuspecting, musically inclined Piper. Brian Ferguson had tried to convince Andy that wrestling was all a big show, that jamming an elbow into an unprotected throat could be fatal. But Andy knew better. Those guys were huge, and as strong as bulls. They could take it. And besides, why would so many people believe it if it wasn't true? When you had a majority weren't you always right? Brian had only shaken his head and smiled in rebuttal, a response that Andy thought was just a half-ass way of saying he was wrong.

But thinking about Brian made him just a little apprehensive. Where had he gotten off to anyway? He should have been here already—unless he'd chickened out. Brian did tell him his dad had a real bad temper. Tomorrow, he thought, Brian's dad would probably get the cops out, although his own dad had said it'd take forty-eight hours before the cops would do anything about anyone who didn't come home when they were supposed to.

With a shrug and another long pull on the now warm beer, Andy shelved thoughts about Brian and concentrated on just why the other guys weren't there yet. He got up, lantern in tow, pulled open the door, which whined on rusty hinges, and drew the light in an arc from side to side. "Shit," he said agitatedly, closing the door again when the light revealed nothing except their recently carved path and the dark expanse of woods. He sat down again, wondering if he shouldn't finish off the bottle of beer, and mumbled, "They're gonna get theirs; just wait'll I see those guys, just wait!"

Suddenly a knock sounded, then another, heavy enough to rattle the door. Andy sat up, eyes round, remembering the quiet, empty woods. "Yeah!" he said, his voice assuming the soprano pitch that snuck into it during times of stress.

From beyond, a man's voice asked, "Can I come in, Andy?"

Andy froze.

"You wanna let us in, son?"

"Dad?"

"Yes, it's your father! Who'd you think it was?"

A great river of relief surged through Andy. He got up and opened the door and saw Brian's dad standing beside his, the prologue of worry on his face.

Len Swartz ducked and entered M.T.D. Headquarters followed closely by his neighbor.

Swartz took a deep breath, looked around, and said, "Okay, son, where is he; where's Brian?"

Andy's look of surprise was genuine; Ben Ferguson could see that. "Dad, he ain't here. He ain't even been here."

"Look, son, we know how boys stick together, but it's very important that you consider Mr. Ferguson, not to mention Mrs. Ferguson. She's worried sick. We had a very difficult time finding this place and I—we—are not in very good moods. Where's Brian?"

"I don't know. No one's been here, Dad, no one 'cept me."

Ben Ferguson stepped forward and touched Len

Swartz on the arm. "Last night, son," he said patiently, "did he come here last night?"

"No—honest. I ain't seen him."

A half-mad smile suddenly fixed onto Ben Ferguson's face. He gave the fort the same perusal that Len Swartz had, looking for anything that might belong to his son, and also becoming a little annoyed with Andy's uncooperative attitude. *If he were my boy!* He had to have seen him—this was the only place he could have gone. And they had found his METS ball cap on the tracks just a short way down. "Listen, Andy," Ben Ferguson began patiently, "don't lie to us." He took a menacing step forward and stopped when Andy took a step backward.

"Whoa, hold on, Ben," Len Swartz said, sticking his arm out.

Ferguson wheeled on his neighbor and snarled, "He's lying, can't you see that? The little son-of-a-bitch is lying! They all lie! Christ, it's as plain as the nose on your face!"

Andy took another step backward and braced himself against Roddy Piper's bagpipes, slightly crinkling the paper. His father put his hand out like a traffic cop, sending an invisible steadying ray across the ill-lit room, and confronted Ben Ferguson. "Listen, if Andy says he wasn't here, then he wasn't here. I'm sure he's out there somewhere, but he's obviously not here. Let's keep searching."

Ben Ferguson swore under his breath and threw up his arms in exasperation. "Yeah, okay." He looked at Andy, sucked in a large breath, and let it out noisily. But still, the anger hadn't left his face. "Sorry,

Andy," he said. "I didn't mean to scare you."

Andy looked at his father, the large, muscular, Rowdy Roddy Piper physique. Ben Ferguson could beat on his own son, but not on him—his father wouldn't let him, not ever. "That's okay, Mr. Ferguson. If I see him, I'll send him home. Okay?"

Pausing briefly, Ben Ferguson reached out, ruffled Andy's hair too briskly, then turned and left, not bothering to leave the door open for Len Swartz, who looked at his son and said, "Steal any more beer from me, Andrew, and you won't sit down for a week! You got that?"

"Beer?"

"Andrew!"

"Yes, sir."

"Good. We understand each other. Now, you got another half hour; then I want you home."

"A half hour, c'mon, Dad, the guys—"

Swartz held up his hand again, bricking back any further protests. "Half hour, son," he said with quiet strength.

Andy nodded and then shut the door as his father ducked and left. Out of curiosity he listened for their footsteps as they walked away. He heard nothing; the spongy, pine-needled ground and the wind weaving through the treetops muted the sounds of footfalls just as surely as the cloaking woods hid M.T.D. Headquarters.

He walked listlessly away from the door and sat down with a *whuump*. Things could be better, he thought, a whole lot better. His dad knew where the fort was, and that he had been lifting his beer. Plus

Brian was missing and the guys were AWOL. He pulled the bottle out of its hiding place and lifted it to his mouth. A few minutes later, as golden, warm liquid slid down his throat, the somewhat nauseating taste making him wonder why in the world he drank the stuff, he heard another knock. He hid the bottle again, cursing as it fell onto its side, the contents trickling out, and pulled the door open.

THE LAST DAY

CHAPTER NINETEEN

The Next Morning

Judd pulled the Jeep into the four-car parking lot belonging to the town's only vet, behind the four corners Methodist church which bordered the park. As yet, he hadn't talked to Steven about what had happened the night before, and Steven—thankfully—hadn't asked. But the boy's first priority was Sam and the extent of his injuries. Later he would ask how someone—a woman, no less—could just reach out and swat away a big, strong dog as if he were a bothersome mosquito. But all Judd could remember was Cynthia coming toward him, a flood of nostalgia, and then Sam flying through the air, Steven rushing to his aid as Cynthia walked away and simply disappeared into the night.

"He's all right, isn't he, Uncle Judd?" Steven asked, his hand wrapped around the door handle.

"I'm sure he is," Judd said calmly. "Give him a couple of months and he'll be chasing around that forest like a puppy."

But when they brought him in the night before, the compound fracture painfully obvious, even in the low light of the forest clearing, Judd had real fears about whether the dog would make it or not. A dog could be overcome by shock as easily as a person, and a compound fracture could definitely induce shock. On the way in, his breathing had been shallow and sputtering, his eyes smokey with pain. Both Judd and Steven had tried their best to comfort him, but their efforts, they feared, had probably been futile.

They had awakened Dr. Sayers from a sound sleep, but because Neal Sayers was a true animal lover, it didn't matter to him what time it was. An animal in need took precedent over sleep, and even over a person's ability to pay—a slip-shod way of operating a business that gave his accountant fits. "He's in shock all right," the tall, balding, bespectacled man with the kindly face had told them. "We'll set that leg and make him as comfortable as possible, but I don't want to hazard a prognosis. Morning might give us a better idea."

"His chances, Doc, what are his chances?" Judd had solemnly asked.

The vet regarded Steven's unflagging interest and said, "Fifty-fifty."

Judd had sighed.

"How did you say he did this?"

Judd had foreseen the question. "Fell, down at the quarry. Guess he got too close to the edge. Anyway, we went looking for him—"

Steven had shot him a questioning look.

"Fell?" Sayers had interrupted, intrigued. "Now,

that's odd. Dog like Sam here has got the balance of a bighorn sheep. Or close."

"He likes to chase things," Judd had added.

Sayers smiled slightly, and Judd thought about those abusive parents who brought in a bruised kid and lied to the doctor in the emergency room, half-knowing they had been discovered.

"Yeah, probably," Dr. Sayers said. "Well, listen, like I said, we'll do what we can. Come back in the morning—"

"Can't we stay, Doc?" Steven had asked.

"Well, son, it really wouldn't do him any good. I'm going to give him a sedative anyway. A sleeping pill. Come back late tomorrow morning. Hopefully the morning will bring some good news."

So now they were back, and they never did receive that dreaded predawn call that Judd felt sure the vet would place.

The keening yelps of bored, barking dogs drifted up to them from the kennels below. A dark-haired girl about eighteen, dressed in a white uniform, her smile warm and sincere, asked them how she could help.

"Is the vet here?" Judd asked.

As if on cue, Neal Sayers, clipboard in hand, appeared behind her. "Sheriff—come on back," he said cheerfully, instantly raising their hopes.

They entered through a white, steel door to their left and found Sam in room two, in considerably better shape than he had been only hours earlier. His eyes were still slightly cloudy, but Sayers told them not to worry about his eyes, that the side effect of the sedative would wear off by noon. Steven hugged

Sam, and a soft mewling sound came out of the dog as he turned his huge head and drew his wet, pink tongue along the boy's neck.

"Can we take him home?" Judd asked.

"Last night I'd have said no, that he'd have to be here at least a couple of days. Today, well, I don't see why not. That dog has amazing recuperative powers, Sheriff. Just amazing."

Judd pulled his hand lightly along the dog's back. "Thanks, Doc," he said. "How long before the splint and cast come off?"

"A while yet. Bring him back in a week; we'll have another look at him. Cost inclusive."

Judd thanked the vet once more and guided nephew and dog out the door.

Today, if events could, in fact, dictate weather patterns, should have been as numbingly cold as any in memory, with a blizzard weaving malefically through the town in search of a few unsuspecting victims to wrap in its breathtakingly icy grip. But storms hardly ever roar during a homicide, and blue skies and calm air just as rarely indicate bliss. Only in the movies, only in bad B movies. What had happened in and around Hunt, and what would happen over the next day or so, had nothing at all to do with rainy days or fair skies. Evil doesn't concern itself with the time of year or the clearness of the sky. Evil—like shit—as the bluntly prosaic bumper sticker proclaims—happens. Regardless.

As they drove slowly down Main, past The Krohbar, Judd's thoughts drifted to Rosemary Hamilton, as they often did when he drove by her store. Days like today, the sun unyielding, the sky clear and wildly blue, usually found the door to The Settler's Post propped open. Although the store was air conditioned, Rosemary preferred fresh air; better for the live plants, she said. Today, however, the store was closed, as it had been the day before. Had circumstances been different, had this been just another summer's day, then Judd would probably not have felt a surge of alarm. And had Rosemary not been an old and valued friend, he probably would not have given the closed store a moment's thought. But she was an old friend, and circumstances were far from being normal.

He pulled over, parked diagonally to the store and stared inside, past the SORRY, WE'RE CLOSED sign. As he looked, he couldn't help but wonder if the evil that had visited him the night before had also visited her, and if she were strong enough. . . .

"Stay here," he told Steven, who was busy with Sam, seeing to his comfort.

He walked to the window and put his hands around his eyes to weaken the glare. The store was definitely closed, despite hours to the contrary posted next to the closed sign. And if she had gone on vacation, which was entirely possible, she had forgotten to leave her sign.

He climbed back into the Jeep and just stared blindly out the bug-spattered windshield.

"What's wrong, Uncle Judd?" Steven asked.

Judd looked at his nephew, then at Sam, then back again. "Listen, I'm going to leave you with Estelle for a while. There's something I've got to check into. Okay?"

"What about Sam? Shouldn't he go home?"

Judd turned and pet the dog. "Home right now, Steven, is wherever you are. We'll put a blanket down for him at the office."

"If you think it's okay, Uncle Judd."

"Yes, Steven, I think it's okay."

Judd parked in front of Rosemary's house, right down the street from Barb and Walt's, got out and just stood on the curb awhile, the sun hot on his face. It was difficult to tell if anyone was home or not, but there were, he saw now, two newspapers lying in a T on the brick walkway. He climbed the steps to the small, open, cement porch and rang the bell, hearing its melodic, but muted song through the closed door. Rosemary had replaced the modest ding-dong with something whimsically musical.

Nothing.

He rang it again, then waited.

Still nothing.

As he was about to open the screen and try the door, he heard footsteps shuffling through the tall grass alongside the house. Seconds later Harry Kroh stuck his head around the corner and waved tiredly.

Judd walked swiftly down the steps toward him. "Harry, what are you doing here?" he asked.

Kroh stepped closer, stopped and said, "Checkin', that's all. Just checkin'," adding with a wry smile, "might ask the same of you, Sheriff."

In his most official voice, Judd said, "Police business, Harry."

Kroh's wry smile broadened. "Yeah? You sure that's all, Sheriff?"

Judd's reply reflected his annoyance. "If I were making a social call, I don't see that it would be any of your business anyway, Harry."

The bar owner allowed this frankness with an almost imperceptible nod.

"And what exactly were you checking on, Harry?"

Kroh shrugged. "I don't know." He thought a moment. "I guess I really *don't* know. I was sitting in the park yesterday, just relaxing, doing a little reading. Well, checkin' out Sandy Furness a little, I guess." A thin grin and a slight shift of his eyes gave him pause.

"And?"

Kroh set his eyes on Judd again. "Well, Rosemary's shop is closed, and there's no sign in the window, Sheriff. I thought that was a little, you know, funny. Unusual."

"So you thought you'd just come by and check it out?"

"Had some free time. She ain't home, though. Back door's open, so I looked inside. There's no one home."

"You know that's trespassing, don't you, Harry?"

"You gonna arrest me, Sheriff?" Harry asked, knowing very well he wouldn't, not with the bloody flood of new business, business that was most certainly more important than a friendly trespass.

Judd strongly assured him that under other circumstances he just might arrest him, a fact Kroh acknowledged with a mumbled apology.

"There was somethin' else, though," he added.

"Other night, at my bar, I saw her leave with Sue Dorsey, you know, her husband, Teddy, teaches at the high school?"

Judd wondered if maybe Harry had been seeing things. Everyone knew about Rosemary and Teddy.

"Impossible."

"Oh, no it ain't! I saw it with my own eyes. And I saw something else, too, that I guess made me worry a little. I saw Bobby All follow them out, no more than ten seconds later."

Judd knew the name and knew it well. "Bobby All's back in town?" he asked, surprise evident in his voice.

"I don't know about now, but he was then," Kroh replied with absurd logic.

"I don't understand, Harry. Why would the fact that Bobby All left at about the same time Rosemary did make you worry?"

"I wondered the same thing. Normally it wouldn't. I mean, that's what bars are all about, isn't it? But there was something about him, something . . . not right. He looked good and he didn't look good, know what I mean? I thought about it, and all I could come up with—now don't laugh—was a bottle of soda pop left open all night and when you went to have a drink the next day all the fizz was gone. All them little gas bubbles had gone out. He looked good and he didn't look good. Kind of . . . flat. Yeah, flat, like old soda pop. My sister, Elaine—now this was strange—she was talking about him just the day before. Described him and everything. Well, I told him how I thought him and your wife—shit, there I go again."

"That they made a strange couple?"

"Well, they did, Sheriff. You and her, you made a real nice looking couple, but him and her . . . like a round peg in a square hole . . . uh, I didn't mean anything sexual. . . ."

"What else, Harry?"

"Well, we just talked awhile, until he left. Sheriff, you don't think. . . ."

Right now, he thought the worst, but he couldn't tell Harry Kroh that. "No, she's just out, maybe buying flowers or something like that."

"Then . . . why are you here?"

"Like I said, Harry, police business."

"What kind . . . ?"

"Dammit, Harry! Just leave it alone!"

There were a couple of messages on his desk when he returned. One was from Elmira, Sheriff Crown.

Judd dialed the number. The other end picked up on the third ring. "Crown, here."

"Judd Lucas, Sheriff. I got your message."

"Listen, Judd, we got us a little trouble down here. Now, I can't say whether your deputy is involved or not." He paused, leaving the line with a faint buzz and a few snaps and chorts because of a bad connection.

"Sheriff?" Judd said.

"I don't think I have to tell you that what I have to say should go no farther. . . ."

"What is it, Sheriff?"

Crown drew a deep breath on the other end. "The Sternmyer girl? She's gone. Someone stole her body. And the morgue clerk is missing, too."

"Shit!" Judd said too quickly.

"My sentiments exactly."

"Someone just came in and stole the body?"

"Yes, Sheriff—unless you got some other explanation."

Sure, he had another explanation, but he wasn't about to talk about it over the phone like they were arranging a golf date.

"None. None at all. Wish I could help you out."

"You're sure?"

"Positive."

"Okay. I'll be in touch."

Judd's mental Rolodex spun, stopped and spit out an image of Gloria Sternmyer. He remembered Harry's soda pop analogy—all the fizz gone. What you saw there on the counter looked okay at first glance, but on closer inspection it was easy to see what was missing—those tiny bubbles that clung to the top, those life-giving. . . . He let that thought gain momentum. Cynthia looked like that, alive but missing something, that spark that made her different. A soul, maybe? Whatever it was that made her human. He also remembered what Crown had said. "Someone stole her body. And the morgue clerk's missing, too." Suddenly what had happened seemed horribly clear. Gloria Sternmyer, probably with Ed Land, had been in the morgue. The clerk must have been ready to piss his pants from fright as they moved toward him. What else had Sheriff Crown said? "Unless you got some other explanation." That sentence rolled through his mind a hundred times, and each time Judd said to himself, *You're damn right I do!*

His phone rang. He picked it up immediately. "Sheriff Lucas."

"Sheriff, this is Ben Ferguson. I've got Len Swartz here with me. . . ."

"What is it, Mr. Ferguson?"

"It's our boys, Sheriff. They're missing."

He glanced at the other message. It had come from Ben Ferguson.

About the same time, Harry Kroh decided to put his deductive powers, powers he thought quite substantial, to the test. Sure, it appeared that nothing out of the ordinary had happened at Rosemary's house, but maybe, just maybe, they hadn't gone to Rosemary's the night he last saw her; maybe they didn't make it, maybe on the way. . . . Or maybe, just maybe, although he couldn't guess why, they went to Susan's. Harry was behind his bar. He picked up the phone book, turned to the "D's." "Dorsey, Dorsey," he muttered, his finger sliding down the short list of "D's" and finally stopping on T. and S. Dorsey. He picked up the phone with one hand, squashed the directory flat with the other, squinted at the number, then dialed. After ten rings he hung up.

Although the required forty-eight hours had not yet elapsed, Ricky Smits—the only available deputy because Estelle was watching Steven, and Ed was missing—was elected to go out to the Ferguson's to take a missing person's report. After he hung up, Judd had had an idea. He pulled all the missing persons files, then concentrated on the ones that involved children. He checked under DESCRIPTION for information about what each had worn the day he disappeared. He leaned back in his swivel chair and thought about the parents, whose hope, like his, probably still smoldered. Well, he thought, quietly damning his authority, he was the goddamn fireman. He'd have to call these people and tell them that their sons were probably dead. Probably hell! They were, dammit, they were dead! Just like Jeffrey. *"Ma'am, we found some dead skin inside a pile of clothing. I checked and that clothing belonged to your son. Well, obviously. . . ."*

"Shit!" he said flatly. This chore, this highly disagreeable chore was not one he looked forward to, not at all. He looked outside, at how cheerfully the day had unfolded, and cursed again.

CHAPTER TWENTY

That Afternoon

Logic and reason still held the town together, but its glue was being severely tested by a host of savagely mutilated corpses. In truth, Hunt was ready to hand itself over to madness, to angry, fear-driven mobs roaming dark streets in search of murderers.

As Judd walked to his car, Jim Arnold walked out of his men's store and stopped him. "I elected you to keep us safe, Sheriff. Come election time maybe I'll undo that mistake."

Arnold was not alone. To the citizens of Hunt, it was pretty much cut and dry. Their neighbors were dead, and for all they knew, they could be next. They wanted the killer caught. He could understand their impatience. They didn't know what was really going on, Judd thought. Would they really want to know?

He took a left at the four corners churches, then another left near the high school. He tried to concentrate on his driving, but the chore he had just completed, that of notifying next of kin, had captured his thoughts. Yes, he had been told by both families, they would come right down and identify the clothing, but after all these years. . . . The thin hope, exposed in each one's tone of voice, made him want to cry out, "THEY'RE DEAD, DAMMIT—JUST AS DEAD AS MY OWN SON. BE DONE WITH IT AND GET ON WITH YOUR LIVES!!" But he allowed them their false hope, their no-body no-tears philosophy. And each had come in promptly, flitting about nervously, not lingering for very long over what they had to know was their son's clothing, as if lingering there made it more true than not, then finally saying, "It certainly does look familiar, but like I said. . . ."

The truth, as it concerned the missing boys—Jeffrey as well—was becoming painfully obvious. The parallels were too easily and too finely drawn. The boys, he told himself with a strangely calm inner voice, had gotten caught in the sunlight. They had been vampires, and they had died a vampire's death. Jeffrey—oh, God, why him? Why Jeffrey?—included. And an unsuspecting Ed Land had gone to the Vasquez home and had probably met one of the boys face-to-face. He pictured Ed roaming the house and finally happening upon the boy, great relief washing over him when he did, and slipping his gun back into its holster because kids were certainly no threat to him, to anyone for that matter. That boy had probably transformed him. Ed had probably gone to Elmira and in a blind frenzy done the same to his girl.

It was all coming together now; this supernatural jigsaw puzzle was starting to make sense. There were some things that still didn't make sense, though. Why hadn't those boys wreaked havoc on the town? And why had each wandered crazily into the sunlight only to meet with a painful and hideous death? Vampires, at least according to his sources, were cunning and ruthless. They were homicidal, certainly, but only for the survival of their species, like any carnivorous beast. They were not normally psychotic. Oh, you could go down to the state hospital and find humans claiming to be vampires, but just try to find a vampire claiming to be human. He remembered something he had read in *Vampires,* a short paragraph about how some vampires had to remain hidden—for one reason or another—for many years and how that isolation—and the accompanying lack of food—could and did cause some vampires to actually go out of their minds and do things they would not ordinarily do. Was that it? Had the boys been somehow isolated? Had they been deprived of food—blood—for an extended period of time? If so, why? And had they spent that period of time here, in Hunt, their presence hidden from an ignorant town? And if that were true—how had they gotten out? What, or who, had set them free? And once free, had they only lived a short while, like goddamn mayflies on a twenty-four-hour sex binge? Still so many questions, so many. But at least now he had some answers to go along with his questions.

He glanced at street numbers, slowed down, stopped and looked at the house and how pin-neat the yard was, how the tan paint garishly reflected the sunlight. "Well, Sue and Ted Dorsey, you home or not?" he said.

The first thing he noticed was that the front door was open, not simply a crack, but at least halfway. He walked up the steps and felt a current of warm relief. They were home. And they might even know where Rosemary had gone.

"Hello?" he said in a loud, friendly voice as a lone figure walked quickly by the sheer-covered bay window to his left. He knocked lightly on the screen. "Mr. Dorsey?" he said, very much expecting Teddy Dorsey to open the door wide and greet him at any second.

"Got me again," Harry Kroh said as he yawned the door open and smiled.

Judd rolled his eyes and shook his head in bewilderment. "Harry, what the hell are you doing here? Are they home?"

"Well, to answer your first question, just checkin', and no, they aren't, for the second."

Judd opened the screen and brushed past Harry, who followed him into the foyer. Without looking at Kroh, Judd said, "You know, I've a good mind to slap irons on you, Harry. Two times in one day! What is it with you? You an apprentice cat-burglar or what?"

Harry snickered slightly. "No, nothin' like that, Sheriff. Truth is, well, I got to thinkin'. . . ."

Judd turned to him. "And because Rosemary wasn't home, you thought that for some reason she might be here. Right, Harry?"

"Seemed to make sense."

Judd's anger was receding now. "Harry, listen.

You can't go around breaking into private homes."

"The door was open, Sheriff."

"Harry, did someone invite you in?"

"Well, no, but no one was here to do that, so technically—"

"Technically, I could arrest you for breaking and entering. Now, I want you to leave."

"Okay, Sheriff, but there's something—"

"No, Harry. Just leave. No explanations. Just leave."

"Sheriff, there's blood—"

"Blood?"

"On the sofa. Sure looks like blood to me."

"Hell!" Judd hurried into the living room and examined the sofa. There were fist-size dark stains on the middle- and left-hand sides of the sofa, stains that he thought could very well be blood, but could just as easily be cherry Kool-Aid. Despite everything, however, he couldn't just rush a team of technicians in here to tear the place apart. Instead he decided to check the place over from top to bottom himself. But first he had to get rid of Harry, who stood by like a curious Dr. Watson.

"Harry," he said, "you're going to have to leave. Now."

As Harry walked down the street, fingers weaving through the clutter in his pants pockets, he suddenly stopped, pulled out three quarters, a dime with a hole in the middle—his lucky dime—a broken toothpick, and in the middle of all this, the man's class ring he had found on the floor of the house, the ring he had casually, almost unknowingly pocketed as he heard Judd's car pull up. He looked back at the house, a half block away now, repocketed the ring and kept walking. Later, he thought, later he'd bring it back. Lucas would probably throw him in jail if he went back there now. It was only a ring anyway, just a class ring. Probably Teddy Dorsey's. He'd meant to tell the sheriff about it in the house, but Lucas had been so damn short with him, so damn official. He shrugged. Pressure did that to a man. And that man back there was under a lot of pressure.

When he got back to the office and saw Steven sitting Indian style next to Sam, Judd wondered if the boy had even gotten up to go to the john while he was gone. "How's Sam doin'?" he asked.

"Okay, I guess. He whines a little sometimes, but I guess that's 'cause his leg hurts, don't you think?"

"If it doesn't, then we've got a scoop, sport!"

He squatted to pet Sam and heard the toilet flush. A few seconds later Estelle Meath walked out of the bathroom and smiled.

"I appreciate your watchin' out for the boy—and Sam," Judd said. "I'll make it up to you."

"My pleasure, Sheriff. Listen, I'm gonna grab something to eat if you're gonna be here. That okay?"

"Well, if you could hold on a minute . . . is Ricky back yet?"

"From that missing person's?"

"Right, the Ferguson's."

"Yep, came back about ten minutes ago. Just

stepped out. You know it hasn't been forty-eight hours, Sheriff."

"I know that, Estelle, but considering what's happened. . . ."

"Yeah, you're right about that. Now that you mention it, have you found out anything? I'm only asking because the mayor called again while you were gone. Seems we got us some irate citizens."

"Irate citizens are at the bottom of my list, Estelle."

The look on his face was unfamiliar to her. He was like a potful of bad news ready to boil over.

"You got something on your official mind, don't you, Sheriff?" she said. "Maybe you oughta unload."

"I have definitely considered that, Estelle. But the words have to come out in the right order."

"Oh, Christ, there hasn't been another murder . . . ?"

"No. No. But there are some things you and I and Ricky and possibly Ann have to discuss. Things that have to do with the case."

Smiling suddenly, as if something he said had rekindled an old joke, she pulled him aside, out of earshot. "There's a rumor goin' round that vampires did it, Sheriff. Vampires, isn't that a hoot?"

All Judd could do was smile a little. This was going to be extremely difficult. Right now he wished he'd been on the debating team instead of the basketball team.

"Vampires!" she said again, astonished that such a possibility would even be considered. "I mean, I know small towns sometimes breed stupidity, but vampires!"

Judd looked at her, hoping the blank expression

on his face wouldn't give him away. "Listen, Estelle, a case like this, the brutality of it, well, a good cop considers all possibilities."

She cocked her head in bewilderment. "Huh?" was all she could say.

Just then Ricky Smits came in. Judd called him over, then took both deputies into Ann Schaffer's office and closed the door.

Estelle stood in the corner, arms crossed. Ricky had his hands on his hips, his fingers just a few inches from the barrel of his holstered gun. Ann remained seated, her face full of wonderment. "What the hell's going on?" she asked after everyone was apparently settled.

Judd remained standing. "Let's just say I think it's time you three were brought up to date."

Estelle fidgeted nervously, then, in an overly calm voice, said, "Please, Judd, don't. Vampires? C'mon, Sheriff!"

"Vampires!" Ricky said, his eyes widening. He had always been fascinated by the occult and considered himself somewhat of an expert on the subject, even if his knowledge was gleaned only from watching Saturday Night Flickers.

Judd held up his hands. This could get out of hand in a hurry. "Ricky, Estelle, Ann. I just want you all to know the facts. Whether those facts do, indeed, indicate something other than what you might consider normal, then so be it. But I've given this a lot of thought, and for your own protection, I've decided to let you in on what's happened, especially to me."

He told them about Cynthia's appearance in the woods, about the human skin found in the clothing, about Gloria Sternmyer and the fact that she was now missing. About Ed Land. Everything he knew, they now knew. And through it all not one of them interrupted, although every now and again Estelle would roll her eyes or a fascinated grin would appear on Ricky's face, as if he were not a sheriff's deputy at all, only some big kid with real six-shooters.

Estelle was the first to speak after he had finished. With her arms still crossed, she said, "Sheriff, because I got a lot of confidence in you, and because I can see where what happened to you might make you believe what you do, I'm going to go on as though it were all true. Every damn bit of it. I'm not saying I like it. I don't. I'm just saying I've got a job to do, and if that job means chasing vampires around with a pointy baseball bat, then okay, I'll do it. I won't like it, but I'll do it."

"I can ask no more," Judd responded, turning toward Ricky, who tried to assume the official air that he had seen Estelle display. On him it looked silly. Finally, a little frustrated with his inability to put into words exactly how he felt, he said, "I'm with you, chief. One hundred and ten percent. No, make that a hundred and twenty percent!"

Judd looked at Ann. "Sheriff, all I do is dispatch. You tell me to send someone to a house to kill a vampire, I'll do it. You tell me to send someone to a house to arrest someone who thinks he's a vampire, I'll do that, too." She looked at the others, then back at her boss. "But I don't mind telling you, this shit gives me the creeps. My skin is crawling right now. If I had my druthers, I'd druther this killer be some looney tune as be a vampire. At least you can shoot a loon. Least a loon lies down and dies."

Judd had the last word. "I wanta be clear about this. All I want is for the three of you to be aware of all possibilities. I'm not going to stand here and tell you the town's been invaded by fang-toothed creatures. Please, don't think that's what I'm telling you. Just keep an open mind. That's all I ask. And do something else. Just one thing, for me." He paused, wondering if his request would be met with hoots and catcalls. Finally, feeling a strong need to finish what he had started, he said, "If you've got a cross, wear it, keep it with you. If you don't, get one. Don't ask any questions. Just do it."

With this strange request firmly in place, Ann Schaffer shivered noticeably, provoking a look of disbelief from Estelle, who quietly suspected that her boss had finally thrown in the towel.

CHAPTER TWENTY-ONE

That Night

A chipmunk scurried across the porch at the All house, his small body lightly illuminated by the half moon. In the trees surrounding the house, birds flitted to and from their nests, releasing vomitus into the mouths of their hungry young. Out front a young couple walked hand in hand, each casting a casual glance toward the house, a thin thread of cool fear scampering up their backs, the same chill one might experience on the fringe of a cemetery. And at M.T.D. Headquarters, just beyond the tracks in the black clump of woods, lay a stale bottle of Old Milwaukee Light beer, its spillage now the object of interest to an army of tiny red ants. The guys had never showed up to meet Andy. And Andy had had no choice but to leave the beer behind.

From his bed Martin eyed the boys, lantern light flickering off their bodies. One cowered, knees drawn to his chest, arms wrapped around them, his whimper constant and infuriating. The other, the taller boy with dark hair, lay unconscious next to him, facedown, his right leg straight, the other forming a triangle, his right arm and hand, palm up, forming yet another triangle. *Maybe Robert brought me a dead boy,* Martin thought. And then his mind began to wander aimlessly. *Am I dead?* he wondered. *Is Robert dead? Is dead dead? No.* Well, that knowledge was old knowledge. There were new meanings for dead now. But then, Aunty Maude was dead, just as dead as she could be, her old bones up there on that hill just rotting away tra la tra la. He wondered if the boy who was awake—doing all that damn whimpering—was going to try and wake the other one again, like he did every five minutes or so. But he didn't know five minutes from five years now; so that thought quickly died, and he simply went back to watching them, breaking the routine with a dig of his terribly itching knee, his long sharp nails raking along like tiny knives.

He had become, over his many years of confinement, prone to severe mental lapses, but often those lapses would be followed by the antithesis. During those periods when he thought clearly, he would try to determine exactly how he could help himself out of his situation. He thought of the movie, *Charley,* with Cliff Robertson. *Just a pill, Charley, just take this pill and presto, chango, you're a genius! But, mind you, take that pill or we'll just have to send someone to the john with you, won't we? Just to make sure you don't mess on yourself and ruin everyone's day with your stench.* Poor Charley, fell in love then failed the test. Poor, poor Charley. He dug his fingernails deeper into his damned itching knee, gouging out skin and flesh like tiny scoops of vanilla ice cream. Poor Martin, poor, poor Martin.

At his request, Robert had brought him a stubby little pencil and a pad of wide-lined first-grader's paper to write on. "What if I think of something that might cure me, Robert, what about that?" Martin had said. "And what if I forget it, huh, what if I forget it? If I write it down, then I won't forget it, not really."

Robert had obliged Martin purely to humor him. There was, of course, no cure. Martin would just grow older and older and older. Even Robert wondered when it would all stop—if it ever would. Would he go into that basement one day and find a dry, cracking, bowling-ball-size lump of alabaster-white modeling clay with dark fizzures oozing wispy trails of smoke where human features had been? And would that lump of modeling clay still have little, pointy, tearing teeth?

Martin clutched his stubby yellow pencil in his left hand and prepared a thought. Curved around his left knee was a blank piece of the lined paper, moist from the dampness of his basement home. Beside him, on the floor, was a scattering of pages, his "memoirs." One of those pages, written the day after the boys were set free, lay faceup.

It said: *They're gone. They left before Robert gave me these writing utensils. It saddened me to see them go, but Robert said they could be replaced. Sometimes I wonder though, what good does it do? What good did they do? Is there a cure?*

The page then showed a long, jagged scrawl to the

next notation, a notation that obviously lacked the clearness of thought apparent in the first.

bugs therr naste but they tast good xcept wen they dont stay down xcept when I thro them up Rats Rats are naste to.

Another, even heavier, more meandering scrawl led to yet a third notation on the same page. It said simply,

fod ned fod.

In its own way, this last passage was the most clear, more to the point. Clearly declarative.

Food need food.

And so each page of his memoirs reflected the three most highly distinct phases of his mental awareness. Sometimes those phases were in reverse order on the page, and sometimes a whole page was given over to one state of mind. These fluctuations made strikingly evident the seeming ease with which Martin slipped from "Charley the genius" to "Charley the retard," with a small, semi-lucid stop in between.

So as his hand trembled above the limp piece of lined paper on his knee, as his dulling eyes shifted slowly from that paper to the boys, an observer might be tempted to guess just where Martin's head was now; what exactly was he thinking? What exactly went on in there? His hand moved downward, and seconds later graphite met paper, the letters going down with preschool preciseness, jaggedly filling up three lines. When he was done, the paper slid off Martin's knee and fluttered like a butterfly onto the top of the pile. He momentarily stared at it, then stood and started slowly across the room, his feet dragging along the floor.

On the paper was Martin's very latest thought.

fod ned fod

Judd was on the phone, so Steven stood by and waited. His intention was to talk with his uncle—finally—about what had happened last night, and why his uncle had lied to the vet. His eyes took in all the things on his uncle's desk, the Puzzler, an empty in-and-out box, a black pen holder with a felt bottom—sans pen—a mess of papers that made Steven wonder how his uncle ever got anything done—his room at home had been neater than this—and fourteen—he had counted them—fourteen paper clips on his blotter. That was about it, except for the photographs of a woman and a boy, one next to the other. Written on the woman's picture were the words, "For Judd, Love, your wife, Cynthia." There were, he knew, other pictures of her at the house, the painting over the mantel, of course, and one on the nightstand in the loft. Jeffrey, Steven thought, looked a lot like him; but they were cousins, so that explained that.

He heard Judd say, "Look, Harry, just bring it here. It probably does belong to Mr. Dorsey; but they still haven't come home, so I think it best that I take care of it." Steven noticed a trace of annoyance in his uncle's tone. "Do it now, Harry."

As soon as his uncle hung up, Steven said, "Uncle Judd. Can I talk to you?"

Judd turned toward him, knowing full well what was coming. He had put it off long enough. Now he'd have to confront the boy about what had happened the night before. But how would he do it? Could he tell him his aunt was a vampire? That definitely wouldn't work. Would he lie? Should he lie? He had denied himself the pleasure of a rehearsal for this moment, and now he was cornered by a bright kid with fried-egg eyes who could easily detect a lie, and had the nerve to tell him he was lying, too. But then, maybe a partial truth, embellished slightly, would work. A blatantly related series of facts wouldn't do at all. With adults, like his deputies and Ann, the truth was necessary, with Steven it might be harmful.

"Steven, that person last night, well, that was someone I knew a long time ago. She, well, she's sick. She's mentally ill. Do you understand?"

"That's why she hurt Sam?"

"Exactly. She didn't mean to, but she gets real mad, real easy."

"Where is she now, Uncle Judd?"

"We're looking for her, Steven."

Steven looked at the slumbering Sam then back at Judd. "She must be real strong, huh?"

"What do you mean, Steven?"

"Well, Sam's a real big dog, and she just hit him and made him fly right through the air!"

"Well, Steven, some people, when they get mad, they get that way. Have you ever heard the word adrenaline?"

"Sure."

"Well, when people get angry or real worried—okay, here's an example. There have been cases where one person, because he or she is very worried, has been able to lift a car right off a person, usually someone they love. It's the same with people who are very mad, for whatever reason. Do you understand?"

"Yeah."

"You do?"

"Uh-huh."

Uncle and nephew just looked at one another then. Finally Steven smiled and said, "Thanks, Uncle Judd."

Judd hugged the boy—for the first time—and felt better than he had for quite a while. But quietly he wondered if the boy's curiosity had really been satisfied or whether the next unspoken question might be one too many.

In the worst of nightmares, those fraught with intersecting avenues of monsters and gargoyles, those laced with mountains of wasted, stinking human flesh and goblins immersed in the entrails of victims, Brian could not have foreseen what was taking place before his eyes. Andy was being eaten. Brian had watched Martin lumber over, stopping briefly to look at him, then again at Andy—almost, Brian thought, like someone picking sides for a ballgame. But finally, after settling on Andy, he dropped to his knees, made a protracted study of Andy's legs, then sank his mouth into the back of Andy's right thigh, biting through his jeans and tearing off a huge chunk of flesh and fabric while Andy, still unconscious, let go with a series of unconscious high-pitched yelps, as if he were only fighting some nightmare demon, the pain punching a jagged, searing hole in the surrounding darkness. Brian found himself hoping with all his might that Andy wouldn't suddenly wake up, because waking up to see a monster eating your leg would surely be worse than simply being unconscious. Even death. . . .

As soon as Martin had torn open Andy's leg, blood gushed, and spurted like water from a loose faucet. The warm blood splashed onto Brian's face and brought him partially back to reality. He crawled off, as far away as he could get, wiping the blood with the back of his hand, but unable to take his eyes off Martin, who alternately chewed and impassively turned to watch while Brian found what he thought was the darkest corner and curled his small body into a tight, sobbing ball.

It was as Martin swallowed, the gut-wrenching gulping sound echoing in the basement room, and was preparing to bite into Andy's other leg that it happened. With a suddenness akin to someone choking, he rose to his full, hunched-over height and brought his hands to his massive stomach as it began bellowing in and out, the skin stretching then retreating like air being let into then out of a huge, white balloon. A look of utter surprise grew on his old face, his eyes, Brian thought, almost pleading for help. Finally—and very much like someone who had had too much to drink—Martin opened his mouth wide and in a series of wretching, heaving motions vomited his meal onto the floor, the fabric and flesh almost unrecognizable now. This vomitus had not been touched by stomach juices; no digestive process had left it glossy with fluid. It was still dry. Of course, this was not something Brian noticed, not at all. His eyes only briefly grazed what Martin had sent from his stomach—but the sight was more than enough to make him close his eyes so tightly that his head immediately began to throb with the sudden pressure.

His stomach again empty, Martin began to sob heavily, a confused, aching cry that set his grotesque, misshapen body in motion. Some minutes later, the stench of new death hanging heavy in the room, Martin stopped crying, walked back to his bed, haltingly picked up his pencil and paper and wrote: *Maybe the answer lies in not simply having them around, but in ingestion.* He seemed to think a moment before he added another long scrawl to the entry:

rats et rats

The paper then fell from his hand, and he looked at Brian, who was still futilely attempting to forget what he had just seen.

"Did he go?" Steven asked as Estelle closed the door behind her, having just taken Sam out to "do his business" in a thickly weeded area behind the office.

"He sure did. I wouldn't go walkin' barefoot back there any time real soon if I were you."

Steven smiled. "Sorry about him smellin' up the place like that," he said. "My uncle says that kind of dog food makes him fart like an old car."

Estelle grinned and led the limping Sam back to

his old, tattered army blanket, where the dog circled once painfully, whimpered and then lay down as softly as his mending body would allow.

"Dark out there," she said. "Only half a moon and a lot of stars, and they don't do much to light things up." She regarded Steven with a lingering eye. "I'll bet you're a little tired."

Steven shrugged.

"Well, your uncle went home to get Sam's food. He'll probably be back soon, but if you want you can lie down in one of the empty cells."

"Naw, that's okay. I'd rather stay out here with Sam if it's all right?"

"Sure, just thought you might like to close your eyes. Kids need their sleep, you know."

"My mom used to say that. . . ." His words trailed off.

Estelle carried on with the conversation as if no change in the emotional atmosphere had occurred.

"Well, moms always say stuff like that. Tell you what. I'm going to move Sam into the sheriff's office. There's a great big chair in there that would probably fit you real good. That way you can doze off if you like and still be there if Sam needs you."

"Okay," Steven quickly replied. "Where are you gonna be?"

"Doing some paperwork the sheriff asked me to do."

Steven brought his hands to his hips in mock exasperation. "Do you work all the time, Miss Meath?"

"Only when I'm needed, Steven. And please, call me Estelle. Okay?"

Calling adults by their first name somehow made

him feel older. "Okay, Estelle," he said.

She smiled at him and, as gently as humanly possible, moved Sam into Judd's office, laying the blanket right next to a big, black leather chair. The dog looked up at her as if to say, "Give me a break, lady, I'm a sick dog," then laid his head between his paws.

Steven slid onto the chair, rocked it back, and lowered a hand onto Sam's massive head.

Vampires! Estelle thought. *Next it'll be garlic on the door or some such foolishness!* To her, anything that wasn't black and white wasn't really worth the thinking effort. The plain fact of the matter was, each killing, although surrounded by a set of admittedly bizarre circumstances, had been done by a human being, a flesh-and-blood, honest-to-goodness human being, not some weird black-caped son-of-a-bitch who turned into a bat or slipped through keyholes to make his getaway! And as far as the sheriff's wife was concerned, well, she, obviously, was as dead as George Washington, and poor lonely Judd just reincarnated her with some supernatural garbage and a lot of hopeful hocus pocus. And why not, she allowed. He had loved her. That much was as clear as the picture on a Sony Trinitron. In some distant corner of thought, she wondered if someday a man would love her that much. Sure, she was middle . . . approaching middle age; but nowadays people lived longer, so her chances were a hell of a lot better now than—

A knock at the door yanked her from her thoughts.

She listened, wondering why in the world someone would knock on the door of a police station, then heard it again, soft yet efficient.

She put down the folder she'd been staring at and got up from the desk, casting a glance at the now sleeping Steven and the dog next to him. As she walked to the door and pulled it open, she half expected to see a couple of kids run off, snickering with this great cop station joke.

Looking back at her was Cynthia, although Estelle did not immediately recognize her. Instead, she noticed the quiet, cool beauty and the overly white complexion that gave her a moment of envy. Then their eyes seemed to lock, and a feeling of great peace began to wash over Estelle, as though she had been cold and a large quilt had been settled over her. She heard Cynthia speak, her words echoing through the long, round corridor of her mind. "May I come in?"

Floating dreamily in the warm calm of the moment was an unspoken warning, an awareness stimulated by Judd's discussion concerning the events of the past few days; but Estelle was so positive that her black-and-white philosophy was the correct approach that she quickly relegated that unspoken warning to a part of her consciousness where it would go unnoticed. Unheeded. She even smiled slightly, although she didn't know she had, and stepped aside, saying "Of course," her tone friendly, devoid of the official tone it most always took with civilians.

Cynthia studied her. Having always been amused by the weight of her mental suggestions, she said, "The other deputy sent me here. He needs your help.

He's in the cemetery and he needs your help. Do you understand?"

In the cemetery. Estelle heard those words, and although she wondered why Ricky was at the cemetery, another long look into the wells of Cynthia's eyes convinced her that Ricky was indeed there and that if this woman said he needed her help, then she should most certainly go. She turned to her right, pulled the car keys from the rack on the wall, car number two, and left as hurriedly as though word of a murder had reached her. She closed the door behind her, remarking to herself as she hurried to the car, that Steven would be all right. An adult was with him. As she inserted the key and brought the engine to life, her thoughts revolved totally around Ricky Smits and what he might have found.

As often happened, reality snuck into Steven's dream and altered it to the point where dream and reality were almost one and the same. He had been dreaming of his mother—as he often did—and of the last time he had seen her alive, in the front seat of the car just before the storm. Of course, during that ride, their dog, Rags, had stayed home. But with the changeability of dreams, Rags was now in the car, right next to him. And as he watched in disbelief, Rags, a black and white springer spaniel, changed into Sam, right down to the cast. And Sam was growling, his canines bared, his eyes bright with fear while the hair on the back of his neck bristled. Steven snapped his eyes open. Sam was in his line of sight, standing as best he could, the hair on his back indeed bristling. Out of the corner of his eye he saw her. He turned his head just slightly, to see all of her, and he instantly saw that it was Cynthia, his uncle's wife. The likeness between the pictures he had seen and the woman standing in the doorway was striking. His thoughts became suddenly tangled, just a mass of curling wire. Why was Sam growling? He wanted to say, "Does Uncle Judd know you're here? He should know. We should go tell him! He'll be so happy!" But he didn't.

As she looked at Sam, her eyes grew huge with rage. Even with a broken leg the dog looked vicious, Steven thought, and she was just a lady. . . .

"Quiet, Sam!" he ordered.

Sam turned toward him and stopped growling for only a second, running his tongue along his mouth to wipe away an accumulation of drool, then continued growling, just as menacingly.

"Quiet, Sam!" Steven said more forcefully.

The dog whined and stepped backward, beyond his blanket; but although he had stopped growling, the hair remained bristled on his back, and he kept a wary eye on the woman who only he knew was not human, who only he knew lacked the human scent he had become accustomed to over the years. This woman smelled of the things he found in the woods, the animals that didn't move when he pawed and sniffed at them, the ones that filled his mind with mystery and awe and fear. She had that smell. He felt the boy's hand on his back and looked at him, wanting to warn him somehow, wanting to tell him that this woman belonged in the forest with the things that didn't move. But there was no way he could tell him, no way he could warn him. All he could do. . . .

Steven saw the hateful look on her face grow suddenly larger, saw it contort and, not quickly enough, saw Sam hobble across the room as best he could and lunge weakly, fangs bared, in defense of his young master. But even in the woods, without a broken leg, he had been no match for her. Again she effortlessly reached out and gave the dog a hammer blow to the side of the head, sending him reeling into Judd's desk with a sickening thud, before he fell in a broken, whimpering heap.

Steven rushed to him and lifted his head. "Sam, please, Sam, don't die, Sam, don't die!" he pleaded.

The dog's breathing was shallow, almost non-existent, his eyes half-closed and glazed with approaching death. Steven looked at Cynthia and knew instantly that she was the same woman who had been in the forest clearing, the same woman his Uncle Judd said was crazy. But although he was as afraid as he had ever been, even as afraid as when his father's car had gone out of control, he was also as mad as he had ever been. He wanted to do to her what she had done to Sam. He wanted to kill her. He put his head down and ran at her like a charging bull, his little fists flailing into her with all the strength he could find, with all the vengeance available. And in the blue-black color of his anger, he heard her cry out. At first he thought he had hurt her, and it made him feel good; but then he realized that what he was hearing was not crying. She was laughing. High-pitched and cackling. She was laughing. "Stop laughing, stop laughing!" he ordered, his fists still pounding into her. "Stop it, dammit! Stop it, stop it, stop it!"

CHAPTER TWENTY-TWO

At The Cabin—
Preparatory Work

The tight, mechanical sound of the Jeep's door closing seemed somehow more defined in the hollow night air. Judd stepped toward the cabin, the crunch of sole against stone echoing lonelily against the surrounding trees.

There was work to be done. There were rules to follow. It was time to summon up that part of him that acted only out of instinct, that emotionless little bastard that said, "Time to eat," or "Time to sleep," or, more appropriately, "Time to blow that sucker's head off because he's got a great big gun pointed right at your forehead!" That guy. That instinctively protecting part of him that lay dormant until survival was in doubt.

He opened the door and flipped on the light switch. Then he walked toward the couch and picked up a three-by-five photograph in a simple brass frame from the end table. The picture was of him and

Cynthia. They had been making angels in the crusty snow, and Jeffrey had rushed onto the porch and snapped their picture with Judd's 110. He remembered that moment, how the cold had hardened the snow until it felt like a mattress in a cheap hotel. But God how they had laughed when Jeffrey said, "I just had to get a picture of this. Old people playing in the snow! You guys are weird!"

He looked at the painting of Cynthia above the fireplace and experienced a hollow feeling in the pit of his gut, the same feeling he always got whenever he looked at a picture of someone he knew was dead.

He scanned the cabin, up and down, nooks and crannies, all those little spaces that were only waiting for Cynthia's distinctive touch.

Cynthia, he knew, would never come to this place, her mind filled with decorating schemes or just how to surprise Jeffrey on that day when he finally reached manhood—that over the precipice eighteenth birthday. And Jeffrey would never walk into a quiet, dark house and then act surprised—whether he was or not—when a bevy of friends and relatives yelled, "HAPPY BIRTHDAY, JEFF!" when the lights were thrown on.

The future didn't have these things in its little satchel of premade moments. The future was foggy and red-stained and waiting out there like some hungry vulture.

As he continued to look around the cabin, he felt an urge to go out to the tool shed, get his gas can, and strategically sprinkle a gallon or so around the place. Then maybe he'd be rid of her; then maybe Jeffrey could die, too.

But he knew that burning this place wouldn't get rid of her. She—at least this new Cynthia—would probably roast weenies over the flames. No, burning this place wasn't the answer. He was only feeling sorry for himself. He had built a shrine to her, a place for them to come home to when they finally got back from wherever it was they had gone. And now he realized, finally, that they weren't coming home. So what good was the place?

What good, for that matter, was hope? His was as dead as any cancer-sodden, bed-ridden lump of reeking flesh who still snuck a cigarette when the nurse wasn't looking.

There was really only one hope now, only one more thing he could do for her. He could take away the blackness of her death and the darkness of her life. He could go on around back, get some of that ash firewood he had been trying to age, and sharpen it up. Then he could get his simple claw hammer and then. . . . But when he pictured himself actually going through with it, that little guy inside of him, that schizoid companion to stoic detachment, reared up his conniving little head. How could he bring himself to hurt her? How? What if, after it was over, he found out that this was all some big, stupid mistake? What if she had only been drugged or had somehow been hypnotized? What if, after he had done the deed, she didn't just shrivel into a pile of human-skin dust. What if she just lay there bleeding through her chest, her eyes pleading with him, begging for an answer to his homicidal act?

Maybe Estelle was right after all. Maybe all those library books were dead wrong. Maybe vampires did *not* exist.

He felt his body drain of strength. He could rationalize until his head throbbed—but there was only one answer.

So he packed up his emotions and went around back, flashlight in hand, mosquitoes droning in noisy abundance. He'd sharpen up some stakes; four was a good number—just in case. Then he'd do something about another cross, something a little larger than the one on the chain around his neck. Size, after all, at least with most things, made a difference. Maybe something good and big would be wise. And after this, maybe a Tupperware container full of blessed water, pilfered from Father Sloan's church. Sloan wouldn't mind anyway—all for a good cause. For the cause of Good.

The stack of firewood stood behind the cabin, just before the tree line, where the smell of Sam's droppings was just negligible. Judd picked out four stout, but thin pieces of ash, fished out his boy scout knife, sat down on the pile and started whittling.

The woods, he decided as chips of ash arced through the air, sounded normal tonight: the whine of insects, the silly baritone song of bored bullfrogs. Cynthia wasn't around right now. He would be able to fashion his pointy instruments of death in peace.

CHAPTER TWENTY-THREE

At four in the morning Judd found Estelle on her knees next to Sam, crying. And Steven was nowhere to be seen. He rushed into the office, glanced at Sam, who looked more dead than not, then pulled Estelle to her feet. She was teary-eyed and red-faced, an emotional mess.

"Steven—where is Steven?" he asked, not really expecting an answer. First he'd have to get her attention.

Estelle could only open her mouth and gesture feebly at the dog, then look toward Judd. The only intelligible sounds that came out of her had something to do with Ricky and Cynthia, which, Judd thought, didn't make sense at all. The only thing that made sense right now was the fact that Steven was gone, that he had left Estelle with the boy and now he was gone.

He shook her, trying to bring her back. "Estelle, was Cynthia here?" he yelled. "Was my wife here? Did she take Steven?"

Her heavy sobs became more fitful. She nodded her head yes.

He set Estelle down in the big leather chair next to Sam and tried to calm her down, which, he knew, would take more effort than a mere "It's all right, take it easy," as if she'd only been stung by a yellow-jacket. She wasn't herself, not the person he knew and in whom he placed great trust. He had never seen her like this, so out of control. Hell, he thought, he'd never even seen her cry. Something had happened to her, something that had broken down the wall of disbelief she had so boldly displayed while he had talked with them earlier. He felt sorry for her, and in the back of his mind the phrase "I told you so," began to take shape. He clipped it short, chastising himself for his childish reaction. The truth, he thought, had jumped up and scared the hell out of her. Now, maybe, she'd be able to defend herself.

But she'd certainly have to regain control. She was of little use to him this way, gibbering nonsense to herself, lost in a nightmare world created by a being whose existence, only hours earlier, had made her laugh.

After he had covered Sam with his blanket—not entirely sure if the dog was dead or not—he went into the bathroom and brought back a cold glass of tap water in a Dixie cup. Estelle took it from him cautiously, her weary eyes trying to gauge his purpose, and then, satisfied that it was only tap water, drank it down. When she was done, she gave it back and said, "Thanks," even that one word showing her fear and confusion. Judd looked down at the dog, saw one eye flutter and then turned his attention back to Estelle, who seemed to have regained a shaky, but workable control.

He measured his words carefully. "Steven, Estelle. Where is Steven?"

She looked at him like someone who'd been caught in a wrong, and said, "I don't know. I don't know. I think . . . your wife was here, Judd." She looked away and just stared with frightened eyes. "She was so—" she looked back at Judd—"what is she? What the hell is she?"

"What did she say to you, Estelle?"

". . . Ricky."

"Yes, you said that. . . ."

She breathed deeply, trying to calm herself. "She said he was at the cemetery." She smiled wanly. "That he needed my help."

"So you went to the cemetery and left Steven. . . ."

Her face slowly suffused with this truth. "ALONE!" she said, "YES . . . GOD, YES! I LEFT HIM ALONE! What have I done? What have I done?" she begged.

She buried her face in her hands and cried, again given over not only to her grief for Steven, but the horrid, black confusion that had grown out of her confrontation with Cynthia. Judd left her alone and checked on Sam.

Although Steven's primary concern was with his own well-being, he couldn't help but wonder about Sam. Even when Cynthia carried him screaming out the door then around back and through the weeds, he had a fleeting image of the dog, reasonably healthy, reasonably happy. He prayed he was all right, that she hadn't killed him this time, even though a small yet clear inner voice told him she probably had.

He remembered how many times he had hit her—hundreds, he estimated, maybe more—and not once had she even so much as gasped, not once. Sure, he was a kid and he didn't hit real hard, but he had been so mad—so full of adrenaline. But, he reasoned, if she was crazy, like his uncle said, then he could probably hit her with a great big club, and more than likely she wouldn't even feel it. Her adrenaline was probably stronger than his—she was an adult, a crazy adult.

Clearly, there was little he could do to escape. He had come to that conclusion earlier. She moved so quickly—without so much as a crack of a twig—that it didn't even seem possible that someone would see them, someone he could yell to for help. They had traveled through backyards to get to where they were now, standing on the porch of a boarded-up house near the canal. He had seen yellow squares of light from the kitchens of a few homes along the way, but they had passed so quickly he hadn't really had time to cry out. Eventually he just lay still in her arms, forsaking any defense, forsaking any cries for help, opting to see where they were going and then, once there, doing what he could to escape. It was, he thought tiredly, the only option he had.

She put him down and looked at him, her eyes glistening with a strange dull light, even in the darkness. "Welcome," she said, just the trace of a smile on her mouth. But as she let him go, as their bodies no longer touched, he saw an opening, maybe the only one he would get. He turned, pleased with himself for waiting until now, and bolted. In a heartbeat she was there, arms spread, blocking his escape.

He ran right into her, but she didn't wrap her arms around him or try to stop him. She simply stood there. He thought about ducking under one of her arms and decided against it. She moved too quickly—she'd probably just wait until the last second and then snare him like a scared cat.

He backed slowly away from her, toward the front door of the house, and suddenly remembered his voice. "Help! Help. Help me!" he yelled. Suddenly there was a sound from above. On the porch roof. Steven canted his head back and listened. *Yes. Oh, God, yes.* There was someone up there walking slowly toward the edge. He lowered his eyes and looked at Cynthia, who, unlike him, didn't look at all surprised by the fact that there was someone on the roof. She was smiling. Then, the footfalls stopped, and just a scant second later, behind Cynthia, Steven saw a figure—neither man nor woman, amorphous in the darkness—flying soundlessly through the air in a big, swooping arc and then landing on the sidewalk just as soundlessly. Steven could see now that it was a man, a big, stupid-looking man. He walked up the porch steps, past Cynthia, who didn't even turn her head to greet him.

Robert All reached into his pocket, fetched the key, and unlocked the door.

"Take him downstairs," he said. "I'll meet you inside."

Neal Sayers looked down at the broken body and said, "Christ! What the hell did this?"

Ricky Smits looked at him. "Can you do anything?" he asked.

"I'm a vet, not God," Sayers answered.

Ricky remembered Judd's exact words: "Have him do everything in his power."

Sayers looked at him. "You're probably better off putting him to sleep," he said, his tone blending pity and professional opinion.

Ricky thought about that—discounted it. Judd would never forgive him. The dog deserved at least a fighting chance. It wasn't as though he had an infection or a disease, something radically terminal. He was broken up pretty badly; but broken bones healed, eventually, and the dog was strong. Judd had told him that if any animal displayed a will to live, it was this one. He stroked the animal's head, getting no response, and then left, wondering if he would ever see the dog alive again, and wondering pretty much the same about Judd's nephew.

As Judd drove, not really sure of where he was going, he wondered how Estelle was getting along. She was like a little kid who'd had a nightmare and wanted to curl in beside her parents for the remainder of a dark, mysterious night. He hadn't wanted to leave her alone, but he had had no choice. The dog needed medical attention, a job he had given to Ricky, and somehow, someway, he had to find Steven, which all added up to leaving Estelle alone, at least until Ricky got back from Sayers' office.

A short while later, realizing that he was, indeed, driving aimlessly, he pulled over, got out and leaned against the Jeep to think. Fumbling nervously through the contents of his pockets, he fingered the class ring Harry Kroh had given him to hold for Teddy Dorsey—wherever the hell he was. He pulled it out, then turned it around so that light from the street lamp sharply glittered in the stone, and then slipped it onto his finger, remarking to himself how large it was. He remembered the family picture in the living room at the Dorsey house. The man was barely as tall as his wife. But then, size didn't really matter. Judd had been in the army with a man about average size who wore a size fourteen ring, the size of most men's thumbs. Thinking that, he dropped the ring into his pocket again and forgot about it.

As he drove, his thoughts centered on just where Cynthia could have taken Steven. The clearing was a possibility, even the cabin, but he didn't think so. Most of all he wondered what to do next, his worry focused primarily on his nephew, who was out there with someone whom Judd had once loved and who was now someone—something—he didn't know, who would probably just as soon kill him as make love to him.

He remembered what the mayor had said about bringing in the state cops to help. That wouldn't be wise, he concluded, not now, not under these bizarre circumstances. He would have to explain everything to some lieutenant or captain who would come in here with a mind about as receptive as Estelle's had been. Or he'd probably have to lie. Probably? Hell, he would have to lie! He'd have to say Steven had been kidnapped, and then they'd ask if he knew by whom, and he'd have to come up with something. Then he'd have to bring Estelle into the ruse, and in her own gibbering way she'd probably say something that would make them look like they were all crazy. He could just imagine them snickering behind his back and politely informing him that it would probably be best if the state police went it alone.

No, this was his fight, his alone. She'd hurt him the most; she'd taken his son and she had taken his nephew. Hell, she had probably even had a hand in Barb and Walt's deaths. Somehow he knew that if he didn't end it tonight, if he didn't find Cynthia and—as Estelle had said—run some pointy baseball bat through her heart—then tomorrow would be too late. She'd have him. Just like she'd had Jeffrey. And there was only one thing he could do—drive these dark streets and hope to find something, anything. It wasn't much, but for now, it was all he had.

CHAPTER TWENTY-FOUR

Martin wrote *no more wimpers,* then raised his eyes and remembered how the second boy had fought and fought, his little fists flailing ineffectually. He smiled, although with difficulty. His face had lost most of its elasticity now; smiling, even opening his mouth to feed, was not easily done.

He remembered the second boy's screams of agony as he sunk his teeth into his belly and tore it out, hoping a different part of the body would produce different results. It hadn't. He had only thrown it all up again, and the boy had died almost instantly. His face, even in death, was still fixed with horror. His hands, flexed like huge spiders, grabbed where his stomach had once been while the life pumped out of his body. Of course, he couldn't feed off of them while they were . . . not alive. The Assyrian legends were clear on that—or were they? Yes, he concluded, the victim had to be alive. Of course, no one had said anything about the ingestion of a living victim being a cure for aging, but it seemed to make sense; young, living tissue ingested into an old, and growing increasingly older, body. Simply having them around hadn't worked, so he had searched for alternatives. But he hadn't been able to keep that flesh down—and there had been the pain, the excruciating pain as he catapulted the vomitus. Now he was alone again. The two boys were dead, and he was alone in the lantern-lit basement room with the bodies of his victims scattered about as if someone had thrown a bomb into a crowded morgue. The stench of them was almost unbearable.

A look of emptiness flashed suddenly onto his face. He picked up his pencil and paper again and wrote: *There were little rabbits on the cards and a picture window and Aunty Maude. . . .* He sighed and continued to write, ramblings mainly, until he heard the door open. Standing in it was the woman, Cynthia, and Robert and, between them, another boy, who turned and tried to run as soon as he saw Martin, only to be stopped by Robert's huge hand on his collar. He pulled him around to face his future, the boy's little legs running in place like in a nightmare. Finally he settled down and began whimpering.

Martin thought about whimpers, how easily they were stifled. And next to random thoughts about Aunty Maude and the quietness of her eternal sleep, he wrote, *fod more fod,* and ended that thought with an overlarge, imprecise exclamation point.

Judd pulled his car in front of Rosemary Hamilton's flower shop and cut the engine. The windshield had fogged over. Cooling down, he thought. He opened the driver-side window and just sat, glancing up and down the deserted street. Seconds later, almost driven to panic by the realization that he was getting nowhere, he flipped on his overhead and looked at his watch. 5:15. The sun would be up in another hour, hour and a half. He looked down the street at The Krohbar and remembered what Harry had said about Bobby All, that he had followed Rosemary and Susan. He tried to picture that: Susan and Rosemary stepping into the night, turning—right? Left? Bobby All maybe thirty seconds behind. But why? He thought of what Kroh had said, about he and Cynthia being right for each other and just the opposite about Bobby All and Cynthia, and his mind drifted to a time long ago, to a ballgame that had dramatically altered his life.

As he stood in line to shoot jumpers during warm-ups, he watched them out of the corner of his eye. They sat on the top right bleacher, Cynthia, Bobby All and Martin Crouper, who was easily twice their age—as weird a threesome as anyone could possibly imagine. Watching them he had an attack of the guilts. Rosemary was his girl, but late at night, while he lay awake in bed, as the awakening dragons of sexuality roared and spit hellfire, Cynthia snuck into his thoughts. Rosemary had been so positive that what they had would last forever that she had even mentioned something about marriage—after college, of course, only after their careers got going. Judd never told her he was as confused about his career as he was about their relationship.

As he secretly watched Cynthia and her entourage, he thought there might be something troubling her. She seemed preoccupied, introspective. Even when they scored, she didn't seem to care. He waited around after the game, intending to say something to her—what, he didn't know—just something to get the ball rolling. But while he stood near the double doors, he saw first Martin leave, then Cynthia and Bobby. He stood out of sight around a corner but still within earshot and listened to their conversation, feeling profound elation when All said something about Judd and about how she couldn't take her eyes off of him. But, hidden around an intersecting corner as he was, he hadn't bargained on Bobby All almost running him down after the conversation ended. All even stopped for a moment and glared at him, something shiny in his palm as he said, "She doesn't want this, Lucas; she wants you. So go on, take her!" his tone layered with a thick frost. Laughing lightly he added, "I'll loan her to you." Then he fisted the shiny thing in his palm and walked away like a salesman who had just finalized one hell of a deal.

The shiny thing in his palm, Judd now mused. He hadn't dropped his gaze to look back then—Bobby and his angry, gleaming eyes had transfixed him. He had only seen the glitter out of the corner of his eye. That shiny thing in his palm. He fumbled with the memory, almost hypnotizing himself to bring that moment into sharper focus; why, he didn't know. But if there was a connection, somehow a connection between Bobby All and Cynthia—a ring? He thought about it. It had to have been! A ring, a goddamn ring! Sure, what else could it have been? She had given it back to him, and he had taunted Judd with it . . . or maybe he had wanted to give it to her that night. They had only dated a little while, so maybe he had wanted to make it a steady thing by giving her a ring. Out of sheer curiosity, and only because he could think of nothing else, he shoved his hand into his pocket and pawed out the ring Harry had given him. He held it under the overhead. Just a typical class ring, he thought, studying it, just your everyday, one-in-a-million—wait, wait. He held it up to the light, slanted so that it caught the light more sharply. There were initials on the inside. He squinted, silently chastising himself for leaving his glasses at the office. All he was able to make out was the first initial, an R. *R . . . R,* he thought, *of course, Robert, Bobby!* He squinted tightly at the second letter. Could be an A, could be an H or a B, too. But he knew it was neither. This ring belonged to Bobby—Robert All—and it had been found by Harry Kroh at Susan Dorsey's house! Somehow, All's ring—that Cynthia might have worn years ago—had made it to the Dorsey house on the same night Harry had seen Bobby All following Susan and Rosemary. Obviously, he had been in the house. And—he gave this thought a wide berth—maybe Cynthia had been there, too. Then, suddenly, even as his mind mulled over these new developments, disappointment shoved revery aside. He had a ring—Bobby All's class ring—but so what? What the hell good would it do? How could it help him find Steven? He squeezed it tightly and banged his fists into the steering wheel.

Then it dawned on him. "Christ, how could I be so goddamn stupid?" he said. "She gave him Steven, just like she probably gave him Jeffrey." He remembered more passages from *Vampires*, those referring to vampire masters. Supposedly, a vampire was more or less a slave to the vampire that had caused the transformation, forever in their spiritual debt. It was all coming together with great clarity now. Cynthia had been transformed by Bobby All, and Bobby All had done something to Susan and Rosemary, probably even Teddy Dorsey, killed or maybe transformed them, like Gloria Sternmyer. And Cynthia had taken Steven as some kind of gift or sacrifice or offering. But why? Just to hurt him again, like she had hurt him ten years earlier? Why didn't they just kill him when they had the chance? And if she had given Steven to him—her master—then where was he? Where was Robert All?

He tried to think of places a vampire might hide, realizing, as he thought, that just about any place would do, as long as that place offered protection from detection and the rays of the sun; any basement in any abandoned building or house. His face brightened, his eyes opening wide. "His house—she took Steven to All's house! Of course!"

He shoved the door open, ran down the block to a phone booth very near where Walt Higgins had often stopped to rest on his way home, and turned to the A's. The name All was not listed.

"Shit!" he said, shutting the door to the booth behind him and glaring up and down the empty main street of town, his frustration compounded by the fact that it had been a very long time since Steven had been kidnapped. Anything could have happened to him by now—anything. He could be dead; he could be . . . changed. And, yes, he could still be alive, still a vital human being with a future. Somehow, in the middle of the goddamn night, he would have to find the house, with only a general location to go by. Somewhere by the canal.

CHAPTER TWENTY-FIVE

Steven wanted to go to sleep. More than anything he wanted to sleep. At least then he wouldn't have to be here—with the smell so bad that it made him want to puke, and the old, old man sitting on the bed over there with a blanket wrapped around him. At least asleep he could go to another place. Even a nightmare place would be better because at least nightmares weren't real. And this was definitely real. There were real dead bodies stinking it all up—other kids' dead bodies. And there was the man and woman over there in the darkest corner of the room who seemed to want to hurt him, but didn't; didn't because the old, old man had sat up and hissed at them real loud when they had moved toward him. And ever since then, they just kept looking at the old man to see, Steven thought, if he was asleep, then back at him, almost like animals trying to steal food. And, of course, there was the old man and his blanket and his pieces of paper that he sometimes wrote on and sometimes didn't. Steven had studied one boy, about ten feet away, after he had finally stopped crying. He wondered mightily why that boy was holding his stomach like he was and why his mouth was open and his eyes weren't shut. He was dead. Steven knew that. He had seen death before, not very long ago. Up close and personal. He had seen his parents die that rainy day on that slippery road. He had seen his father's head ram against the driver's window, blood flying everywhere like movie ketchup. He had seen his mother's body lying pretzel-like around the steering wheel, her head caught between it and the dashboard. But both of them had closed their eyes. Or dying had. So why weren't this boy's eyes closed? The answer was probably because when he died he had been awfully, awfully afraid. Like a dead animal in the road who's just been run over. Whatever had killed him—probably that man or woman over there—had probably scared him enough so he couldn't close his eyes. Steven wondered if perhaps the old man had killed them, but thought not. Old men didn't hurt people. Old men just said wise things and gave away money. The old man was probably a prisoner here, just like he was.

Judd rang the bell, waited, then rang it again, pressing even harder on the button, as if that would somehow send an extra surge of electricity charging through the wires, powerful enough to yank Harry from a deep sleep. Still nothing. With growing frustration, he banged on the door, then backed away and gazed hopefully up at Harry's apartment above The

Krohbar. "Harry, goddammit, wake up, Harry. I need your help!" he yelled.

In the east, meanwhile, the first hint of morning diluted the darkness and produced a deep purple haze, lighter near the horizon, but progressively darker as it moved upward to where the stars, like stationary flakes of snow, were still visible. "Harry," he yelled again. Harry didn't answer. "Shit," Judd seethed, "I'll have to do this myself!" He piled back into the Jeep and brought the engine to life with a roar that sounded obtrusively loud in the solitude of early morning.

Fifteen or so minutes later, after he'd driven around like a drunken madman, he slammed his foot onto the brake. To his right was the All house. It gave off a kind of mutated electrical charge, like he had just read his own obituary. This was the house. If it wasn't, then All could use this one as a goddamn spare.

He parked in front and simply sat for a moment to compose himself, think things out. Across the street lay a thick clump of woods over which the sun would soon rise. Years earlier, those woods had been intensely searched three separate times, once for each missing boy. Neighbors back then, and on three separate nights, had heard noises one had described as "fearsome screams" coming from this general area. So fearsome, so frightening had been the screams, that the only direction the people who had heard them could give was "You know, around here somewhere," and they'd gestured with their hands, each one of them in a different direction.

The street was basked in the soft, shadowy flush of

predawn, but the near-white color of the All house was easily distinguishable, the tan-colored plywood over the windows appearing for all the world like giant Band Aids. From the Jeep, Judd saw a glint of light off the circle of brass that formed the lock—*probably a damn sturdy one, too,* he thought.

He got out, went to the back of the Jeep, opened the tailgate and pulled back the blanket he had used to cover his arsenal. Under that blanket lay a huge wooden cross strung tightly together at the intersections, four wooden stakes fashioned from ash firewood roped together like a clip of bullets, and a plain claw hammer. He shoved the hammer into the left side of his belt, the cross into the right, and cradled the bundle of stakes under his arm. The final weapon in his supernatural array was the holy water pilfered from Father Sloan's church. It sloshed innocuously inside a small white Tupperware container with a red, snap-on top. As he put the container into his shirt pocket, a fleeting image of Cynthia screaming in acid-gouging agony, her face wreathed in sinuous tendrils of smoke, passed before his eyes—and he didn't even flinch. He was running on pure instinct now, pure automated instinct.

Fully armed, flashlight included, he closed the rear gate and climbed the stairs to the porch. Getting in, he knew, would not be easy. He noticed that the huge helping of confidence that he had felt just seconds earlier, confidence strengthened by anger and fear, had weakened considerably. It was not a pleasant feeling. Not at all. And now was certainly not the time to feel defenseless and insignificant.

Breaking in with only the claw hammer would

probably take a while, but, he decided, setting his mind to the task, the hammer would have to do. No matter how long it took, no matter how much noise he had to make, he'd get in there—eventually—and confront whatever needed confronting in order to rescue his nephew.

And free Cynthia from her "curse"—if that was the right word.

He put the bundle of stakes down, mindful of the business end. Blanks wouldn't do him much good later—and that's all they'd be if he dropped them hard on their tips, just blunted, harmless pieces of firewood.

As he pushed the claw end of the hammer in between the door and the jamb, he heard from behind him, "Try this."

Judd wheeled, his heart catching in his throat, the hammer raised high, and looked into the startled face of Harry Kroh. His grip weakened, and the hammer came down. Judd grabbed at his chest, his breath rushing out.

"Sorry," Harry said. "Didn't mean to scare you."

Judd thought about chewing him out, but not for very long. This was not the time for sheriffing. He looked at the crowbar in Harry's hand and grabbed for it. Harry watched while Judd slipped the crowbar in between the door and jamb and pried. Finally, his face red from the strain, he said, "Christ, Harry, help me!"

Harry mumbled, "Yeah, sure," put his hands on the middle of the crowbar and pulled. The door gave haltingly, only centimeters at a time, the wood straining to hold. Eventually, however, it popped open with a huge splintering crack, both men losing their balance.

Judd caught his breath and looked at Harry. "Stay here," he ordered. "If I need you for any reason, I'll call for you. You got that?"

He picked up the bundle of stakes, and Harry glanced at both the bundle and the makeshift cross. "What the hell are you hunting, Sheriff?" he asked, somewhat amused.

"Never you mind, Harry, just never you mind. Just stay here."

Judd didn't bother to ask Harry what he was doing here, or even how he knew to come here. But Judd concluded Harry had also taken a close look at the ring and recognized the initials. Harry, Judd thought, had gone to a lot of trouble, not to mention a great deal of personal danger, to find out what had happened to someone he supposedly barely knew.

"You sure you don't need my help, Sheriff?" Harry asked.

Judd held his hand up and simply shook his head.

Harry shrugged. "Okay. I'll wait here," he said. "I'll wait here and listen for you. You call now if you get into trouble. You do that, Sheriff!"

Judd said, "All right, Harry," and stepped inside.

The darkness here, even with the reflected light of approaching dawn and punctured by the flashlight's beam, seemed to close in around him as if he were a claustrophobic surrounded by a huge crowd of strangers. Along with the normal lack of light was another, far more sinister darkness. The smothering, consuming darkness of death was here, all around him, crushing in, stealing his sight and his ability to reason. And there was the odor—a coppery, almost unbearably sour smell that was reminiscent of decomposing flesh, an odor that really had no direction, but that was growing stronger with each halting step. Reflexively he yanked the cross from his belt and held it stiff-armed out in front of him, the beam of light falling onto sheeted furniture, a stove, and boarded-up windows. At any second he was positive that Cynthia or Bobby would appear in the beam, teeth jocularly bared, ready to rip him apart. But as he thought that, he wondered if perhaps the lateness of the hour might not have them all sleeping, or whatever it was vampires did when the sun was up, or nearly up, like now. In his haste, it was a circumstance he had given little thought to, but now the possibility that they were all bedded down restored a little of his lost confidence. For reassurance he grasped the bundle of stakes and gave them a squeeze, silently counting as he did, to make sure he still had the four, and then walked into the kitchen.

Near the cupboards now, he drew the flashlight in a semi-circle and stopped. There was a door behind him, open an inch or so. Seeing it, he had an urge to call out, "Steven, where are you? I'm here. Uncle Judd's here to rescue you!"

But he didn't call out. Surprise was his ally. He couldn't go charging willy nilly through the house. Even if they were "asleep," who was to say how deeply they slept?

He stepped haltingly toward the door and then stopped abruptly, as though an impassable wall had been suddenly built in his path. In effect, there had been. In front of him were ornately carved sarcophagi guarded by circling, flying gargoyles and huge, hooded snakes slithering around and over them. The sarcophagi themselves, well over ten feet in height, smashed through the kitchen's ceiling and rose into the second floor like newly formed islands. Upon seeing this, the feeling of being extremely tiny in a land of giants, the feeling that had overwhelmed him as soon as he had entered this house, grew even stronger. He felt suddenly weak and fragile and terribly frightened. He staggered backward, his face contorted with fear, and he looked at his crude weapons and passed judgment on them. They were now only children's playthings. Useless. He had been silly to even think. . . . The tendons in his calfs felt suddenly hot, the musculature rubbery. His legs buckled, and it was all he could do to keep himself from falling. He dropped the bundle of stakes to the floor by his feet and looked at them almost scornfully. He could see it now. Cynthia and Bobby would merely laugh at him as they easily tore them out of his trembling hands and turned them against him, jamming one of the lethally pointed stakes through his chest; their faces alight with the stupidity of his task as they raised the hammer and brought it down time after time until he had finally been impaled into the floor like a collector's butterfly.

It was almost enough to make him turn and run, his tail tucked securely between his legs—a coward, yes, but a live coward, not a dead, worthless hero.

But he didn't run. He fought this vision that he knew could not be real and watched as it finally shimmered and then disappeared, leaving his path clear. With a deep sigh of wonder and relief, he stepped forward, pushed open the door and played the light down the stairs.

What he saw then made his heart hammer against his chest wall. They were down there, at the bottom of the stairs—a crowd of slavering vampires, naked and white, the genitals of the males grotesquely oversized, the breasts of the women strangely nonexistent. Their hands were joined, and they were skipping a circle around his stinking, steaming remains. While he watched disbelievingly, one of the females broke hands, squatted and ripped off a fresh handful of his flesh and then gazed up at him with feigned pity, her mouth gaped exaggeratedly wide as she devoured him.

And all Judd could do was watch until, repulsed to the point where his stomach was ready to revolt, he had to turn away and brace himself against the stove to catch his breath. His strength, he thought, was draining quickly. They were having one hell of a laugh on him, one hell of a laugh. They were so unbelievably strong. Even simply being in the same house with them, let alone the same room, was physically and emotionally fatiguing. He hadn't felt this weak in the woods, with only Cynthia . . . with only Cynthia. Suddenly he raised his head as a vague sense of victory grew within him. They—Cynthia and Bobby—had arranged these visions as some kind of defense mechanism. Given the power of their minds, it was entirely possible that they were able to fill a trespasser's thoughts with the visions he had just seen, with the feelings of deep inadequacy he had just experienced. He turned and ran the light down the stairs again. He smiled. Now, after having regained a small amount of control, the visions, although still there, were not nearly as powerful, as though he had, indeed, just gotten through some first line of defense. He sighed with relief: it was all just a jumble of mental barbed wire, just a shitload of mental hocus pocus! With that thought, he couldn't help but smile even wider. He was stronger than they had expected. Hell, he was stronger than he had expected. He had survived the first two tests. He picked up his clutch of weapons and threw back the door.

From here, he could see two doors, one on his left—barricaded?—and one on his right, apparently closed.

He stepped onto the top riser and remotely heard Harry Kroh say, "Sheriff? You all right in there?"

He didn't bother to answer, and Harry said, "Upstairs, Sheriff, you look upstairs yet?"

Judd silently cursed Harry Kroh's big mouth and stepped onto the second riser, noticing with each step that the ring of vampires was growing less and less distinct, like a weakening mirage. And as he reached the bottom and boldly stepped into the middle of them, where his pellucid remains lay, they disappeared altogether.

He drew the light from left to right. *A choice, again a choice. So many choices,* he thought, *so goddamn many choices. Big cross, little cross, left door, right door! Shit!*

Games—more games!

He drew in a deep breath, exhaled and felt better. The door on the left was indeed barricaded. A six-by-six, slotted on either side, had been placed across the middle. Obviously the door opened outward. And just as obviously, he thought, someone could be imprisoned behind it. But as he pondered that possibility, he wondered if perhaps this door hadn't been chosen for him—that barricade just another mirage. Realizing what he thought was another small victory, he choose the door on the right. Placing his hand just above the brown, ceramic knob, he pulled just hard enough to creak the door open about a foot, the flashlight pointed toward the dirt floor inside. On the right, as he raised the flashlight, he saw wood racks piled high with dust-laden, unlabeled canned goods. The fruit cellar, he thought, pushing the door open a little farther and running the light up the racks. On the top shelf were what looked like cans of paint, although on most the labels hung in limp half circles or had fallen off entirely. The remaining shelves held only the canned goods and a few glass jars with what looked like tomatoes inside, although the layers of dust made it difficult to determine what they held, only that the contents were tinted a dull red.

Judd stepped inside. On the left were more shelves and still more canned goods, although mixed in with these were a few bundles of strung-together Indian corn and some empty wicker baskets. On the bottom left shelf sat a pile of old, yellowed newspapers, neatly strung together and tied in a bow. The headline beneath the neatly tied bow read simply, "DEWEY WINS!" There was a small window at the far end, barred on the inside and covered on the outside by a small piece of plywood. The ceiling here, only six inches or so above his head, a line of vertical one-by-fours supporting the hardwood floor above, was littered with the razor-sharp tips of at least a hundred stalactitic hardwood nails. It was a small room, only eight by ten, he guessed, and there definitely did not appear to be anyone—or anything—here. He kicked disappointedly at the dirt floor, raising a small cloud of dust that hung limply in the dank, turbid air.

But then, just as Judd was about to leave, he heard chuckling, deep throated and filled with rising amusement, as if from the bottom of a well. From behind him? He wheeled and brought the circle of light to bear on the back wall. Nothing. He took a step, then another, overcome by frustration and anger. *Shit! Where? Where?* Judd turned back, light burning through the dimness. And it was then that he saw him, a broadly grinning dwarf dressed in a black vest and trousers and a crisply creased, long-sleeve white shirt.

His nose was huge and round, taking up most of his face, and his eyes were almost nonexistent. Glitz ran the length of his butterfly-shaped bowtie, harshly reflecting the light. In his mouth was a long, fat cigar. Tipping his jauntily cocked bowler, he bent sharply at the waist, as if in introduction. Upon seeing this, a sound escaped from Judd, a sound that was more surprise than fear, and in the dwarf's hand there suddenly appeared what looked like a choke of dollar bills. He momentarily studied this sudden windfall, chomped down harder on the cigar, sending a squirt of blood out the end, looked back at Judd and in a voice that because of its rock-scraping-rock quality, strongly suggested cancer, said, "A dollar. You got a dollar, maybe we can do some business here. Of course, you ain't got a dollar. . . ." He smiled like someone who had a deep, moldy secret and then seemed to study the dirt floor beneath his tiny feet. Again he chuckled. "Of course, you ain't got a dollar . . . ," he repeated. His gaze shot up again, his buglike eyes fixed and hard. "How about that, boy, you got a dollar? Four bits and a holler?"

And Judd felt himself actually begin to mentally explore the contents of his wallet.

The dwarf cupped a hand around his ear, pretended to listen, and said, "What's that, boy? Speak up, boy. Can't hear you, boy." He paused, as if waiting for a response, then laughed loudly, leaped into the air, did a flip, and landed at Judd's feet. After steadying himself with a pinwheel of his arms, he winked up at Judd and, with a curling finger, beckoned him down to his subbasement level. Despite himself, Judd bent at the waist. The dwarf cupped his hands around his mouth and whispered into Judd's ear, "No dollar, huh? Well, for those that ain't got a dollar, we got a special prize."

More chuckles, thin and obscene, and the dwarf stepped backward, Judd querulously appraising him as he penguin-walked to the right, bent at the waist, wiggled his fat rear end a couple of times and then shoved his stubby fingers under what appeared to be a large piece of plywood on the earthen floor. He looked up at Judd again, light reflecting off the glitz on his tie like individual lasers, and with one giant effort flipped the plywood over to reveal

(Cynthia! Oh, God, Cynthia!)

the sleeping vampires beneath. Cynthia and

Robert, side by side. Grinning. Asleep? On a bed of black silk.

The dwarf winked at Judd, penguin-walked a few steps toward him and whispered, "Now look what you've done! You've woken them up. Oh, they are gonna be pissed! They are really gonna be. . . ."

Leaving his sentence unfinished, the dwarf turned sharply. As he did, Robert pushed himself up . . . and up and up and up. He was—but how could he be; he had never been—as large as the room, his shoulders, even as Judd watched, widening to the confines of the fruit cellar. The dwarf stood beneath him, the look on his face like that of an amused child as he nodded exaggeratedly and said, "Oh, sure, he's pissed, mister. He is really pissed!"

Sleepily, Bobby All studied Judd while at the same time, Cynthia pulled herself up, wrapped her arms lovingly around Bobby's waist and smiled drunkenly at Judd. "Oh, sure," she said, her head nodding with the gravity of her warning, "he is really pissed. If I were you, I'd get while the gettin' was good! If I were you!"

Reality, Judd, reality!

But right now, reality had all the quality of a television melodrama. Judd hurriedly fumbled out a stake, fisted the cross and stiff-armed both out in front of him, his elbows locked hard enough to make the joints ache. Robert raised his hands protectively, backed away slightly and said mockingly, "Save me, please save me!" grinning all the while, the power of his plea smacking onto Judd's ears with sledgehammer efficiency. He laughed derisively, as did Cynthia, while the dwarf put his fingers over his mouth and only chuckled. But with exaggerated abruptness, they stopped laughing, and the two vampires slowly stepped out of the pit. The dwarf, seeing this, said, "Oh, shit!" and scurried penguin-style to the back of the room, where he covered his head and peeked out, then covered himself again while Cynthia and the towering Robert advanced on Judd, their fangs growing steadily as they did, reaching almost walrus-size by the time their black, stinking breath blew into his face.

"I said you could only borrow her, Lucas," Bobby All said, his face no more than a foot away now, and twice as large as it should have been. As if blown by some internal gale, blood sloshed and waved in his eyes, but only to mid-point. And Judd could see something—someone—thrashing about, drowning. He looked more closely. It was him! This huge, room-size vampire had swallowed him whole, and he was drowning in an eyeful of blood! He screamed, groping for the edge of sanity, his hand curling tightly around the stake.

Bobby All grinned. "How's the water?" he asked.

"NOOO!" Judd screamed, bringing the stake sharply upward and finding the giant's heart with it. And although it took Bobby All a few seconds to realize what had happened, he finally stumbled backward, shrinking steadily and clutching madly at the thing in his chest while Cynthia brought her hands to her mouth, her eyes wide with surprise. The stake sucked even deeper into All's chest, and his mouth grew cavernous with his pain, his shark eyes opening to saucer-size, his flat death screams echoing in the small room like gunshots in a closed cylinder.

Judd, his chest heaving in and out, looked at his wife, and she at him.

No, Judd, no, don't look, don't look. . . .

But she wasn't ready to draw him in. The mystical, unflinching pull was missing, unlike what he had experienced with her vampire lover. And on her face there even began the whisper of a smile. But as he looked into her dark eyes, Judd knew what she was up to—she was trying to vex him with memories, with the life they had had. *But, God, it had been such a good life, so rich, so filled with love.* Surely he wouldn't—couldn't—do to her what he had just done to Bobby.

And maybe, he allowed, as he looked even deeper into the pools of her eyes, he could even save her.

She reached out to him lovingly, as if profoundly thankful for her rescue, as if all along she had only been waiting for him to find her, to take her away from this awful place. No longer did her face reflect harsh angles. No longer was her skin washed with a deathly white pallor.

She was—as she had been long ago—the woman he loved.

Joy surged through him. A prisoner, yes, she had only been a prisoner here, with that, that thing dying in the pit! He looked at the still-cowering dwarf and yelled triumphantly, "She's mine now! I'm going to take her home, and we're going to be a family again!"

She drew nearer.

"We're going . . ."

Her breath was the black, burning exhalation of hellfire.

"We . . ."

She was death.

"CYNTHIA!" he pleaded.

The dwarf pointed and laughed, deliciously amused.

Her face did not change expression. She moved closer, her fangs bared, her eyes smoldering with purpose. Judd's face swelled with tears of anguish as he groped blindly for another stake.

Only inches away now, she said, "Welcome, Judd."

Having found one of the stakes, Judd drew it quickly up, gripped it tightly in both hands and, as she tickled his carotid with her fangs, plunged it deeply into her chest and raised her off the ground as if she were weightless.

The surprise on her face as she looked deep into his eyes, her hands still gripping the back of his neck, and then, as she vainly tried to disengage the stake, made Judd want to reach out and help her. But he didn't. He could not. He would not. And before she lay down in the pit, there was one extremely brief moment when there actually did appear before him the woman he had married, the woman he had loved for so long.

And then she died, her screams weak and discordant, until finally there was no scream at all, leaving only her skeleton, the skull of which separated at each portal, her jawbone clicking onto her breast in a grotesque rictus while the bones of her fingers drew along the silk bed. Eventually, her blond, curly hair turned gray white, disintegrating into puffs of fine, yellow-white dust, completing the process, leaving only her clothing and the black silk bed, skin-dust scattered about it in a vaguely human silhouette.

Judd let out a deep breath. His thoughts were of her, only of her, not what had just died, but what she had been, what he could now put to rest, finally put to rest.

But there was more to do, lots more; there was Steven. Lots more. He turned, stepped toward the door . . .

. . . and heard it again—the dwarf's maniacal chuckle.

He wheeled, his scalp tingling, and again played the light along the racks of canned goods and bundled newspapers until he realized that the dwarf was standing just to the right of the beam. Judd drew the beam over, laid it on him and, as if that were his cue, watched as the dwarf again tipped his jauntily cocked bowler, as he again bent sharply at the waist, and as he again said, "A dollar. You got a dollar, maybe we can do some business here. Of course, you ain't got a dollar. . . ." He smiled down at the earthen floor.

Harry Kroh played his flashlight down the cellar stairs and started down, still wondering what the hell he was doing here—those screams, those god-awful screams! Surely that hadn't been Lucas screaming; humans weren't capable— He stopped. There was a door on the right, open slightly, and one on the left, barricaded.

"Sheriff?" he whispered.

Christ, Harry, you can do better than that!

"Sheriff Lucas!" Louder.

Noises—from both rooms. Harry stepped backward, positive he had done a really stupid thing by coming down here.

Judd Lucas stumbled into the hall, his face milk-white.

"Jesus H. Kerist!" Harry mumbled, stepping cautiously toward him. "You okay?" he asked, reaching out with a steadying hand.

Judd could only rake his fingers through his wet hair.

"What the hell was that goddamn scream, Sheriff? Christ, sounded like a herd of banshees!"

Judd turned jerkily, looked at the door from which he had just exited, then looked back at Harry. "Later . . . we gotta come back . . . later." He grabbed Harry by the collar. "Steven, gotta find Steven. Gotta find Steven!"

Harry pulled Judd's hands away. "Yeah, sure, whatever you say, Sheriff."

Judd, wild-eyed, saw the other door, still barricaded. He reached over and, smiling crazily, ran his fingers over the wood.

"Look, maybe we oughta get some help," Harry offered.

Judd, still stroking the wood, shook his head rapidly, like an overzealous child.

"Dammit, Sheriff!"

Judd ignored him. Eventually, without Harry's help, he lifted the six-by-six from its slots and threw it down. It thudded twice and lay still.

"Shit!" Harry said.

Judd rubbed his hands over his thighs, glanced at Harry and then pulled the door open, instantly releasing a raft of dead, noxious air.

And lantern light flooded the hallway.

Standing no more than a foot away was Martin Crouper, with Steven, apparently unconscious, under his arm. A blanket was wrapped around Martin's body, four white fingers holding it closed in front, a clutch of crumbled grade-school paper stuck between his thumb and forefinger like used hankies, the handle of a lantern hanging from one crooked finger. His face had the texture of old, severely depressed pottery with, it seemed, only deep, black pencil lines in place of features. His ears were too large, the lobes grotesquely huge, and his bald head was almost pointed. His fangs protruded only slightly below his upper lip. Seeing this, Harry clutched at his chest while a dull, thick pain roared into it. He dropped the flashlight and fell to his knees, his face masked with agony.

By now Judd had regained a modicum of control, but it was only shaky at best. Was this real? Did this—thing—actually exist? He vaguely heard Harry moan.

"Steven?" Judd said.

Steven didn't budge.

He reached out and touched his leg. *He is real!* Martin grunted. He looked into Martin's eyes, into the slits that were his eyes, and softly pleaded, "Please, give me the boy. Give me the boy."

And much to his surprise, Martin did, hesitantly, as if he were handing over an extremely fragile package. Judd took Steven and pulled him close while Martin backed slowly away, their eyes still locked.

And as Martin backed farther into the room,

lantern light flickering, Judd saw movement toward the back. He looked more closely. Ed, still in his uniform, and the Sternmyer girl were walking toward him, their faces wild with confusion, their eyes rotating first clockwise then counter clockwise, as if the muscles had atrophied. At the same time Martin flung the lantern away, instantly sending a shower of burning lantern fuel onto a wooden pillar. The flames spread rapidly while Ed and Gloria stopped and watched, and Martin rushed toward a startled Judd and then whisked past him up the stairs.

The house was easy prey for fire, old and mostly wood, the flames rocking and rolling through the basement at a furious pace. He had to get Steven and Harry out of here—now! He bent and pulled Harry up by the arm, Harry still clutching at his chest with spiderlike hands. With one last look behind him at the other room, he took them both quickly up the stairs and to the street, only catching a glimpse of Martin, seated in the rocker, as they made their way to the street.

Night and day were in balance now, and Martin, at long last, admired the beauty of morning: bands of yellow-topped clouds floating lazily on the horizon, a pink-blue sky, the grass glistening with dew, the air freshly scrubbed and new, just waiting for the life-giving warmth of the sun. He had, these past years, missed fine warm mornings like this.

And behind him, the fire began to build.

He looked up and down the street and wondered

about the humans in the houses, the sleeping, unsuspecting humans, and he thought of the few times he had actually scratched at a window and caught the gaze of someone in the shadow of sleep; how, upon catching that gaze, he would ask—to satisfy the rules, the damnable rules—if he might enter. They would hesitate a moment, fighting with what their mortal eyes were showing them and what their time-honored impressions of reality said could not be there. Eventually, though, they would walk across the room, their feet dragging as if through mud. Then they would shove the window up and step away, awe and fear in combination on their faces, but mostly awe, he thought; he was, after all, an awesome being. Once in, the rest was simple. Rarely would they fight. Mostly they would simply cant their necks slightly and sometimes even smile wanly as if they knew the peace of a vampire's kiss. Sometimes, however, someone who was especially strong would turn quickly away and recite something from the Bible or shove a cross in his direction and say things like, "Begone, Satan!" or "Away with thee, dark one!" That kind of nonsense. But he wasn't Satan. He had never wanted to be Satan. He had only wanted to live forever—but vitally, not like Aunty Maude. Immortality—life as a vampire—had seemed to offer that. And now, it had been taken away. He thought of the last boy and smiled, his cracking old face wrinkling with it, his squinting, tiny eyes glinting in the feeble glow of early morning. And he remembered how Aunty Maude had died so well—nary a peep. Brave one, that Aunty Maude. He remembered Father Unu and the night he had taken him. Even he went well, although the recitation of his prayers had amused Martin. He even thought of the boys he had recently cannibalized and how they—even the sleeping one—had done well in their final moments. And he wished. . . .

The fire licked at the first floor, seared the wood that covered the windows, and slipped brazenly through any available opening. Meanwhile the top quarter of the sun crested the woodline and sent a long shaft of warm sunlight onto the sleeping town and onto the roof of the porch where Martin sat, a slender tentacle of which reached onto the porch, stopping scant inches from his leg. Martin watched it like he might a poisonous snake and grunted as it moved toward him, as the sun rose slowly in the eastern sky.

Watching this, Martin had an almost overpowering urge to seek shelter. But where could he go? He had lit the fire himself. Purposely. There was nowhere to go. Nowhere at all. He had made his choice. Life was no longer worth living. He watched as a thread of sunlight fell onto his leg and immediately provoked a pain that wrenched from him a scream that seemed to come from hell itself.

The scream traveled the neighborhood, waking humans and beasts alike, and all Martin could do, his mouth gaped wide, the blackness within screeching his agony, was sit and bask in it, knowing full well that soon he would not have to face an eternity of lifetimes. And he even felt a certain pride at having spared the third boy, even though he had only spared his life because it hadn't been necessary to take it. Certainly under other circumstances. . . .

Judd watched from the road, Steven still in his arms, while the sky awakened totally, while flames licked through the roof of the All house. By now Martin had stopped screaming. The sun had taken that ability, leaving him with only an open mouth and eyes floating in the blood he so loved, the life-giving blood. And although his body twitched electrically as the sun completed its hideous work, and although his limbs were turning to dust, on his face there appeared a feeble, pain-filled smile. Finally, as death neared, he thought of Aunty Maude and wondered if she would be there waiting for him when he arrived at wherever he was going, a nickel in her arthritically clawed hand, a nickel for a creamsicle down at the country store. . . .

The last few pages of his memoirs fell to the porch. And Martin was dead.

Judd clutched Steven even closer as he felt him grope for consciousness. Harry, better now, sat in the Jeep while flames engulfed the house, roaring toward the morning sky.

It's over, Judd thought. *Over. Finally over.* But as his body went limp with that supposed truth, as he finally allowed himself a moment of rest, the blazing front door smashed open, and onto the porch stepped the dwarf, his fat cigar still clenched between his thin lips, while off to his left a tall, large man hefted a huge sledgehammer and slung it easily over his bare shoulder. On the screen of his mind Judd pictured himself at a carnival, raising that huge sledgehammer high over his head. . . . *Christ!* he thought, *a carnival—what the hell?* As if he'd read Judd's thoughts, the dwarf grinned at him, reached into his pocket, looked for a moment at the contents, and then pulled out what appeared to Judd to be a dollar bill and waved it like a flag of surrender, the air alive with the snaps and pops of burning wood and punctuated by the dwarf's maniacal, cackling laugh. Reflexively, Judd pulled Steven closer, expecting that at any moment the dwarf would march down the steps, his large friend—and his hammer—close behind. But that didn't happen. In what was either an extraordinary coincidence, Judd would later think, or simply the death throes of trapped and burning vampires, both the dwarf and his large friend disappeared in a flash of white light at precisely the same time that the house exploded in flame.

At the same time, Steven woke up and knuckled his eyes, and both watched as the All house—and whatever lay inside—was consumed by fire, a fire intense enough to level the structure before the Hunt fire department could lock in a hose.

CHAPTER TWENTY-SIX

The Next Day

As Judd braked to a stop in front of Rosemary's flower shop, he once again thought of Cynthia. Had she been killed by the fire? Had she somehow miraculously escaped? He remembered the dwarf, his little penguinlike walk, his catlike flip, how, after appearing on the burning porch, he and his pal had finally popped into nonexistence. He had killed the vampires, sure, he had killed them; he had jammed his crude sticks into them and watched them die, but they had only died in his mind, only there. He hadn't actually lifted those floorboards and trained his weapons on living tissue. But he had chosen to leave, to come back later and finish the job. Well, he hadn't had to come back; the fire had seen to that. But still, they had been alive right up until the house came down, right up until the dwarf—their hallucination—had disappeared, the dwarf's death coinciding with their own.

He drew in a deep breath, then let it slowly out. Fortunately others hadn't seen what he had seen. Had the house not burned, they would have, and most definitely suffered for it. Inside that house there had been nightmares just waiting to be discovered. Estelle had had her nightmare, and Ricky, well, no telling how he might have reacted. Now the bodies of Rosemary and the others were unrecognizable, just masses of charred flesh that Ben would have to somehow identify. Dental records probably.

He shrugged and thought that after a while, after a long while probably, this would all blow over. Normalcy would again fall over the town. The old boys down at the hardware store would unwittingly arrange daily contests to see who could out bullshit the other, and Rosemary's flower shop would house some other business, a pizzeria or maybe another video store. By then maybe even Sam would have recovered. Sayers said it would take time, but eventually the dog would make it almost all the way back. He'd retain a small limp, but that would be it. That and maybe some bad dreams, Judd thought.

Sitting there, the sun high and hot overhead, the day warm and filled with new hope, he drew in a hearty lungful of air and remembered a back-to-school-sale sign he had seen in the window at Murphy's Department Store. Maybe he'd pick up a few pair of jeans for Steven, some sweaters. To the north, he knew, far to the north, there lay a mass of cold air. It would get here soon enough.

EPILOGUE

The state police came in right afterward and claimed what was left of the bodies, none of which were readily identifiable, even by sex. But after they left and long after the CRIME SCENE trappings had been removed, a few people, those not frightened by the rumors about what had happened here, began to see the property in a more normal light. Some, like Stanley Crimmons, even began to use it as a short-cut. But Stanley, whose five-buck-a-week stipend to keep the lawn mowed had at least given him the chance to catch the weekly feature at the Strand, would never see the property in a normal light. He had been, after all, the caretaker, more or less, and had had more intimate contact with the All house than almost anyone. His wonderment did not stem from any physical thing; the house had not smelled evil, had not given up strange sounds. Not at all. Stanley's relationship with the All house had been more subtle than that. While he mowed the lawn—which he still did, even though the house was gone now—he always pushed the mower a little faster on the back passes, and more slowly while he walked toward the house, at least while the house had been there. If pressed, he would probably have said something like, "Tell you what, you ever think someone was checkin' you out when there wasn't supposed to be no one home? Weird feelin', man, weird feelin'!" Of course, it had been no surprise to him to hear that people had died in there. He had even known one of them, the Hamilton woman. Well, his mom had known her at least, and that was close enough.

But even at that, there came a time when even Stanley began to use the All property as a shortcut, it and the Tyler property right behind. And it was while he was doing just that, the ninth of May, a Saturday, to be exact, that he found it. At first he thought he'd found a dollar bill, all crumpled and caught up in the hedges, but still folding, spending green, so he plucked it out and ironed it flat on his shirt, thanking his lucky stars all the while. But after he flattened it out and after he took a good look at it, he realized that he hadn't been so lucky after all. It was some stupid coupon thing, some Halloween prank. And even though Halloween was still a long ways off, wasn't this a good place to hide something like that—where the killers had lived. Where the killers had killed! Sure, it looked like a dollar bill; there was old wooden-tooth George on the front, and it was green and white and about the right size. But in the place of IN GOD WE TRUST, the phrase, IMMORTALITY—ONE DOLLAR had been substituted, and on the flipside, the phrase, REDEEMABLE AT ALL PETRY BROS. CARNIVALS.

Stanley studied it awhile longer, crumbled it up again and was just about to throw it away when he realized that the PETRY BROS. CARNIVAL was "over to Geneva" this week, at least according to his best friend, Al. *Well,* he thought, *maybe I'll check into this. Probably some scam though, just another scam. Probably get there and someone carves your name in a rock or somethin'. Somethin' stupid like that.* But Stanley was never one to pass up a freebee. Never. And hell, a carnival sounded kind of fun.

So after checking out the horizon to see what kind of weather was headed their way, he pocketed the coupon and went off in search of his friend, Al.

Al was older and Al had a car.